Tangerine Marmalade Murder

by

Meg Benjamin

Luscious Delights, Book Three

Copyright Notice
This is a work of fiction. Names, characters, places, and incidents are either the product of the author's imagination or are used fictitiously, and any resemblance to actual persons living or dead, business establishments, events, or locales, is entirely coincidental.

Tangerine Marmalade Murder

COPYRIGHT © 2023 by Margaret Batschelet

All rights reserved. No part of this book may be used or reproduced in any manner whatsoever without written permission of the author or The Wild Rose Press, Inc. except in the case of brief quotations embodied in critical articles or reviews.
Contact Information: info@thewildrosepress.com

Cover Art by *Tina Lynn Stout*

The Wild Rose Press, Inc.
PO Box 708
Adams Basin, NY 14410-0708
Visit us at www.thewildrosepress.com

Publishing History
First Edition, 2024
Trade Paperback ISBN 978-1-5092-5471-2
Digital ISBN 978-1-5092-5472-9

Luscious Delights, Book Three
Published in the United States of America

Dedication

To my editor, Dianne Rich, and all the nice folks at Wild Rose Press. And to my hubs, Bill, for tasting my jams and putting up with my hours.

Prologue

We settled down at the dinner table for some general conversation about the Merchants Association, blueberry jam, and just how much snow we were likely to get from the latest storm, which was still stalled somewhere on the Western Slope. I'd just gotten up to see what ice cream I had in the freezer when someone hammered on my door.

Herman whimpered, and Uncle Mike pushed himself up from the table. "What the hell?"

I started for the door, where the hammering was still going on, but Uncle Mike grabbed my arm. "Let me open it. You hold onto Herman."

That was a good idea, since Herman had moved from whimpering to growling along with stalking toward the door as if he'd actually protect us. In fact, it was more likely we'd protect him, but I wouldn't tell him that.

Uncle Mike threw open the door. "What the hell…" he started, then paused. "Donnie?"

I moved closer to the open door and saw Donnie McCray, Dolce's dad and Uncle Mike's foreman, standing on my doorstep. He's a big man, but right then he looked like he was ready to collapse. "Come inside." I grabbed his arm. "Sit down. What's wrong? Are you hurt?"

Donnie dropped onto my couch, gasping. "There's

a woman," he began and then stopped to catch his breath.

"What woman?" Uncle Mike said. "Where?"

"Up by the road. In a car." Donnie gasped again, and I dropped to my knees beside him.

"What about her, Donnie? What's wrong?"

"She dead," he blurted out. "She's dead up there in the car."

Chapter 1

"Hey, Roxy, you got any more of those curly things with the cheese on 'em?"

I'd never considered the Shavano Garden Club to be a hard-drinking bunch. Not until we'd been hired to cater their Start the Season party. Now I regarded a man who apparently knew me, but whose name didn't leap to my mind. His eyes were bloodshot, and he seemed to have a little trouble wrapping his tongue around the word *curly*. Given the crowd around the full bar in the corner—a crowd that had stayed large all evening long—I guess I shouldn't have been surprised that several members of the group were getting soused. Particularly when it was an open bar.

Robicheaux Catering was supposed to take care of any problem with drunks by providing food and plenty of it. But the heavy hors d'oeuvres we were pumping out weren't enough to counter the rivers of booze being pumped out by the bar.

The guy with the *curly* problem was watching me hopefully, and I yanked myself into the game. "Cheese straws. Yes, sir. Coming up right away." I spread a new layer of cheese straws on one of our serving trays and expressed them to the food table.

I heard Nate make a disgruntled sound somewhere behind me. Technically, I was supposed to stay in the kitchen warming food and getting it plated up. But the garden clubbers were zeroing in on the food trays like ants at a garden party, and Donnell, tonight's waitress, was having a hard time keeping up, even with Nate's help.

I put the cheese straws in a prominent place on the table then stepped away to let the famished hordes get by me.

"How much more do we have in the kitchen?" Nate muttered in my ear.

"Not a lot. How much longer does this thing go on?"

Nate checked his watch. "Thirty minutes, supposedly. Tony Babbitt was saying something about hiring us for another half hour a couple of minutes ago."

I gritted my teeth. "He can hire us for another half hour, but that won't mean we have any more food in the kitchen. We made as much as they said they wanted." Plus a dozen or so more of each hors d'oeuvre just to be on the safe side.

"I know that," Nate snapped. "I've already told him as much." The stress of watching our food disappear like wheat fields in a locust attack was making us both irritable. Particularly since it didn't seem to be slowing down.

"I'll go down to the kitchen and bring up everything we've got left. It should last for another thirty minutes. If they want more after that they can order pizza."

"Not a great testimonial for Robicheaux Catering." Nate stared darkly at one of the members who was piling multiple appetizers onto his plate.

"However, it's the best we can do." My teeth were

gritted again. "Unless you want me to run over to City Market and grab some chips and dip."

Nate put his arm around my shoulders. "Nope. It's okay. Give Donnell the rest of the crudités to put out and bring up the last of the hummus. I'll grab the cheese puffs and Coco's mini-quiches. We've still got a few Swedish meatballs to warm. It is what it is."

What it was was a minor crisis, sort of a bump in the catering road. We'd relied on the estimates the guy from the Garden Club had given us, and he probably hadn't taken the open bar into account. Even with the few extra we'd added to the count we'd been given, it hadn't been enough. Maybe they'd had a last minute rush for tickets and hadn't bothered to let us know. Regardless, I didn't see how they could blame us.

But they probably would.

I'd been working with Nate Robicheaux as part of Robicheaux Catering for around three months now. The business had been more successful than anyone anticipated, except possibly Nate's mom, Madge, who'd come up with the idea in the first place. Winter was the slow season for my jam business, Luscious Delights, which meant I could devote more of my time to helping Nate prepare the menus he'd come up with. I wasn't sure what would happen when the Shavano Farmers Market got going again and my jam production picked up. I figured we'd cross that bridge when we came to it.

In the kitchen I got the final platters of food ready to go. Donnell had already taken up the containers of veggies to add to the crudité platter, not that we had all that many veggies left, or dip either. I arranged the last of the mini-quiches Nate's sister Coco had made. They were delicious but tiny. Maybe for our next heavy hors d'oeuvres order we should go with something bigger, like sliders or ham salad pinwheels.

Or pizza.

Our garden club contact, Tony, came down to the kitchen, looking a little panicky around the eyes. "Any more of those cheese straws? People love 'em."

"Glad to hear it, but that last platter was the end of them. We're getting the other refills up as quickly as we can." And I really wished he'd get out of the kitchen. Civilians were supposed to stay in the dining room.

Nate stepped through the kitchen door, frowning when he saw Tony, then switching to a quick smile. "We'll get everything out on the table, Tony. We should make it to seven." Which was when this so-called cocktail party was supposed to end. I only hoped the garden club had come well provided with designated drivers.

"Oh, okay." Tony glanced around the kitchen again. "I guess I underestimated how much people would eat. The last catered party we threw ended up with a lot of leftovers. They're really going to town on your stuff."

This was great. And also awful. Would the club members realize their problems stemmed from having Tony Babbitt make decisions about how much food they needed? Or would they think we'd somehow screwed up and brought less food than we should have?

Nate's jaw tightened, and I guessed he was thinking the same thing. "Glad it was a hit."

"Oh, definitely." Tony stared around the kitchen a little absently. "So I guess that's it for the food."

"Yep, that's all you ordered and all we brought.

You can check the invoice and the order form," Nate said a little stiffly.

"Oh, I know, I know. My fault entirely. Great food though. Great food." Tony wandered back to the dining room.

"Cleanup?" I asked. Given that we didn't have anything else to put out, cleanup was a good idea.

Nate sighed. "Yeah, sure. Just rinse off the platters and stack everything in the boxes. Tres can run it all through the dishwasher tomorrow."

Since the club had opted for paper plates rather than crockery, the dish cleanup would be minimal. The event space belonged to one of the members—a meeting room in an office building downtown. We'd do a quick swabbing of the counters and the sink, leaving any heavy cleaning to the janitorial staff.

I started rinsing the sheet pans we'd used to warm everything as Donnell came in with a couple of platters. "Those people sure can eat." She paused. "And drink. Bartender's having a hard time keeping up."

The bartender wasn't our problem since he'd been hired separately. "Once the bar closes down they'll be done." I figured no more food and drinks would equal the end of the party.

"Don't know about that. They're trying to pay that bartender to stay another hour."

Terrific. Another hour of booze and no food would not make for a good end to the evening. "We're closing down regardless. We're out of food."

"Right. I'll bring down the platters as the last of it gets taken."

I'd just finished piling the sheet trays in one of the boxes and begun piling the platters in another when

Nate stepped into the kitchen carrying another two platters to be rinsed. He didn't look happy.

"What's the matter?"

He placed the platters onto the counter with a little more force than necessary. "Turns out they took your suggestion."

Huh? "My...suggestion?"

He sighed. "They're ordering pizza."

"Well, crap." I had a feeling we weren't getting a bonus for this one.

I helped Nate unload the pans and platters at the catering kitchen. It was a building next door to Robicheaux's Café that had once been used for storage. Madge had invested in some upgrades like a new floor and a better stove, but it still looked a little drab. Someday Nate wanted to turn it into a bistro restaurant, but that was clearly way off in the future.

We put the boxes on the counter where Tres could find them and take them to the dishwasher in the café. Nate leaned against the counter when we were through, rubbing his eyes. "Well, that was fun. Remind me not to work with Tony Babbitt again in this lifetime."

"Maybe he's learned his lesson. Next time he'll order extra if he gets food from Robicheaux's."

Nate gave me a sardonic smile but didn't say anything more. There wasn't much to say, after all. It hadn't been a triumph, and yeah, it wasn't our fault, but that probably wouldn't occur to the drunks, who'd happily feast on pizza and remember that the catering company hadn't provided enough food.

"You want to come to the cabin? I've got some new IPA from that brewery in Golden." It was Wednesday night, but I figured we both needed to unwind.

Nate shook his head. "Can't. I've got breakfast tomorrow."

I frowned. "I thought the deal was you didn't work breakfast after you'd done a catering job." That was the deal originally, but things changed.

He sighed. "Bobby's shorthanded. Coco's filling a big order for the Merchants Association coffee tomorrow."

Even though their catering business had taken off, Robicheaux's Café was still staffed by the original three Robicheaux kids: Bobby, Nate, and Coco. All three of them were beginning to show the strain.

"You need to hire some more people. The three of you are stretched way too thin."

"Mom agrees with you. She's working on Bobby. I figure she'll start looking for another cook by next month, whether Bobby approves or not."

Bobby was Nate's older brother who hated changes at the café. He'd refused to have anything to do with the catering business, but he couldn't run the café on his own since the number of people they served were more than a single cook could handle. Still, they obviously couldn't go on with Nate working twelve-hour shifts, covering both the kitchen and the catering. Or anyway, Nate couldn't go on doing that.

I stood up on tiptoes to kiss his cheek. "Maybe this weekend."

He closed his eyes, wrapping his arms around my waist. "Definitely this weekend."

"Okay. We can put our feet up and watch a movie. Maybe order out."

Nate nodded, resting his forehead against mine.

"Neither of us cooks on Saturday. Just one thing."

"One thing?"

"No pizza. No pizza at all."

"Agreed," I said. "No pizza until this is all a fading memory."

I drove to the farm, a lot more tired than I'd realized. I was almost glad Nate hadn't been able to come out to my cabin, which, of course, made me feel guilty. Nate was the love of my life. He was the first person I'd ever felt that way about. And even though it sounded a little cheesy, it was the absolute truth.

But working lots of hours with the love of my life in a very high stress environment was beginning to take a toll, no matter how hard we both tried to pretend it wasn't. We'd started snapping at each other now and then, taking out our stress on our nearest and dearest. We both knew it was a bad idea, but that hadn't made us less likely to do it.

Still, I was determined not to let this job become a problem. I liked working with Nate. I enjoyed being part of the process of developing the menu and then finding local sources for some artisan food stuff.

And I won't lie—the money came in handy. I was just getting started with my mail order jam business. After Luscious Delights had been featured on a national TV show, I'd gotten a lot more interest in my website store, and the orders were beginning to pick up.

Launching the mail order part of Luscious Delights had taken a fair amount of money up front, but I was still at the early point where the sales hadn't quite caught up to my expenses. I'd hired a couple of people to help with the jam making and order fulfillment, and I'd had to invest in more jars and specialized mailing boxes and more professional-looking labels than I'd used for my local customers. Not to mention postage and upgrading my website. I could have dipped into my share of the profits from Constantine Farms, but I didn't want to do that unless I had to. I usually took a large part of my share of the business in summer fruit to make my jams. Working for Robicheaux Catering filled some gaps.

And I believed everything was going to be great even if right now it was a little less than. I had a business I loved, a man I loved, a place I loved. I couldn't ask for much more.

I parked my truck in front of the cabin that was the headquarters for Luscious Delights as well as the house I lived in. In the early spring moonlight, it looked sort of romantic—all silvery clapboard with a peaked roof and a couple of rocking chairs on the front porch. I'd even put in a couple of planters made from galvanized steel stock tanks on either side of the entrance, although they were currently full of week-old snow rather than flowers. That was something I'd take care of when the weather got a little warmer.

I loved my cabin, but I knew it could use some work, too. I was co-owner of Constantine Farms, along with my uncle Mike, so improvements to a farm building like the cabin could probably be charged off to maintenance. Still, those improvements wouldn't come cheap, and they'd probably interfere with my jam business.

A business you love, a man you love, a place you love.

I couldn't ask for more, right? I hauled my tired butt into my cabin, repeating that phrase like a mantra. I couldn't ask for much more. Except maybe a beer.

Chapter 2

I got to work on my jam backlog. I was getting a respectable number of online orders, mostly for my standbys: raspberry, peach, apricot, strawberry, and pepper peach. I hadn't checked the orders for a couple of days, but I figured I'd increase the inventory so when my part-time help came to work that afternoon, we'd be ready to go. I'd just gotten the first load of jars into the canning pot when someone knocked on my door.

We're pretty far outside the city limits of Shavano, which means I get very few casual visitors. Most people who knock on my door are people I know, and most of them just walk in after a token knock. This time, however, the person just went on knocking.

I checked the canning pot to make sure it was boiling at the right level, set the timer, and headed for the door.

The woman on my doorstep was a stranger. She looked to be in her forties with blonde hair that had been dyed once too often and sort of nondescript clothes—jeans and a sweatshirt from Arizona State. "Roxy Constantine?" she asked when I opened the door.

"That's me. What do you need?" I sounded pretty abrupt, but I had jam in the canning pot and no time for sales pitches.

"Heard you were hiring," the blonde said.

I stared at her for a moment. In fact, I could have used another part-timer to help with the jam shipping, but I wasn't actively hiring right then. And I wouldn't have hired a stranger anyway. "No, not right now."

"You sure? I'm a hard worker. You won't regret it." Her lips edged up in a sort of sly smile that made my nerves tingle. Right then I regretted even opening the door for her.

"Sorry," I said.

The blonde didn't move, and she didn't lose that sly smile. "Here's the thing…"

"Roxanne?" Uncle Mike stepped up onto the porch beside me, frowning at the blonde. Like I said, we don't get many strangers out here. "What's going on?"

Good question. I had a feeling more was going on there than I knew, but I wasn't sure what was happening. "This lady is looking for work, but I told her we don't have any openings."

The blonde turned her sharp eyes on Uncle Mike. "Nothing on the farm? You don't need help around the house?"

He shook his head, still frowning. "No. We don't need anyone right now."

The blonde looked back and forth between us, and I thought she had more to say. But then she shrugged. "Can't blame me for trying."

"No," I said. "Sorry."

She turned and sauntered away. For the first time I saw a battered green car parked a little distance away from the cabin.

Uncle Mike stared after her. "That was weird."

I nodded. 'Yeah. I don't know what she was after. I don't think it was a job." That sly smile and those sharp eyes didn't seem to go with someone who came to an isolated farm looking for work.

"Keep your door locked," Uncle Mike said. "You never know who's around or what they're after."

"Right." Just then I heard the timer ding in the kitchen, and I remembered the canning pot. "See you at dinner." I moved inside at a trot.

My part-timers showed up later that day. By then, I was sort of in the groove. And sort of not.

"Well...hell."

Normally my language is a lot saltier than that when one of my jams heads south, but I was currently sharing my kitchen with Dolce McCray, and I needed to cool it. For all I know, Dolce swears like a sailor when she's on her own time, but she's sixteen years old and I didn't want her repeating words she'd learned from me where her parents might hear.

My other assistant, Bridget Sullivan, took a moment from printing out mailing labels to give me a commiserating smile. Bridget is a single mom in her mid-forties, with the kind of tough prettiness that comes from hard experience. She could probably teach me a few new curse words, given that she's worked as a waitress for a lot of years. "Marmalade, right?" she said.

I sighed. "Right."

Marmalade is a bitch to make under ideal circumstances. You have to boil the whole fruit and then you have to boil the pulp and then you sieve it and add sugar and the sliced-up fruit rind and then you boil it again. And then, after all of that, I kept ending up with soupy blood orange marmalade. I briefly considered billing it as blood orange syrup, but I figured the orange rind slivers would just clog the neck of the syrup bottle.

"Could you boil it down some more?" Dolce asked. She was currently putting labels on the several dozen jars of raspberry jam I'd finished over the last couple of days.

"I'll have to, but I'm not optimistic. Sometimes jam just has a mind of its own." Particularly when you're making that jam at seven thousand feet altitude where the boiling temperature was below two hundred degrees.

"You want to come up with something else for next month?" Dolce asked.

"I'll probably have to." Not that I had any idea about what that would be. I was working with a digital marketing expert on ways to promote more sales, and she'd suggested a monthly limited special. It had seemed like a great idea at the time, but now, in the middle of March, with no fresh Colorado fruit to be had, I wasn't so sure.

"Blueberries," Dolce said decisively. "They're always in season."

"Not Colorado fruit." But then neither were blood oranges, the current source of my pain.

"It's March. There is no Colorado fruit. Except frozen." As the daughter of Colorado farmers, Dolce knew what she was talking about. She started stacking the jars of raspberry jam—which had, in fact, been made from frozen Colorado fruit—in the nearest carton.

"Right." I could do blueberry jam, but I'd have to come up with a special version. I could always use booze. Blueberries and gin might work. On the other hand, booze was expensive, and I was already jacking up the price for the specials. "I think I've got a recipe somewhere for blueberry jam with Earl Grey tea."

"There you go," Bridget said. "Unusual enough to attract the curious and tasty enough to please the picky."

That left me with a kettle full of runny blood orange marmalade that I'd boil a little while longer in hopes it might firm up. And if it turned out okay, maybe I'd tuck it away on the website to see if I could sell it.

"I've got the labels on all the jars. You need anything else today?" Dolce looked like she was eager to go, since it was Friday afternoon. Maybe she had a pep rally or something.

"That's good for now. Remember to sign out."

"I will." She gave both of us a megawatt smile and stepped toward the door.

Bridget watched her sign her timecard and head outside. "Oh, to have that much enthusiasm for life." She brushed her hands on her knees, then pushed herself up. "I need to get going, too. These orders are all up to date, and I'm on the dinner shift tonight."

Bridget worked at High Country, one of Shavano's few fine dining places. Working for my mail order business was strictly part time during the week for her. For now. If I was ever able to pay her what she was worth, I'd hire her on full time.

"Okay, thanks. Maybe I can get a package pickup on Saturday to clear this stuff out." Always assuming I didn't have more jam disasters to deal with.

Bridget frowned as she opened the door. "You need to take a break sometime, too, Rox. Go do something sexy with the chef."

I gave her a limp smile. "I'm sure we'll figure something out."

"Do that. Bye."

I watched Bridget head for her truck. I didn't envy her having to work a full shift waiting tables after spending the day getting jam orders ready to mail. But, of course, I had my own supplemental job coming up tomorrow with Nate, that sexy chef Bridget had mentioned.

Truth be told, I'd have liked nothing better than to spend some time on a little hanky panky with Nate over the weekend. But our available time for shenanigans had dropped off sharply since I'd become his ever-reliable sous chef at the catering company.

After I dealt with the slightly thicker blood orange marmalade, I checked the printout of mail orders Bridget had left for me along with the stack of address labels. Most of them were one or two jars, although a few were for more. Putting together the small orders was a pain, but maybe those customers would order more next time. I started loading the jars into the boxes, complete with our custom printed *thanks for your order* cards, slapping the mailing label on the outside and checking off the name on the address list.

I was operating more or less on auto pilot by then. I'd spent the day on the marmalade along with doing more raspberry jam since it was my biggest seller. I'd been on my feet since I'd gotten up that morning, and I only stayed upright now by promising myself a glass of wine when I'd finished the one- and two-jar orders. I was about two-thirds of the way through when I heard a car pull up outside. For a moment, I thought about the odd encounter with the blonde job-seeker. I hadn't seen her since, but I'd kept my door locked like Uncle Mike had suggested.

Or I thought I had. I heard the door open as I put the last of the single jars into its box. I glanced up as I felt a pair of arms around my shoulders and a cool nose pressed against my neck.

"Hey, babe," Nate said, "you want some help?"

I turned around and hugged him back. He smelled like Robicheaux's Café, where he'd probably been doing prep work for Saturday lunch, a delectable mixture of scents that made him particularly edible. After a couple of minutes spent enjoying a few mutual nibbles, he asked again. "Want some help?"

"Sure. It's mostly two-jar boxes at this point." Working together we got the rest of the orders done and I stacked them next to the door for pickup when the delivery truck came by. And then I collapsed on the sofa.

"There's no way I can cook tonight. Can we order out? Maybe Thai?"

Nate picked up a sack he'd left near the door. "I've got it already. Chili and corn bread. Leftovers from lunch."

Robicheaux's chili was superlative, and Nate's sister Coco made great cornbread. "Terrific. Want a beer?"

"Sure." He put the sack on the counter, pulling out the cornbread and a restaurant-sized container of chili.

"Want to bring me one while you're up?" I gave him a tired smile. Like I said, it had been a long day, and I didn't feel like getting up again.

"Got it." He brought me a bottle of something cold. I was so tired I didn't even check to see what I was drinking.

Nate dropped down on the couch beside me. "What were you making today?"

"Blood orange marmalade. Or maybe blood orange syrup. Depends on how you look at it."

"Not a success?" He took a swig of his beer.

"It finally thickened up, but it's not one of my triumphs. Maybe I'll see if I can sell it to Bianca." Bianca Jordan ran Shavano's best bakery. She bought some of my less inspired creations to use as fillings for jelly doughnuts and Bismarcks.

"Maybe we can try it on toast tomorrow." Which meant Nate was staying overnight. Which meant the evening was suddenly looking up.

"I'll be glad to let you. Who's our customer tomorrow night?" We usually had catering jobs on Fridays and Saturdays, with the occasional Sunday brunch.

"Name's Arredondo. Birthday party. Out in that new development near the road to Mount Oxford."

"And that's the Bolognese, right?" We had a variety of menus, and the customers usually just chose one rather than asking for something special.

Nate nodded. "I got the sauce done this afternoon. It's sitting in the cooler, hopefully building up flavor."

"So tomorrow it's salad and pasta and appetizers. Did Coco do the dessert?"

He nodded again. "Flourless cake. With candles."

"Good." I stretched my legs out in front of me. I'd probably be on my feet again for part of tomorrow, putting together the salad and the bruschetta appetizers. We were doing stuffed mushrooms, too, but the filling was already made so we'd just need to stuff them and run them under the broiler at the customer's house before we served. "Who's serving?"

"Dorothy and her son. He's just sixteen, but he's tall enough to pass for older."

Usually, we hired a couple of the waitresses from Robicheaux's. Like Bridget, they were glad to pick up a little extra cash on top of their salary and tips. Dorothy was a veteran, but I'd never met her son. "Does he have any experience?"

"Dorothy says she's been drilling him. It's not going to be a tough gig, just a buffet."

"Right. I forgot." We did sit-down dinners, but the buffets were more popular for informal stuff like a birthday party.

Nate turned to me, looping his arm over my shoulder. "Are you going to be okay for this? You look beat."

"I am beat, but I'll be okay tomorrow." And having gotten the packages ready for pickup, I wouldn't have to do much more for Luscious Delights until Monday. I took a closer look at Nate then, which was always a pleasure. Right now, though, he looked almost as beat as I felt. "You look tired yourself."

"Like you said: tough day. But I'll be better tomorrow." He paused. "Actually, I've got some good news to pass on."

"What's that?" I hoped it wasn't a big catering job. If so, I'd have to pretend to be excited since the real thing would probably be beyond me at the moment.

"You remember I put in a bid for the Wine and Food Festival banquet?"

I did, vaguely. The Wine and Food Festival was the local restaurant association's attempt to drum up a little extra business during the spring low season. The banquet was their big finish.

"We got it." Nate gave me a tired smile, and I did my best to return it.

The banquet would be huge, which would be a great payout for the catering business but a massive amount of work for us. Right then it was hard for me to get any enthusiasm going. "What are we serving?" I hoped it was one of our set menus, but I doubted it.

"Well, here's the thing: we're only doing the first course. They've got different people doing different parts of the dinner. I think McKinley's doing the main, since the restaurant association wants meat. Jan Duffy's doing the healthy alternative." He gave me a dry smile. Jan Duffy ran a vegetarian place that was sort of hit and miss, but she could probably come up with a vegetarian main that would pass muster.

McKinley's was an old-line steak house, so it figured they'd be doing beef in some form, probably massive.

"Who's doing the dessert?"

"Don't know for sure. Rumor is it's Grace Peters."

I rolled my eyes, although I don't know if Nate saw it. Grace Peters had recently opened a bakery in town that was competing with Bianca. Or trying to compete with Bianca. Peters came from somewhere in the east and had a stint as a pastry chef at one of the big restaurants in Las Vegas to recommend her. Plus apparently she'd worked at a patisserie in Paris at one point. Her stuff was more on the trendy end of things than Bianca's—cronuts and neon-colored macarons and cookies made with kids' cereals—but she didn't yet have much of a following. Plus from what I could tell, her croissants and brioches weren't even close to Bianca's pastries in quality. Still, Shavano could probably support a couple of bakeries for different tastes.

My shoulders relaxed slightly. "We can handle one course. How many are they expecting at the banquet?"

"They're estimating one fifty to two hundred, based on how many they had last year."

"What are you thinking for the first course? Soup?"

"Maybe." Nate shrugged. "It should be something light. I hear McKinley's doing medallions of beef with duchess potatoes. The restaurant association may get them to throw in a green vegetable, assuming the McKinley's cooks know how to do one."

I settled down a little farther into the couch, resting my beer on my stomach. "You sure you don't want to do a salad? Maybe with marinated artichokes or cold asparagus."

"Yeah, that might work better than soup. We'll want something flashy, though."

"Torn croutons. Shaved parmesan. Maybe pine nuts. We'll think of something."

Nate grinned at me. "Yeah, we will. This is a great chance to show off what we can do to a couple hundred people."

I let myself relax a little more. He was right. It *was* a great opportunity for the catering company and a coup for Nate himself. "Congrats, babe." I leaned over to kiss his cheek. "This is a big thing."

"Yeah, it is." His grin broadened. "But now we've got to come up with a dish that'll knock their socks off."

"Right. And one we can stretch to feed two

hundred or so." No way did I want to repeat our garden club experience. This time we'd have enough to feed the multitude and then some.

Chapter 3

The Arredondo birthday party turned out to be a breeze. The only rough spot was that we'd forgotten to order bread for the dinner. Nate sent me to Bianca's, and I crossed my fingers that she'd have a couple of baguettes left. As I walked up the street to her shop, I saw someone else step out Bianca's door. It was a woman, although I couldn't see her well. She was wearing a jacket that was too light for the colder temperatures we had currently. As I watched her, snowflakes began to drift by.

Then I caught a glimpse of blonde hair.

I increased my speed, but by the time I got to Bianca's, the woman was gone. I told myself it wasn't the woman who'd come to my door, but I had the uncomfortable sense that it was.

So she was still around Shavano. I didn't know why that made me feel uneasy, but it did.

Bianca was at her front counter, which was unusual. She normally spends her time in her workroom. "Hey, Rox," she said. "What's up?"

"Do you by any wild chance have a few baguettes I could get for Nate? He forgot to put in the order." We'd both forgotten, but I figured I could drop the blame in Nate's lap for now.

"Yeah, I've got three left. You want them?"

"Absolutely." I grabbed my wallet, thanking the

bakery gods for coming through.

But as Bianca bundled the three baguettes together, I remembered the woman I'd seen. "Did you notice a blonde woman who was in here right before me? Fortyish, bad dye job?" Even as I said it, I realized how sketchy my description sounded.

Bianca frowned. "I don't remember anyone like that. Sara's assistant was in, but she's younger than forty."

"Sara has an assistant?" Sara was Bianca's daughter-in-law. Bianca's son had a butcher shop a couple of blocks away.

Bianca's expression turned sour. "Oh my, yes. Although between you and me, I've got no idea what that assistant does. Hell, I've got no idea what Sara does."

Relations between Bianca and Sara weren't great. I figured I'd avoid making them worse. "Thanks for the bread. You're a lifesaver."

"Just bring me some jam the next time you come over. We're running low on raspberry."

Bianca sold my jam at her front counter, and she sold a lot of it. "I'll do that next week. Thanks again."

The birthday party was a success so far as I could tell from the kitchen where I hung out. Dorothy's son was a sweet boy who didn't turn out to have much knack for waiting tables. But he was strong enough to heft trays of dirty dishes and he kept the buffet table loaded while his mother brought people's drinks and served them pieces of cake after the candles had been blown out.

The clients were taking care of cleanup themselves, so all we had to do besides cooking was load the dishwasher a couple of times. The husband who'd hired us was so pleased that he gave us a bonus. We divided it with Dorothy and her son, and all of us left happy. All in all, a satisfying evening.

On Monday, I started working on the blueberry and Earl Grey jam, which involved finding enough frozen blueberries without destroying my profit margin and picking up a very inexpensive box of Earl Grey teabags. Bridget showed up after lunch to start work on the next bunch of mail orders that she planned on dropping off at the shipping company on her way home. Dolce came over after school to help me fix the blueberries. She's always more interested in the cooking part than she is in the business side of things, although she's getting pretty good at pricing.

By five I had several jars of blueberry Earl Grey jam sitting out to cool. I planned on letting them set up overnight and then tasting them tomorrow, but my initial impression, based on a small sample with a tasting spoon, was good.

Dolce spent another hour putting on labels and then she and Bridget both took off for the day, leaving me to contemplate what I wanted to fix for dinner. I wasn't as tired as I had been on Friday, but I also wasn't up to a big production, so I decided to grab some leftover chicken and rice from the freezer to warm up for Uncle Mike and me.

The two of us didn't have dinner together every night anymore, but we did manage to hang out two or three times a week. Uncle Mike had taken our mutual dog, Herman, up to the main house to live with him after my mail order business ramped up. Herm is a sweetheart, but he's also huge. Not exactly what you want to deal with when you've got several cartons of jam jars stacked around the living room.

Yet another thing I needed to deal with: getting some kind of storage unit so I wouldn't have to share my cabin with my mail orders. Besides, I missed Herman.

Uncle Mike and Herm arrived a little after five bearing gifts, a half pie he'd picked up from Robicheaux's on his way home from the Merchants Association. I wrapped it in foil and put it in the oven to warm up. "What's new with the merchants?"

"Not much. They're all yammering on about that Wine and Food thing next month." Uncle Mike regarded his fellow members with a jaundiced eye. He sat down at the kitchen table with a beer, while Herman stretched himself across the area between the stove and the sink where I was trying to get dinner ready.

"Move, Herm." As usual he ignored me beyond giving me a soulful glance. "I thought the festival was strictly the Restaurant Association's deal. What do the merchants have to do with it?"

Uncle Mike grimaced. "They're pretty much the same association—they just meet in different places. But the board is trying to come up with some package deals to attract out-of-towners. You know, lodging along with tickets to the festival and maybe a seat at the banquet."

"We're doing a course at the banquet. Did I tell you?" I got the chicken and rice onto a serving platter and put it in the microwave.

"Madge mentioned it," Uncle Mike said and blushed.

Uncle Mike and Madge Robicheaux have a thing

going, although he's still sort of embarrassed about it. Nate and I think it's cute, which is probably annoying for both my uncle and Nate's mom.

I pretended that I hadn't noticed the blush. "We're just doing the first course. McKinley's is doing the main and Grace Peters is doing the dessert. I don't know who's doing the appetizers yet."

Uncle Mike shook his head. "Peters's stuff stinks. They're going to end the meal on a downer."

"Yeah, I don't know why they chose her. Maybe to get somebody new." Plus, Grace Peters had golden hair and big blue eyes. She'd perfected a smoldering look I'd seen her use a couple of times on the town's movers and shakers. And the officers of the Restaurant Association were mostly male.

"Anyway, it's great you're going to do part of the banquet," Uncle Mike said. "Good publicity."

We settled down at the table and had general conversation about the Merchants Association, blueberry jam, and just how much snow we were likely to get from the latest storm, which was still stalled somewhere on the Western Slope. I'd just gotten up to see what ice cream I had in the freezer when someone hammered on my door.

Herman whimpered, and Uncle Mike pushed himself up from the table. "What the hell?"

I started for the door, where the hammering was still going on, but Uncle Mike grabbed my arm. "Let me open it. You hold onto Herman."

That was a good idea, since Herman had moved from whimpering to growling along with stalking toward the door as if he'd actually protect us. In fact, it was more likely we'd protect him, but I wouldn't tell him that.

Uncle Mike threw open the door. "What the hell…" he started, then paused. "Donnie?"

I moved closer to the open door and saw Donnie McCray, Dolce's dad and Uncle Mike's foreman, standing on my doorstep. He's a big man, but right then he looked like he was ready to collapse. "Come inside." I grabbed his arm. "Sit down. What's wrong? Are you hurt?"

Donnie dropped onto my couch, gasping. "There's a woman," he began and then stopped to catch his breath.

"What woman?" Uncle Mike said. "Where?"

"Up by the road. In a car." Donnie gasped again, and I dropped to my knees beside him.

"What about her, Donnie? What's wrong?"

"She dead," he blurted out. "She's dead up there in the car."

Chapter 4

Uncle Mike and I grabbed our jackets and trotted out the front door. I thought about leaving Herman behind, but he was already ahead of us, galloping toward the county road that runs by the farm. "Herman," I yelled. "Get back here. Heel, dammit." Sometimes Herman remembers the obedience lessons he took long ago, but usually not. This time he slowed, but stayed ahead of us, still at a brisk trot.

Donnie came too, moving slowly behind us. After we'd jogged up the drive and onto the highway, we'd come a quarter mile or so from the cabin. I saw a car on the shoulder of the road. "Is that it?"

Donnie nodded. He looked like he'd rather be almost anywhere but here. Snow had begun to fall lightly, giving the frozen ruts in the drive a sort of speckled look. It felt like the kind of snow that would pick up speed and force pretty soon.

As we got closer, I recognized the car. Or anyway, I recognized that I'd seen the car before, but I couldn't remember where. I followed Uncle Mike to the driver's side. He'd grabbed a flashlight before we'd left the cabin. Now he flipped it on to peer into the driver's side window. After a moment, he gasped and moved away quickly. But not so quickly that I hadn't seen the woman in the driver's seat.

She was pushed up against the driver's side

window. Her eyes were open, staring at the car roof. When I realized that the smear on the window beside her was blood, I staggered to the side of the road and worked on not being sick.

It was the blonde, of course. That's why I'd recognized the car. And she looked thoroughly dead. No wonder Donnie had been so freaked out.

"Get back," Uncle Mike said, waving us away from the car. "There might be evidence here. The cops won't want us tramping all over it."

Cops. Until that moment, I hadn't put things together, but now I did. We'd need to call the cops. Actually, we needed to call Ethan Fowler, the Shavano Chief of Police, because this was absolutely going to be something he'd be in charge of.

Unfortunately, I didn't have his number, but I knew someone who did. My best friend, Susa Sondergaard, had had what she called a *fling* with Fowler around Christmas time. They weren't currently together, but they weren't entirely apart either. Susa would know how to reach him.

I grabbed Herman and pulled him down to the cabin. Then I grabbed my phone. Susa picked up after a couple of rings. "Hey, kid, what's up?"

"Do you have Ethan Fowler's number? I need to get in touch with him. Like right now."

"Oh, God, what's happened?" Susa asked. Because the last few times I've needed to get in touch with Fowler it was because somebody was dead. Which was still true, of course. "There's a dead woman in a car up by the county road. Uncle Mike's called 911, but we need Fowler."

"Okay, I'll give him a call. Would you like me to

drive out, too?"

"No, hon, but thanks for the offer. I'll talk to you later."

"Yeah, you will," Susa said dryly. "Count on it."

I didn't want to go out there again, but it was cowardly to leave Uncle Mike at the murder scene by himself. I grabbed a heavier jacket and walked up the twisting drive, after closing Herman in the cabin. It was snowing more heavily now, small icy flakes that pinged against my forehead. Uncle Mike and Donnie stood behind the car with the body, although they both looked like they'd prefer to be inside or somewhere else far away.

As I got closer I heard the distant sound of sirens and saw the reflection of flashing lights in the distance. Shavano's finest were on their way. I only hoped Fowler was with them.

He was. The next hour was sort of chaotic and a bit scary. Fowler sent us to the cabin as soon as he'd gotten a look at the car. "We'll take your statements in a few minutes," he said, moving us politely but firmly away from the scene.

It was a lot more than a few minutes, but I didn't mind. I was much happier in my own house than I would have been out on the county road in a rapidly worsening snowstorm. I got coffee for Uncle Mike and Donnie, and brought out a bottle of whiskey when Uncle Mike asked for it. I noticed the two of them doctored their coffee liberally, and I didn't blame them. I grabbed a cup for myself.

When Fowler finally appeared, he looked half frozen, too. He took me up on my offer of coffee, but I didn't bother to offer the whiskey since he was on duty and all.

Fowler sat down in a chair opposite the couch where Uncle Mike and Donnie were sprawled, taking out his notebook. "Okay, what happened when?"

Donnie leaned forward, placing his doctored coffee on the coffee table. "I had to go to City Market for some breakfast stuff. When I came back, I saw that car sitting on the side of the road. I thought maybe something was wrong, so I parked at the house and walked up to the car. And I saw her. I ran down to the cabin and told Mike and Roxy." He paused, glancing longingly at his coffee cup.

Fowler nodded. "What time was that?"

"Carmen had me go to the store after dinner, maybe around seven thirty or so. I got back around eight or eight fifteen." Carmen was Donnie's wife. My guess was she could tell Fowler to the minute when Donnie left and returned.

"Was the car there when you left for the market?"

Donnie paused to think. "Nope. I'm pretty sure it wasn't. If it had been, I'd have stopped then."

Fowler turned to Uncle Mike. "How about you—did you notice the car earlier?"

Uncle Mike shook his head. "I came down for dinner around six thirty or so. I didn't see anything."

"It was dark, though, right?" Fowler took a careful sip of his coffee then gave me a grateful look.

"Still some light in the sky," Uncle Mike said.

"How about you, Roxy?"

"I didn't go out all afternoon, so I didn't see anything. Dolce and Bridget were here, but they didn't mention seeing a car when they got here."

"Dolce and Bridget?"

"My assistants," I explained. "Bridget Sullivan and Donnie's daughter, Dolce."

Fowler copied down the names, then flipped to another page of his notebook. "Did any of you recognize her?"

Donnie looked a little queasy. "I didn't look at her too close, but she didn't seem familiar."

Uncle Mike and I glanced at each other. Fowler noticed. "What?"

"She was here a week or so ago. She said she was looking for work."

Fowler paused. "Looking for work? With you?"

I nodded. "Yeah. It didn't make sense. I mean, she might have checked at the main house, but I don't know why she'd come to my cabin. She said she'd heard I was hiring."

"Are you?"

"Not at the moment." And I wouldn't have let a stranger into my place without a lot of recommendations from people I knew.

"Did you see her?" Fowler turned to Uncle Mike.

"Yeah. I saw her talking to Roxy, and I was curious, so I walked over. She asked if I needed anyone at the big house."

Fowler narrowed his eyes, glancing back and forth between us. "And you'd never seen her before?"

"That's why it was so weird," I said. "Why would a complete stranger come to my door and ask me for a job? It's not like I've got a sign out front or anything."

"Do you have people coming to the house asking for farm work?"

Uncle Mike shrugged. "Rarely. We use the same crew every year, and I hire them through a contractor.

He's responsible for finding enough people to get the work done. We don't use casual labor. It's too risky."

"What about people who work in the house—cleaners, cooks, like that?"

"Roxy does the cooking." Uncle Mike gave me the ghost of a smile. "Carmen's in charge of the house. I don't think she'd hire somebody off the street."

Donnie shook his head vigorously. "No way. She hires people we know. People's kids and in-laws. Like that." Carmen was one of the toughest taskmasters around, as I knew only too well from my years of working for her when I was a kid. Donnie was right—she'd never hire someone who didn't have several locals to vouch for her.

"Did she give you a name?" Fowler turned to me.

"Nope. We didn't get that far. She said she was a hard worker, but Uncle Mike and I both said we didn't have anything for her. She left right after that."

"That strike you as strange, that she didn't introduce herself?"

I sighed, picking up my coffee again. "The whole thing was strange. The idea someone would come this far out of town looking for a job. The idea she'd heard I was looking to hire someone. None of it made sense." I thought about telling Fowler I'd seen her in town a couple of days ago, but I decided against it. I wasn't sure it was the same woman.

"Did any of you hear anything tonight?" Fowler was carefully expressionless.

"Like a gunshot?" Although it was possible somebody had hit the woman over the head, it was a lot more likely she'd been shot.

"Anything," Fowler said flatly.

Uncle Mike and I looked at each other again, but then I shook my head. "We were in the kitchen. We don't usually hear highway noise." *Highway noise* in this case covered gunshots on the county road.

"We didn't hear anything either. Or anyway, I didn't. You can ask Carmen if she heard anything after I left." Donnie looked like he'd just realized Carmen might have been nearby during a shooting. It wasn't something that made him happy.

"I'd like to ask her what she heard. Is she home now?"

Donnie nodded, as Fowler took a last swallow of his coffee. "Okay, I guess that's it. If you remember anything else about this woman or anything that happened this evening, give me a call." Fowler pushed himself to his feet, then turned to me. "Thanks for the coffee."

Donnie and Fowler left, walking toward the McCray house on the other side of the property. Carmen's concern for Donnie would probably be tempered by curiosity about just what the hell was going on. I honestly wished I knew.

Uncle Mike stepped toward the door himself, then paused. "She say anything else before I walked up the other day?"

"Not that I recall. It was pretty much what you heard."

He nodded heavily. "Damnedest thing. You want to come up to the big house tonight?"

I thought about it. I wasn't exactly scared, but I was unsettled. On the other hand, if I was in the cabin, I could get an early start on jam making tomorrow. "I'll be all right."

He nodded. "Okay. But I'm leaving Herman."

I thought about telling him that wasn't necessary, but in fact, it was. I didn't want to be alone that night even though I wanted to stay where I was. "I'll take care of him."

"And he'll take care of you." Uncle Mike kissed my cheek. "Lock up after me."

"Right." I figured I'd be locking my doors a lot for the next few days. Herman or no Herman.

As I secured the door and pulled the shades across the windows, I found myself thinking about the blonde, something I was pretty sure I'd be doing for the next several days. I tried to recreate our conversation, but it had been too long ago and I hadn't been paying attention at the time.

What she'd said to me probably had nothing to do with what happened to her, but I couldn't quite shake the idea that it did. Was it just a coincidence that she'd died on my front step, more or less?

It would have been comforting to think so. But I wasn't sure I could.

Chapter 5

The dead body at the farm was a minor sensation for a couple of days. But after people discovered we didn't know the victim and we didn't know much about what had happened to her, they lost interest. The prevailing theory was the woman had been killed by a hitchhiker. However, the fact the hitchhiker hadn't taken the car made me skeptical.

Nate was sympathetic. But after I said I wasn't too freaked out by finding a dead body—or rather, seeing somebody else find a dead body—he switched to his major concern: Robicheaux Catering's contribution to the Food and Wine Festival.

The festival had begun to take up more of the public interest along with most of our time. It was a four-day deal, although not much happened on the first two days. The Wednesday and Thursday sessions were all about wine, featuring Colorado and New Mexico vintners. There were tastings and discussions and a couple of wine dinners at local restaurants, including High Country. Bridget wouldn't be coming to work on the mail orders on Thursday because High Country was paying her extra to help with set up.

Meanwhile, Nate and I were up to our elbows in butternut squash, having decided to make roasted butternut soup for our first course. To feed two hundred people, we needed around thirty-five normal-sized squashes. There are two schools of thought about peeling butternuts: you can cut them in sections, roast them, and then scrape the flesh off the skin. Or you can peel them and cut them into chunks before you roast them. Both methods are a pain in the ass, but Nate leaned toward the peel them first option. I was agnostic on the subject as long as I had a nice sharp vegetable peeler to work with. We both dived into the prep, although Nate had more to say about it than I did.

I learned not to pay too much attention to his constant, slightly peevish directions about proper peeling and chunking. He was concerned about making a good impression at the dinner. I understood that, although I was still faintly annoyed that he thought I needed instructions and supervision.

We set up in the catering kitchen in the building next door to the café. It had a sturdy prep table in the middle of the workspace, along with a spiffy new commercial stove. We took turns peeling and chunking, piling sheet pans full of squash and loading them into the ovens.

Midway through our squash extravaganza, Nate's older brother, Bobby, stepped in after he'd finished his own prep for the next day's breakfast. Bobby has never been a big supporter of the catering business, largely because Bobby hates any change in the operation of Robicheaux's Café. Since the catering operation had begun to turn a profit, he'd grudgingly come on board, but he still seemed to regard it as Nate's whim. Actually, the catering business had been Madge's idea. And both Nate and Madge had very thoroughly researched the whole thing before they'd gone ahead with it.

Which Bobby knew, although he never appeared to acknowledge it.

Now he regarded the pile of butternut squash with a skeptical eye. "Think you bought enough?"

Nate nodded. "More than."

"So we'll have to use the leftovers in the café?" Bobby didn't look happy about that either, but then Bobby rarely looked happy about anything.

"Probably not," Nate said crisply. "Don't worry about it." He used a cleaver to chop off the round bottom of one of the squashes. The cleaver hit the cutting board with a very solid *thonk.*

Bobby looked like he was considering a more extensive argument about the annoyance this squash was likely to become for him and the café but decided against it. I applauded his decision, believe me.

Madge came in later in the afternoon. I guessed she'd been at one of the wine events, given her rosy glow. I might not have been interested in hearing the lectures, but I definitely would have liked having a couple of glasses of wine along about then.

"How's the squash coming?" she asked cheerfully.

"It's coming." Nate paused to wipe the back of his sleeve across his forehead. "We should have it all roasted in another hour or so. Then we'll put it in the refrigerator until Saturday."

"You're going to make up the soup Saturday afternoon?"

He nodded. "Chopping up the squash and roasting it is the time-consuming part. Boiling it and pureeing it shouldn't be that hard. And we can take it to the event center in soup kettles."

"What about the pecans?"

"Coco's doing them. She's already toasting a bunch for her tassies."

Madge grinned, leaning against the prep table. "Sounds like you've got it all figured out. Good for you."

"I hear McKinley's doing ribs. Lynn Greenwood said they're using her hot sauce as a baste."

Madge's grimace became more pronounced. "I hope they dilute it some. Hank Greenwood really loves Scotch bonnet chilies."

"Well, if they go too heavy on the hot sauce, that should shorten the evening," Nate said dryly.

Madge snickered. "There's an upside to everything, I guess." She leaned up to kiss him on the cheek, then gave me a hug. "Have fun with your squash."

"Oh yeah," Nate muttered. "Highlight of my day."

When everything had been roasted, we heaped the squash into a couple of industrial-sized soup kettles and put them in the walk-in cooler. We'd use the same kettles to boil down the squash on Saturday morning, which would save us time and dishwashing.

"You want some dinner?" Nate asked as we hoisted the last kettle inside. "I think I've got some pot pie in the freezer."

"Why don't we go to Dirty Pete's?" I countered. "It's Thursday. They're not likely to be too crowded."

Nate sighed. "On a normal Thursday, that would be true. On a Thursday during this double damned festival, I'm not so sure."

I sighed, too. "I forgot about that. But the wine dinner is tonight, so a lot of the tourists and local foodies will be at that. Plus, Dirty Pete's isn't on the beaten path."

"True. Okay, let's get cleaned up and see what Harry's got on tap tonight."

Harry Potter, Dirty Pete's very knowledgeable bartender, had a couple of IPA's and a stout from Montana on tap. I went with the IPA with the citra hops since I love the piney taste. "How are the crowds?" I asked him.

Harry shrugged. "We've had a few tourists wander in, but we're not on the radar for this particular festival." He gave me a dry smile. "Foodies aren't going to stop by for nachos."

Nate and I glanced at each other and shrugged back. "I guess we need to order some nachos."

"My kind of foodies." Harry entered the order on his computer.

True foodies might not have stopped by Pete's, but the people who produced their food did. I recognized cooks from three different places, along with a couple of my fellow farmers market types. Bianca Jordan was sitting at a table at the side. When she saw us, she waved, and we brought our beers from the bar.

"How's the banquet coming?" she asked as we sat down.

"Okay. If you like butternut squash. Which I may again six months from now." The smell of butternut squash had worked its way into my skin over the past day. I was declaring a moratorium on all winter squash, and possibly extending it to kabocha and delicata.

Bianca gave me a sympathetic smile. "Yeah, we make butternut soup about twice a year then freeze it. I figure I'm only going to go to all that trouble a couple of times."

"We got the prep work and the roasting done today," Nate said. "All we have to do on Saturday is boil it and puree it."

"And add cream, and pour it in the bowls, and garnish it." I took a swallow of my beer. "At least we don't have to serve it."

"What else is on the menu?" Bianca asked.

"Ribs from McKinley's with a mop featuring Lockwoods' blackberry hot sauce. I don't know what sides they're doing, but probably potatoes in some form."

Bianca grimaced, a lot like Madge had. "Lockwoods' stuff specializes in pain. I'm all for chilies, but they need to be used for flavor, not punishment." She took a sip of her own beer, her eyes taking on a calculating gleam. "What's for dessert?"

I'd forgotten that Bianca had been frozen out of doing dessert for the banquet in favor of Grace Peters. I glanced at Nate. "I've got no idea."

"Chocolate decadence cake," he said without looking up.

I wondered simultaneously where he'd heard what Grace Peters was making and why he wasn't looking at me, but I wasn't sure how to ask him either question.

"Holy heartburn," Bianca muttered. "After incendiary ribs, a heavy chocolate cake is the last thing people need."

"I don't think Grace Peters knew what the main course was going to be," Nate explained. "We only found out because Roxy heard Lynn Lockwood talking about it. The festival board didn't tell any of us what the other cooks were making."

That seemed to be a natural opening. "How did you

find out what Peters was doing?" I asked, all wide-eyed innocence.

"She was at the Blue Spot when I was playing pool with Spence last week." Nate took a swallow of his beer. I checked for some sign of guilt but didn't see anything.

Spence was the chef at High Country, and the Blue Spot was a dive where a lot of line cooks hung out. It wasn't surprising that Grace Peters had been there, too, although she wasn't exactly a line cook.

"Coco says Grace's chocolate decadence cake is her signature dish. Maybe that's why she went with it," Nate went on.

Bianca snorted. "Signature dish, my ass. Chocolate cake only takes you so far. She'd better have more than one string to her bow if she expects to make it up here." Bianca, it went without saying, was a multi-hit wonder. People lined up for her muffins and seed bread. And on the infrequent occasions when she did bagels, the news flashed around town like Paul Revere's ride. She didn't do many cakes, but her cookies and brownies were superlative.

"As I understand it, she's sticking with pastry," Nate said. "She didn't say much about bread."

Bianca looked like she was considering some choice comments about the advisability of not baking bread in a town like Shavano. But if Grace confined herself to pastry, she wouldn't be competing with Bianca, so maybe it behooved her to be generous. "Let me know how decadent her cake is."

I contented myself with wondering just what Grace Peters had been doing in a dive bar frequented by the rowdier line cooks. And how she'd gotten into a conversation with Nate, but that was really none of my business.

Which is to say it *was* my business, but I wasn't sure how to ask Nate about it.

Caroline, Dirty Pete's wizard of a waitress, brought us a plate of nachos, which we shared with Bianca. "You need to bring me more jam," she said midway through the platter. "I've had a run on your stuff since the festival started. I'm almost out."

Bianca sold a lot of my jam, no doubt driven by the smell of her fresh-baked bread. "Okay, I'll bring you a load tomorrow when I get a minute."

"That'll do it. Tourists love to bring home exotic foods from the provinces." Bianca's smile was dry.

The evening wound down, and I tried to pull my brain away from speculation about Grace Peters to consideration of what we had to do over the next couple of days.

Nate walked me to my truck, both of us hunched against the cold breezes of the evening. He put an arm around my shoulders, pulling me close so that I could cuddle up next to him and share a little body heat. "You want to stay with me Saturday night after we finish the banquet?" he asked.

"Sure," I said a little absently. We usually spent the weekend together because we didn't get to spend much time together during the week.

Except Nate had had time to play pool with Spence and hang out with Grace Peters.

That isn't fair, and you know it.

I did know it, but I still felt vaguely grumpy.

We stopped at my truck, and I put my arms around his waist, staring up at him in the frosty night. He leaned down to press his forehead against mine. "Thanks, Rox. We got through a hundred pounds of squash today. I couldn't have done it without you."

I sighed. "Yeah, and if I don't touch or smell a butternut squash again for the foreseeable future, I'll be very happy."

The next day I stopped by Marcus Jordan's butcher shop on the way from dropping off the jam at Bianca's bakery. Marcus is Bianca's son, which gives him a leg up in the Shavano food world. His stuff is better than any other meat you can get in Shavano, and the prices reflect that fact. Still, Marcus's bacon is Best of Breed.

I didn't see Marcus when I came into the shop, but his wife, Sara, was behind the counter in her Jordan's Meats apron. Sara and I don't get along, but then Sara doesn't get along with anyone, so I didn't take it personally. "What can I do for you?" She gave me a slightly suspicious look.

"I need a pound of the bacon, and maybe a pound of your stew meat, too." We hadn't had stew in a while, and I was up for anything I could toss into the slow cooker.

Judging from Sara's expression, measuring out two pounds of meat ranked as a major imposition on her time, but she did it anyway. "Heard you had some excitement out at your place," she said as she wrapped the bacon.

I'd been so concentrated on butternut squash soup for the past couple of days that it took me a moment to understand what she was talking about. "More upsetting than exciting, but yeah, we did."

"Who was the woman who got killed? Anybody I know?" Sara went on weighing out my order.

"Not that anyone has mentioned to us." If Fowler did discover the blonde's identity, I hoped he'd tell us, but I figured there were no guarantees.

"Kind of weird, I'd say. Stranger coming out to your place and getting killed." Sara gave me a skeptical look, like we'd somehow arranged for the murder to take place at the farm.

I gritted my teeth. "We're in the country, a long way from everybody else. Maybe they thought she wouldn't be found."

"Maybe." Sara looked like she thought that was unlikely. She had a point.

I decided a change of subject was in order. "Bianca said you had a new assistant. How's she working out?"

Sara stared at me for a moment, eyes wide. Then she shoved the packages over the counter. "She's gone. She didn't work out. That's twenty-two fifty."

That was a little abrupt, even for Sara. But the whole conversation had been sort of bizarre. I paid up and left with my purchases.

"Did Fowler ever find out who the murder victim was?" I asked Uncle Mike at dinner that night.

He shrugged. "If he did, he didn't tell me. She should have had car registration or something."

Assuming the car was hers and registered in her name. Assuming she was carrying identification when she went out that night. Assuming all kinds of things I didn't know if we could assume. "I still don't understand why she was out here."

"Probably never know. Unless they find out who killed her." Uncle Mike didn't sound particularly interested. It was a puzzle, but not one we could solve. I saw his point of view, but I couldn't shake the sense that something was happening here.

And it was something we needed to know more about.

Chapter 6

On Saturday, I met Nate at the catering kitchen around eleven. He'd had to work breakfast at the café and do his prep for Sunday brunch, so this was the earliest we could get started. It made no sense that he was still doing breakfast, given that he had a major dinner that evening, but that was the way things were. At the moment, anyway.

He seemed harried and a little snappish, although we'd have ample time to finish before the banquet. He studied the pans of squash with something like resentment.

"What time are we supposed to be there?" I asked, just to be on the safe side.

"Five thirty or thereabouts," Nate said. "Dinner's at seven and we'll need to get set up and dished up. Ready."

Set up and *ready* meant laying out two hundred soup bowls in a more or less logical arrangement and then filling them as quickly as we could, while still making everything look good. Cool, cool, cool as they say.

Nate grabbed the first pot with the roasted squash. "We need to get the cooking done ASAP. We've got no slack time."

We seldom had slack time, and boiling down the squash wouldn't take that long, but I let it go. No point in making him even more stressed and grumpy.

One by one, we wrestled the soup kettles out of the refrigerator and onto the stove, then added equal parts water and chicken stock. While we waited for the squash to soften, I went next door to the restaurant to get the pecans from Coco.

Nate's sister was in charge of desserts and salads at the café. She was a gifted pastry chef, and she could throw together some sumptuous rolls in less time than it took me to find the yeast. Unfortunately, Bobby kept her on a tight budget, which meant she didn't get a chance to do as much as she wanted to. The catering company had given her a lot more room to maneuver, and the list of possible desserts on our sample menus was one of our major draws.

I found her working on cinnamon rolls and muffins for the Sunday brunch, one of the meals where she got to spread her wings a bit. "Hey," she said. "How's the squash?"

"Yellow. And mealy. I'm pretty much off squash for the time being."

"Works for me. You want your pecans?" She pointed toward a five-gallon tub on the other counter.

I sighed. I'd likely be doing that a lot today. I hefted up the tub. Or I tried to.

Coco sighed. "Get Nate. Or get a wagon or something. That thing weighs a good fifteen pounds. I've been throwing toasted pecans into it all week."

Bobby was on the other side of the kitchen, but asking him for help was out of the question since he considered the catering business to be strictly Nate's affair. I finally found an aluminum shopping cart. Coco helped me load the tub of pecans into it and I wheeled it to the catering kitchen.

Nate blinked when he saw me. "Good grief. I guess we've got enough pecans."

"I guess we do. Where should I put this?" Needless to say, we were going to have to parcel the pecans out into smaller portions, but I didn't know if we'd do it at the banquet hall or here.

Nate shook his head. "I don't know exactly. Let me see if I can find some other jars we can use."

That was typical of the way the day went. First we had to get the pecans divided into smaller containers. Then we had to start pureeing the squash, taking turns running the café's huge immersion blender in the soup kettle before adding the cream. By mid-afternoon, my shoulders were aching, and my hands had a permanent cramp. "How many more pots are there?" I asked. I was hoping Nate would say we were done.

"There's one more, but I can do it. Why don't you go home and put your feet up until it's time to go to the banquet hall?"

That sounded wonderful, but I wasn't ready to abandon him to his fate. Not when his mood was already turning south. "What about you? You need to get off your feet, too."

"I'll go home as soon as I finish this pot." He picked up the immersion blender, ready to go again. "Meet me here at five, okay? We'll load up the kettles for transport."

I nodded. "Okay. I can do that." I left more quickly than I probably needed to, but I was looking forward to putting my feet up and then taking a shower. Once again I had butternut squash in my hair.

I did wash up, and I did rest for an hour or so, but I

headed back sooner than I wanted to.

I drove my truck to the café because I wasn't sure the SUV Nate was using would be big enough to carry all the pots of soup. As it turned out the SUV could carry the stockpots, but it couldn't carry both of us as well. I followed Nate as he drove very carefully to the banquet hall.

We parked near the door to the kitchen, and I helped Nate tote the stockpots in. There were three of them, twenty-four quarts each, which should have provided more than enough for two hundred. I went to my truck to grab half the pecans and a gallon container of chopped green onions. Nate had the rest.

The banquet hall kitchen had a large island for plating, and we managed to set up a hundred cup-sized bowls. We didn't yet have the final count of people, but we were still working with the initial estimate of two hundred.

Nate hefted the first kettle onto the stove while I finished laying out the bowls. Once the soup had come to a simmer, he ladled it into a container he could serve from and started dipping, one cup per bowl. I followed along behind, placing a small pile of chopped pecans in the middle of each bowl. Nate would step back to refill the container whenever he ran dry, giving the bowls a critical gaze and pointing out pecan piles that were nonstandard. I gritted my teeth, adjusted pecans, and kept going.

We finished in decent time. When most of the bowls were filled, we did a second round, me sprinkling a few green onions and Nate doing an artistic dribble of olive oil. He did one more pass with his kitchen towel, wiping up any dribbles of soup that had landed on the rims and muttering imprecations against banquet service. I couldn't blame him. I felt sort of the same.

After we emptied the first kettle, Nate hoisted the second one up in its place.

We were sliding into our "well-oiled machine" routine, which we did regularly when we catered a meal. The difference here was that as we worked, we were surrounded by chaos. The cooks from McKinley's had shown up with their racks of ribs to be warmed in the oven. The blackberry hot sauce made the meat look a little dark, and I wondered if people would think they were overdone. I wondered if they *were* overdone. Ribs were tricky under the best of circumstances, and these definitely weren't the best.

Wait staff hurried by with trays of appetizers that looked like bruschetta and something resembling meatballs on a toothpick. I'd never found out who was doing the apps, but these looked like they might have come from one of the other catering companies in town. Their lack of imagination was one of the reasons Madge had decided Shavano was ripe for another caterer.

Before I could ask who was in charge of hors d'oeuvres, Nate returned with more soup. We finished filling the first hundred bowls and Nate glanced up at the clock. Ten after seven. He frowned as he watched the wait staff hurry by with their uninspired apps. "They should start putting these out so we can get to the next hundred. They're cutting it damn close."

"Everything's running late," one of the other cooks explained. "The guest of honor was late getting here. Greeting his adoring fans." The guest of honor was a TV chef of questionable skill, but the crowds loved him.

Nate's jaw firmed. Something else to be pissed about. If the soup had to sit out too long, it would get cold. I was about to suggest moving it to the warming table, when the head waiter pushed through the swinging door. "Okay, we can get started with the soup. People are beginning to take their seats."

The wait staff began loading up their trays, and we worked quickly, replacing the full bowls on the worktable with empty ones. The second hundred bowls would have to be done a lot faster since the waiters would be coming in to refill their trays as soon as they were emptied. Nate picked up his pace, trying to fill the bowls with enough precision that we wouldn't have to do too much cleanup. I tried to keep up with him, making sure the pecans were centered but not obsessing over the shape of the piles. Green onions, olive oil, cleanup, and another rank of bowls disappeared, leaving us to set up again.

We couldn't pause to see how things were going. Instead we kept dipping and pouring and sprinkling and dribbling. Nate's olive oil squiggles became less artistic and my pecans became heaps rather than clusters, but the bowls went out without pause, which was the major thing. Finally, the head waiter leaned into the kitchen again. "Soup's done. Clear off for the main."

Nate and I stepped away from the table as the squad from McKinley's began to lay out the dinner plates. I couldn't tell what the sides were, since at the moment they were struggling to get the ribs on the plate without splattering blackberry sauce over everything.

I leaned my head on Nate's shoulder, catching my breath. Catering for parties of twenty or thirty was nothing compared to this. My hand still felt cramped from grasping pecans, and butternut squash soup was dribbled all the way down my apron.

"We did it, babe." I gave him a squeeze. "You're a star."

"Damn that chef," Nate muttered. "The last bowls looked like crap."

They hadn't, not really. But I sensed this wasn't the time to argue. Maybe later I could get him to accept that we'd done a good job.

The wait staff were bringing trays of empty soup bowls in now, always a good sign. You don't want to see half-empty bowls, indicating that somebody took a few bites and decided not to finish eating.

I stepped back to get out of the way of the McKinley's cooks, and my cell phone vibrated in my pocket. I found an unoccupied corner of the kitchen and checked the number. Uncle Mike. Who should have known I was in the middle of service, so he shouldn't have called me.

Unless it was something important.

I connected quickly. "Hi, we're in the middle of service, so I can't talk long. What's up?"

"Fowler's here. He's found out something important. You need to come home. ASAP. He'll wait for you."

I frowned. "What is it? What's happened?"

"Not over the phone. Come on home. As soon as you can get here." He disconnected, as ice water dripped down my spine.

I shoved my phone into my pocket and trotted across to where Nate was watching the trays of soup bowls return to the kitchen. "Uncle Mike just called. I have to go. There's an emergency of some kind."

Nate frowned. "What happened?"

"I don't know. He said he didn't want to tell me over the phone. But I need to go home."

"All right. Help me with the clean-up, and then you can head out." He gave me an unsmiling look.

I was tired. Very tired. And frankly, I was sick of the attitude. I knew Nate was tired, too, but he was being a pain in the ass. I figured he could load the empty soup kettles and the other containers on his own. He was a big boy.

My jaw firmed. "I can't. Sorry. I've got to go now." The more I thought about it, the more worried I was about Uncle Mike. He wasn't the type to cry wolf. If he said I needed to be there, I needed to be there.

Nate's jaw hardened. "Come on, Roxanne, I need your help here. Part of the job. It won't take long."

"I have to go. Now." My own jaw felt pretty hard all of a sudden. I'd been putting up with his bad temper for several days, and I was short-tempered myself.

"You're going to leave me to do the rest of it on my own?" Nate looked outraged, which was ridiculous. He didn't have that much to do.

I nodded. "Yeah, that's exactly what I'm going to do." I pulled off my apron and sprinted for the door without looking back.

I might apologize at some point, or I might not. Mainly I needed to get to the farm and find out what had gone so ominously wrong. And Nate needed to chill.

When I got to the farm, Fowler's car was parked outside the main house. I guessed that was where he and Uncle Mike were. I pulled my truck in and trotted up to the front door.

I grew up in the main house, and I still have a bedroom there if I need another place to sleep, but I don't spend much time there these days since the cabin is where I live and work. I pushed open the front door and trotted up the hall to the living room, only to hear Uncle Mike's voice from the kitchen.

He and Fowler were seated at the kitchen table with cups of coffee. They both glanced up when I came in—neither of them looked happy, but neither of them was bleeding so far as I could see.

"Okay." I grabbed a chair and pulled it up beside Uncle Mike. "What's going on?"

Fowler glanced at Uncle Mike, then reached toward a pile of items in front of him on the table. "We finally identified the woman who was killed out here. Her name's Muriel Cates." He dropped a New Mexico driver's license encased in a plastic bag in front of me.

The woman who stared back—Muriel Cates, based on the name on the license—looked sort of like the blonde who'd knocked on my door but mostly not. I guessed that the picture had been taken a few years ago, since she looked both younger and less tough. Then again, driver's license photos weren't exactly glamour shots.

I glanced back and forth between them. "Is that it? So far as I know, I've never heard of Muriel Cates."

Fowler shrugged. "I didn't expect you to have heard of her. But we also found this in her room in town."

He dropped another plastic bag in front of me, enclosing another New Mexico license along with some other cards and papers. I looked at the picture on the license, but it didn't appear to be Muriel Cates. I turned to the name.

And froze.

Linda Constantine it said.

I stared at the picture again, trying to see if it was the blonde, but it still didn't look like her. My hand closed into a fist as I looked up at Fowler. "That's my mother," I said softly. "Linda Constantine. That's my mother's name. Only I haven't seen her in thirty years, so I'm not even sure what she looks like."

Chapter 7

"It's not the same woman," Uncle Mike said. "That license is Linda's. But that blonde was somebody else."

I didn't look at him. All of a sudden, I couldn't take my gaze off that license.

I don't really remember my mother. She left my dad and me when I was around three years old. I have some vague recollections of a woman who might be her, but I'm not sure they're real. I didn't know what had happened to her after she left, and I'm not sure my dad did either. After he died when I was sixteen, I helped Uncle Mike go through his things. I found a few photographs that were probably taken early in their marriage, and that was all I had of her.

I'd never wanted more. She left, we moved to Colorado to live with Uncle Mike and Aunt Rhoda, and that was the end of it. So far as I knew, she'd never tried to get in touch with either my father or me.

"She's not Linda," Uncle Mike repeated. "Linda would be older, closer to my age. And she was a tall woman—not as tall as Roxy, but tall. That Muriel Cates was short. She wasn't Linda."

"No, I agree," Fowler said. "It's unlikely that she was Roxy's mother. But could she have some other connection to the family? Why would she have Linda Constantine's driver's license, along with the other documents?"

I looked at the plastic bag again. Along with the driver's license, I saw what looked like a gas card and a couple of letters. "Did my mother write those?"

Fowler shook his head. "They were written to her. Dated several years ago."

"Linda's maiden name was Murphy, not Cates. Of course, she could have gotten married again later on. Steve didn't have much contact with her after the divorce." Uncle Mike rubbed his forehead.

"You think Muriel Cates might be related to me? My half-sister?" My throat felt tight all of a sudden. I'd never thought about the possibility I might have half-siblings out there somewhere.

"Based on her driver's license, Muriel Cates was older than you are," Fowler said. "She's most likely not your half-sister, unless Linda Constantine was married before she married your father."

Uncle Mike shook his head. "No. She and Steve were barely in their twenties when they got married."

"Did Linda have any siblings? Could Muriel be related that way?"

"Why does she have to be related? Maybe she got all this stuff some other way. Maybe she stole it." Uncle Mike sounded annoyed, and I could see his point. But I could also see Fowler's. And I wanted to know what was going on.

"If I gave you a DNA sample, could you test it?" I asked. "Could you find out if Muriel Cates was related to me?"

Fowler frowned. "I could do that, if that's what you want. It might help us find out more about her."

"That's nuts. Why would you want to do that? She's not your mom. I know that for a fact." Uncle

Mike gave me a fierce look.

I had no idea why he was so upset, but I knew I had to do this. "I know she's not my mom, but maybe she's related to me some other way. What can it hurt to find out?"

Uncle Mike still looked fierce, but he subsided into silence.

I turned to Fowler. "Where do I need to go to give the sample?"

"As it happens, I brought a DNA kit with me. It's pretty easy to do." Fowler's expression was bland, but I figured he'd been hoping I'd volunteer.

The sample was basically a swab of my cheek, awkward but painless. Fowler tucked it away, then pushed to his feet. "I'll let you know what they find out. Shouldn't take too long."

I wasn't sure how long *too long* was, but I figured I could wait. Once Fowler was out the door, I turned to Uncle Mike. "Are you okay?"

He snorted. "Damn fool thing to do, Roxanne. Why would you want to know?"

"I don't know anything about the Murphys. I don't know anything about Linda Constantine, as far as that goes." I stared down at my hands. "Maybe I need to find out a little more."

"Like what?" Uncle Mike glowered at me. "She walked out on Steve, didn't want to be a farm wife. Don't know what she thought she was signing up for. Steve was a farmer. Did she think he was going to get a job in town or something?"

"Dad never talked about her. I don't even know where she came from."

"Clayton, New Mexico," Uncle Mike said. "Just

like Steve and me. That's where we all were from. Steve inherited some land from our grandparents, and that's what he was working. After Linda left, he sold it and came up here, invested his money in the farm."

"Did my mother stay in New Mexico after Dad left for Colorado?"

"No idea," Uncle Mike said shortly. "I doubt it. She wanted to move to the city."

"Albuquerque?"

"More like Los Angeles. Or maybe Chicago. She wanted to put some distance between herself and the mountains. She was supposed to pay Steve child support, but that stopped after a couple years. Not that we needed it." He gave me another dark look.

I knew the bare bones of the story. My mom walked out. Uncle Mike gave Dad the chance to buy in on a fruit orchard in western Colorado. Dad packed up everything and moved us to Shavano, where we stayed and prospered.

But I knew next to nothing about the other half of my heritage, the Murphy half we'd left behind in Eastern New Mexico. "Did my mother have sisters and brothers?"

Uncle Mike shrugged again, stiff-shouldered. "A sister. Don't remember her name. Their folks weren't around. I think their mom died and their dad moved someplace else."

So I might have some cousins. And one of them might have been Muriel Cates. I still felt a little queasy about that. "Muriel Cates may turn out to be no relation. If that's true, the only mystery would be how she got hold of my mother's stuff."

"Probably stole it, like I said." Uncle Mike's jaw

firmed. "How was the dinner?"

It took me a minute to realize which dinner he was talking about, and then I felt a sudden flush of guilt. I'd walked out on Nate because I'd thought there was some emergency I had to deal with. As it happened, it wasn't so much an emergency as a puzzle.

"It was okay. We got the soup out, and they seemed to like it." That was one thing I'd missed—feedback from the diners.

"I guess you had to leave in the middle of things." Uncle Mike looked a little embarrassed but only a little.

"Yeah, I did. But we were through serving, so there wasn't much left to do."

"I just…" He paused for a few moments, then he shrugged. "It threw me for a loop, seeing those things of Linda's. I know she wasn't Linda, but it was sort of a gut punch."

"It's okay. I'm glad you called. I needed to be here." That might or might not have been true, but I'd always go if Uncle Mike called. Considering all he'd done for me in my life, I could put up with a little inconvenience.

And if Nate couldn't understand that, then he had bigger problems than just having to do some work on his own.

I went back to my cabin with Herman. I needed some reassurance, and since I obviously wasn't going to be spending the night with Nate, Herman was the best I could do. In fact, I should probably have called Nate, but I didn't. I was more tired than I'd expected, probably from stress and delayed reaction. Whatever the reason, I just didn't feel like talking to him right then.

Maybe tomorrow.

I woke late the next morning, a little groggy. Herman was making whimpering noises to let me know he wanted to go out. I pulled a jacket on over my sweatshirt and took him into the front yard. The day looked misty turning toward rain. A good day to spend looking at jam recipes and ignoring the fact I hadn't heard from my boyfriend.

By mid-afternoon I was bored enough that I decided to try making some whiskey flavored peach preserves. I usually use fresh fruit for those, but I had some frozen fruit sitting around, and I figured I might as well give it a try. I freeze the fruit in season, and I add the amount of sugar I need for jam, so it usually works out. On the other hand, peaches have an unholy amount of liquid even when they're fresh, so you need to be careful with the boiling step, and you need to add more pectin than usual.

I was trying to judge how well the preserves were setting up, and whether I needed to add more pectin or not, when the phone rang.

Nate!

I let it ring a couple of times while I turned off the burner. But it wasn't Nate, it was Susa.

"So what's up with you and Nate?" she said as soon as we'd gotten through the hello's.

"What do you mean?" It was unlikely Susa could have heard about my walking out of the banquet, given the chaos that was going on in the kitchen last night.

"I mean I saw him sitting with Grace Peters and a bunch of other people at the Blue Spot last night."

My heart promptly dropped to somewhere around my toes, and I found myself clutching the phone so hard my knuckles went white. "What were you doing in the Blue Spot?" I asked, stalling for time.

Unfortunately, Susa knows me too well to be distracted. "Having a beer with Wilson. Don't change the subject. What's up with you and Nate?"

"I had to leave the banquet before we did cleanup. Uncle Mike had an emergency."

"An emergency? What happened?"

I wasn't sure how much to tell Susa, but Fowler hadn't asked me to keep things quiet, so I gave her an outline.

Susa was silent for a moment. "That's…weird," she said finally. "I mean really weird."

"Yeah. Uncle Mike was shaken up. So was I."

"Do you think she wanted to talk to you about your mother?"

"I don't know. She didn't act like it. I mean, she didn't say anything about my mom the one time we talked to each other."

"Why else would she have your mother's ID? It sounds like she wanted to prove to you she knew your mom."

I paused. That honestly hadn't occurred to me until then. "Yeah, I guess it does."

"Did you tell Nate about it?"

I sighed. "No. At the time I was just in a rush to get home. Uncle Mike didn't tell me what was going on, just that he needed me. And afterward I didn't feel up to it."

"And he went out with Peters?" Susa snorted. "That sucks."

No kidding. "I don't know what he did after I left. So you're going out with Wilson Krebs again?" That was a pretty ham-fisted attempt to change the subject, but Susa let me get by with it.

"Yeah, for right now. So should I come over?"

I thought about it. As an independent, self-reliant woman I shouldn't need to vent. But this was Susa. We'd been venting to each other since second grade. "Sure. I'm making peach preserves."

"Be there in a few."

I gave Susa a more detailed explanation of what had gone on at the banquet and afterward while she snuggled with Herman. When I'd finished, she sighed—I was afraid she was going to tell me I'd screwed up, which I'd already begun to suspect. But she surprised me.

"What do you remember about your mother?"

"Nothing really." I returned to my jam. "She left when I was little. And she never tried to contact me. So far as I know, that is. It was just me and my dad. And Uncle Mike, after Aunt Rhoda died. And Carmen and Donnie. And, you know, lots of people." Including Susa's mom, who'd been a kind of surrogate aunt until she and Susa's dad had retired to Phoenix.

"I know. I remember. I always thought it was sort of cool that you had two dads looking out for you. Your dad was a stand-up guy."

"Yeah, he was." I started the jam pot again so I wouldn't be tempted to think about my dad too much. It always made me sad.

"I take it Mike wasn't a big fan of your mom's."

I grimaced. "Definitely not."

Susa walked over to the counter where I was working. "What are you going to do about Nate?"

"I haven't decided. I feel like it's sort of his move.

We're still working together in Robicheaux's Catering until I hear otherwise. If he doesn't get in touch with me about future jobs, I guess that tells me where I stand." Although my heart dropped a bit as I said it.

Susa took a spoonful from a bowl of the experimental preserves. "You could call him."

"The only reason I'd call him would be to apologize. And right now, I don't feel like doing that. My leaving didn't hurt him. And I needed to go. And he'd been sort of a jerk for a couple of days before that." Constantine pride was a pain in the neck, but it was my family legacy.

"For what it's worth, I don't think he was *with* Grace Peters. He was sitting next to her, but there were a lot of other people. Maybe cooks from the festival." Susa shrugged. "She appeared to be a lot more interested in him than he was in her."

I wanted to ask her how he'd looked, if he'd seemed mad or sad or…I didn't know exactly. But that sounded too much like high school. We were all adults here, supposedly.

"What about you and Wilson? I thought you were going out with Fowler." Susa had connected with Fowler last winter. They'd seemed like a great couple. But even great couples could have rough spots.

Obviously.

"I thought we were, too, for a while. He's hard to read. I think he's the type who doesn't give much away as far as feelings go. Anyway, Wilson asked me out and Fowler didn't, so we went to the Blue Spot and then we went to his place." She took another spoonful of preserves. "And a good time was had by all."

Susa gave me a smile that wasn't one. We both

were going through some communication-in-the-relationship problems.

Susa stayed for dinner, which pleased both Uncle Mike and Herman. We watched a movie together afterward, after we found one we could all tolerate. She left around nine. Uncle Mike went to the big house at ten, and he took Herman with him this time.

Nate still hadn't called.

The next day, Monday, I was on my own. Bridget was working a private event at High Country, and Dolce had an after-school meeting. To tell the truth, I wasn't too unhappy to be working alone. I was upset about Nate, and I didn't know what to do to make it right. Or even if I could make it right. My Constantine pride still kept me from needing to apologize, but I wanted to talk to him anyway, maybe offer a few explanations. The Grace Peters thing put me off, though. I didn't think Nate would cheat on me out of spite. On the other hand, he might decide I wasn't worth the trouble I was causing him and call it quits.

So I should have called him, but I didn't. And he didn't call me. It was a lot like high school, after all.

Sometime after lunch, I heard a car pull up outside. I'd given up thinking that every random visitor was Nate, but I still had my hopes up when I opened the door.

Of course, it wasn't Nate. It was Fowler. When he showed up at my place, it usually wasn't good news. Particularly when he showed up in uniform as he was currently. I wondered if he had the DNA results already, but that seemed unlikely.

"Hi," I said, "what's up?"

He raised an eyebrow. "Can I come in?"

I stepped back and waved a hand. "Sure, come on in. You want some jam?" I gestured toward the stacks of cases that still hadn't been picked up. "I've got lots."

"A peanut butter and jam sandwich would be great. I missed lunch." He took off his Stetson and tossed it on my coatrack.

"I can probably do better than that. I've got smoked turkey and cheddar from the creamery in Geary if you want something more substantial."

Fowler pulled off his jacket. "Actually, I'm in the mood for PB and J if you've got it."

"Like I said, I've got it."

I dug out some peanut butter and an open jar of peach preserves, along with a loaf of Bianca's whole grain. Fowler took a seat at my kitchen table as I started slapping together a sandwich.

Frankly, I was curious. When Fowler took the time to drive from his office downtown to our farm on the outskirts of town, it was because he wanted something. Most frequently that was information. He made me nervous, but I would never have admitted that to anyone, least of all him. Sometimes it felt like something was going on between us, but I absolutely ignored that possibility.

I handed him a plate with the sandwich. "You want a beer or a soda?"

"A soda would be great, thanks."

I grabbed a Dr. Pepper from the refrigerator, then sat down opposite him at the table. A polite hostess would have waited until he finished his sandwich before grilling him. I was not that polite hostess.

"So why are you here?"

Fowler gave me one of his standard half-smiles.

"You don't think I just dropped by because I was in the neighborhood?"

I shook my head. "Doubtful."

"I need to ask you some questions. After I finish this." He took a couple of bites of his sandwich. "Good stuff. What is it?"

"Whiskey peach. Made with frozen fruit. I was experimenting."

He gestured toward the stack of cartons in the living room. "Mail order business going okay?"

I nodded. "Picking up." Unlike the delivery driver who'd apparently missed me again, although he might swing by later.

Fowler took the last bite of his sandwich, which had disappeared quickly. "You want some chips?" I asked.

"I'm good. Thanks for the sandwich. Hit the spot." He took another swallow of his Dr. Pepper.

And now for the interrogation.

Fowler wiped his fingers on the napkin I'd provided, then he leaned back in his chair. "What do you know about Linda Constantine?"

"My mom? What do you want to find out?"

"As much as you can tell me. Mike's a little touchy on the subject, so I thought I'd try talking to you when he wasn't around."

Well, that was direct. Also smart. "My dad was really hurt when my mom walked out—or anyway that's what Uncle Mike always said. I don't remember it myself."

"You don't remember her at all?"

"Some hazy half memories maybe. I'm not even sure they're my mother. I mean, Uncle Mike was married, too. His wife died young, and I don't remember her all that well either." A lot of people passed through my life when I was little. I hadn't thought about that until now.

"So two single guys raising a little girl on their own?" Fowler arched an eyebrow.

"They did a great job. And they had help. Donnie's wife Carmen cooked and cleaned and looked after me. She was around to answer any questions I didn't feel like asking my dad or my uncle."

"Okay, point taken. What do you know about your mother's family?"

"Very little. My dad's family, the Constantines, were and are farmers. My dad had some land outside Clayton, New Mexico. He wasn't rich, but he wasn't poor either. He was solid, with prospects."

"Attractive to someone like your mom?"

"Probably. Her family were further down on the economic ladder. My mom waited tables in a diner in town. That's where my dad met her. He was smitten, and he thought she was, too. They got married after they'd dated a few months. She got pregnant with me a year or so later."

"He was still farming?"

I nodded. "Oh, yeah. She moved to the farm, worked on it with him until I came along. Then she divided her time between looking after me and taking care of chores around the house. Pretty much what every farm wife does."

"Your dad ever say why they broke up?"

"Not exactly. He didn't talk about her much, like I said. Based on what Uncle Mike said, she probably expected more out of life than keeping a farm running.

She left him after five years and gave him full custody, so I guess she wasn't crazy about motherhood either." That sounded a lot more flippant than I felt, but it had been too many years for me to spend much time agonizing over my missing mom.

"You don't know anything about her family?"

"Just what Uncle Mike told me. I guess she had a sister. He said her folks weren't around anymore. My dad's folks moved to Tennessee when I was a kid. They died while I was in high school."

"Do you know if your mom came from Clayton?"

"Not for sure. Uncle Mike would know. It sounded like she did from the way he talked."

"Okay, thanks." Fowler stood up, then paused. "Were you ever curious about her? Did you ever try to get in touch?"

It was a question I had a hard time answering. "I was curious about her, sure. But I couldn't ask my dad anything without making him sad. And Uncle Mike would just ask me why I wanted to know. As far as he was concerned Linda wasn't worth talking about. She hurt my dad and that was that."

"I guess I can understand that." Fowler took his hat from the rack. "I'll let you know the results of the DNA test when I get it. If you think of anything else about your mom or her family, give me a call."

"Okay," I said. But I was pretty sure I wouldn't be doing that. The few hazy memories I had of my mother weren't enough to build a solid investigation on.

They also weren't even enough to build a solid sense of who Linda Constantine had been. Or possibly still was.

Chapter 8

Uncle Mike came down for a coffee break the next morning, something he only did occasionally. I figured something was up. "Saw Fowler's car here yesterday. He got the DNA results yet?"

"Not yet. He just wanted some information."

Uncle Mike narrowed his eyes. "Information about what?"

"About my mom and her family. I told him what I knew, which wasn't much." Uncle Mike knew a lot more, but he hadn't been forthcoming with Fowler before.

He sighed. "Okay, I'll get in touch with him. You talked to Nate?"

This was a subject we'd both tap-danced around. He knew we'd quarreled over my leaving, but I wasn't sure how Uncle Mike felt about it. "No," I said.

By now the silence had stretched over almost two days. Nate and I appeared to be locked in a battle of wills, and I didn't know how to get out of it. Or even if I could get out of it.

"Idiot," Uncle Mike grumbled. "He needs to get off his duff and call you."

I wondered if he'd talked to Madge, but I didn't want to ask. If he hadn't, I didn't want to inspire him to try. Once again that sounded like high school.

"Guess I'll go on up to the house," he said.

Tangerine Marmalade Murder

After lunch I drove into town to make some deliveries. The packages had finally been picked up at seven the previous night—late, but at least they'd gotten off. I remembered Bianca telling me she was running low on jam, and since a healthy part of my sales came from her bakery, I loaded up a few cases and drove into Shavano.

I found a parking spot down the street from Bianca's shop and hefted two of the cases. As usual, she had a kid working the main counter, ringing up the last couple of diners. "Bianca in the back?" I asked, and he nodded.

Bianca's ovens and working space spread across the back of the bakery, and I found her kneading a couple of loaves of what looked like pumpernickel. "Brought the jam," I said, hefting the two cases. "I've got another couple in the truck. Where do you want them?"

She paused, rubbing her nose with the back of one hand. "Maybe in the storeroom." She nodded toward a door at the side, and I pushed it open. I stacked all four cases among the bags of flour and sugar and cans of nuts and dried fruits. It was the best smelling storeroom I'd ever been in, and I thought how nice it would be to just stay there and breathe for a while.

When I came out, Bianca had dumped the pumpernickel into the proving drawer and was washing her hands at the utility sink. "So what's the latest on the murder at your place?"

I wanted to protest that statement, since the murder wasn't exactly at our place, just the body. But maybe that was splitting hairs. "They still don't know what happened. Is it a hot topic around town?" I hoped the gossip was dying down. I didn't want people to hear my family might be involved in this some way.

Bianca gave me an incredulous look. "Are you kidding? It's the slow season. Everybody wants to know what happened."

"I guess so. Even Sara was asking me about it, and she usually doesn't say more than how much I owe them."

Bianca grimaced. "Don't take it personally. She doesn't talk to anybody."

"She said her assistant quit."

"Oh yeah?" Bianca raised her eyebrows. "News to me. Not that her assistant had all that much to do anyway. Let me give you a receipt. I'll get Jason to enter these into my database so I can keep track of inventory."

If Jason was the teenager glued to his phone behind the counter, I didn't have high hopes for his accuracy.

I tucked the receipt in my backpack and headed for my truck, musing about where I might be able to get an out of season flat of raspberries if I ran out of frozen, which it was looking like I might do. I didn't trust commercial frozen berries. With my current stuff, I'd done all the freezing myself, and I knew what was in the bags.

When I turned the corner, I saw Nate leaning against my truck, arms folded. He wasn't smiling.

My stomach did a quick clench, along with my shoulders, but I managed to keep my chin up. "Hi," I said.

"Hi. We need to talk."

The four most ominous words in the English language. I took a breath to calm my nerves and leaned my shoulder against the truck, facing him. "Okay."

"Not here. Can you come to my place in ten minutes or so?"

"I guess." I could always go down and check Made In Colorado to see if they needed more jam the next time I came to town.

"Okay, see you then." He pushed off from the truck and walked toward the café. Or anyway, I thought that was where he was going. I made it a point not to watch his retreating figure.

For a minute I considered driving over to Susa's office to get her advice on how to handle whatever Nate tossed my way, but I decided that was dumb. If Nate was breaking up with me, I needed to take it like an adult. I'd had romances end before, and I hadn't buckled. I wasn't going to buckle now.

Even though the relationship with Nate was a hell of a lot more serious than anything I'd had with anyone else.

Around fifteen minutes later, I pulled up at Nate's place. Yeah, I had timed it to add in the extra five minutes. Not the most mature thing to do, but I hadn't been too mature lately.

Nate was sitting on the picnic table in his backyard, and I walked over to join him. Staying outside struck me as a good idea right then. The weather was cool but not cold, and I had my jacket and my hiking boots to deal with the muddy ground. The picnic table had a scattering of pine needles and cones but it was snow free, and I brushed them out of the way as I stepped up beside him. I sat down, folding my arms across my bent knees. And then I said nothing because I couldn't think of the right thing to say. *What's up? What did you want to talk about? What's on your mind?* They all sounded way too jaunty and unspecific.

He turned toward me, still not smiling although his expression seemed more friendly than it had downtown. "Mom told me about the woman having your mother's driver's license. How are you doing?"

I shrugged. "I'm okay, mostly. How are you?"

"Okay. Mostly." He paused, and I wondered if either of us would be able to figure out a way to get beyond this.

He picked up a pinecone, turning it between his fingers. "I was really pissed at you Saturday night."

As an opening shot, that was pretty good. "Yeah?"

"Yeah." He stared down at the pinecone in his hand. "You took off and left me scrambling. I had to get all the pots and implements out to the SUV while the McKinley guys were working around me, trying to get the main ready to go."

My jaw firmed. I felt sort of guilty about that, about leaving him to tote everything out on his own. "I didn't know how serious things were. Uncle Mike sounded upset. He had a right to be." Maybe I didn't need to be there instantaneously, but it had turned out to be an important discovery, one that had shaken me up almost as much as it had Uncle Mike.

Nate stared out across his backyard. "It couldn't have waited another thirty minutes?"

I shrugged. "Maybe. Maybe not. I didn't know how serious it was at the time." I drew myself up a little more. I wasn't the only one at fault here. Time for a counter thrust. "Did you go out to the head table and get congratulated?" Which probably took another ten minutes or so.

I thought his cheeks flushed a little, but his voice was steady. "Yeah. Didn't take long." He tossed the pinecone to the ground.

The aspen trees were still bare in his backyard, stark white trunks against the deep green of the pines and the patches of snow still dotting the ground. A breeze rattled through the branches, and I pulled my jacket closer.

I needed to do a little apologizing. "I'm sorry I left you to clean up on your own. That was a lousy thing to do. But like I said, I didn't know how serious the problem was."

Nate was watching me. I couldn't tell if he looked sympathetic or annoyed, but whichever it was, I couldn't help him. I'd left the banquet hall kitchen because I felt like I had to. If he still didn't understand that, I didn't know how else I could explain.

"You didn't call," he said finally.

"Neither did you." Because apparently both of us were still in high school. Scratch that. We were both still in middle school. And we were each waiting for the other person to give in.

The silence stretched between us again, then Nate sighed. "I've got a catering job. Next weekend. Corporate. Tony Aldo's insurance company. Celebrating some company milestone."

That sounded like an important order. "What do they want for a menu?"

"They're taking the buffet option. Meatballs. Smoked salmon. Mostly heavy hors d'oeuvres, but classy. Cookie ice cream sandwiches for dessert. They're supplying the bartender. I'm guessing this group will be heavy into celebrating. We'll have to work around it."

That *we* was encouraging, assuming I wanted to be encouraged. I hadn't decided for sure yet. "Sounds like the Hiatt Brothers thing we did in February."

"Yeah, like that. Only a lot bigger. Fifty to seventy-five people."

It *was* a good order. Up until then, most of the catering jobs had been for twenty or thirty, with a few in the ten to twenty range. And Tony Aldo's company was a big deal. Chances were if Robicheaux Catering did well with the job, it would lead to others. This might be a springboard to the kind of prestige Nate and Madge had been hoping for.

"Do you want in?" Nate asked. He looked at me squarely for maybe the first time since I'd joined him on the picnic table.

I nodded. "Sure." A job was a job. And this one might help us iron out our issues. Or not.

"Okay. I'll text you the schedule so we can figure out when to do what. There are a lot of small dishes to do, but they can mostly be done in advance."

"All right." I stared out at the pine trees again, wondering if I needed to say anything else. Normally, we'd be making plans to get together, but this situation wasn't normal. Obviously. And there was no way on God's green earth that I was going to mention Grace Peters. Not until I had more concrete evidence that something was happening between them.

Nate didn't say anything else, and I pushed myself to my feet. "Guess I'll go home," I said. "See you."

Nate didn't say anything for a moment, then he glanced at me. "Yeah. See you later."

I walked toward my truck, with my heart aching

and tears prickling at the corners of my eyes. It felt like we'd broken up, although you couldn't tell from what had just transpired. If that was the case, if we were no longer a couple, I wished Nate had just gone ahead and said so.

Why was it Nate's job? If you're through being a couple, why can't you say it as easily as Nate?

From a power perspective, that was absolutely true. I could end things just as easily as Nate could. But I hadn't done that. And neither had he. So maybe neither of us wanted to be the one to drive a stake in the heart of our relationship. That could be a good sign. Or it could be a sign that neither one of us had enough courage to do what needed to be done.

I sighed and climbed into my truck. I didn't think I wanted this relationship to be over, but I wasn't sure how to go about mending it. And I wasn't sure Nate was similarly inclined. At this point, the best thing I could probably do would be to throw myself into the next catering job and see what happened after that.

That was not only the best thing, it was probably the only thing.

Chapter 9

I decided I needed to get a project going, one that would take my mind off the situation with Nate. A new jam usually got me thinking, so I decided to see what kind of jam I could find that involved citrus. It was the end of winter and it would be a couple of months still before I could start getting any fruit from the Southwest, let alone fruit from Colorado. The blood orange marmalade debacle had pretty much soured me on oranges, so I decided to look for something with limes or lemons. Lime or lemon jam would have the advantage of being unusual, which might appeal to my mail order customers.

Having decided that, though, I discovered that jam and jelly recipes featuring lemons and limes weren't all that common, and the ones I did find struck me as problematic. There were recipes for lemon curd (requires egg yolks and refrigeration; non-starter for mail order); preserved lemons (great for north African recipes, but probably not in high demand among my clientele); and a few sketchy recipes for lemon jam that I had such serious doubts about that I wasn't willing to try them.

And then there were recipes for marmalade. Lots of recipes for marmalade. I began to wonder just why my blood orange marmalade had been such a disaster. Citrus fruit has natural pectin, lots of it. My marmalade should have thickened up nicely. Maybe the problem wasn't with marmalade itself. Maybe it was with my version of it. Maybe I just hadn't cooked it right.

I found a recipe for tangerine marmalade that looked doable and involved powdered pectin, which would probably ensure that it actually firmed up enough to spread on a biscuit. I made a quick list of ingredients and decided to go to the grocery store. Or rather, I decided to go there before I looked outside and discovered the sky had turned dark. I checked my watch and found it was supper time.

The jam recipe had done what it was supposed to do—distracted me from my distress over Nate. Of course, now I needed to fix dinner for myself and possibly for Uncle Mike if he chose to come down and join me. I grabbed a bag of frozen leftover rice from the freezer—I always make twice as much as I need for just these situations—and a couple of cans of tuna. It wouldn't be gourmet, but it would be filling.

Uncle Mike did show up around thirty minutes later. He narrowed his eyes, and I waited for him to ask if Nate had called. But he held his peace as far as Nate was concerned.

Dinner conversation was a little stilted, given that we were avoiding conversations about Nate and Fowler and my dead possible relative. But we finally settled down to talk about next year's crops and what I wanted or needed in the way of fruit. Uncle Nate had a lot of fields planted in strawberries and raspberry bushes, and I took my share of the harvest. But he only had a small peach orchard, another of my big sellers. We talked about which growers would be best to get flats from, and if it would make sense to try and get some orders in before the season started. The big guys had standing contracts with growers, but I wasn't that big. The mail order business might push me in that direction, though.

It was a good conversation in that it didn't hit any hot buttons or make me want to go curl up in the fetal position. Uncle Mike was less enthused about the tangerine marmalade.

"Thought you already went that route. What's going to be different about this batch?"

"Pectin," I said flatly. "I'll add it. The stuff will gel. QED."

"Why can't you just do something with frozen fruit? Those peach preserves were pretty good."

Leaving aside the fact that *pretty good* was a lukewarm endorsement, I wasn't ready to use frozen peaches for a special feature. "I don't want to do anything that's too similar to my summer jams. I'll be selling whiskey peach as soon as the season starts. I don't want to rush it now."

"You'll try this tangerine stuff out first, right? Let us taste it?"

"Absolutely." Uncle Mike had tasted every jam I'd ever made, and he'd given me his honest opinion each time. Strawberry rhubarb, big thumbs up; blackberry lemon verbena, not so much.

He pushed himself to his feet, snapping his fingers to Herman who was lying in the corner with one of his rawhide chew toys. "Guess I better get up to the house." He leaned down to kiss my forehead. "You call me if you need anything, okay?"

"Sure," I said, fighting down a sudden and totally unwelcome prickle of tears. Every once in a while my uncle would say something that reminded me how much I counted on him being around. It had been that way since my dad had died. I didn't figure it was going to change any time soon.

I hoped not, anyway.

The next day I decided to head to the grocery store in town to pick up some tangerines and sugar. I was still going to try that marmalade and hope for the best. The need for a special jam wouldn't become critical until the end of the month, but I wanted to be ready before then.

I'm a true Type A. Sue me.

I was slightly concerned about running into Nate or one of the other members of the Robicheaux family in town, but I figured the chances were slim at that time of day since they'd be hip deep into the transition from breakfast to lunch, and nobody would be able to leave the café until mid-afternoon.

We have one of the large, national chain grocery stores in town, but we also have a smaller sort of neighborhood place where I go to get good produce. They don't always have much variety available, but they're more likely to have something outstanding than the big guys are. I only needed a few tangerines for my first experimental batch, and I wanted the most flavorful ones I could find.

I pulled into the parking lot, noting that there were few cars at this time of day, and walked in, waving at the manager, whom I'd gotten to know during my annual search for last-minute sources of good fruit. True to my expectations, they had a nice selection of tangerines, and I picked up a half dozen that looked promising.

As long as I was there, I decided to grab a few

more things for the week. I needed some sugar for the recipe, plus I was low on rice, and they carried an obscure brand of tortilla chips I liked. I worked my way across the store, which didn't take long since it was pretty small. I had started to cruise down one aisle when I caught sight of a familiar face. Or if not familiar, at least a face I'd seen before.

Grace Peters wasn't particularly beautiful. She had light brown hair she wore pulled into a classic chef's ponytail, brownish-green eyes, and a sort of typical chef's build. Not fat, not thin, muscular arms. But she was also something I absolutely was not: petite. I'd estimate she was a little over five feet, with the kind of delicate features that went with small bones.

I'm not particularly self-conscious about my height. I was taller than everybody in my class, almost from the moment I entered school until some of the boys had their growth spurts and finally caught up with me. I endured the usual teasing about being super tall, but I was also decent at sports, which made up for a lot. Being a volleyball star silenced the talk, and nobody ever tried to bully me. I had friends of both genders, and I did all the usual teenage things, including some I'd rather gloss over in any future discussions. A six-foot Amazon in the Colorado Rockies fit right in.

But Grace Peters made me feel large and ungainly, maybe because I mentally compared myself to her at Nate's side. He and I were about the same height. Grace would probably come to his shoulder, if that.

If he wanted dainty, I was out of the running. Of course, he'd never indicated *dainty* was a requirement before.

As if she sensed I was watching her, Grace glanced

up and smiled. "Hi, it's Roxy, isn't it?"

"That's right. Good to see you again, Grace."

She nodded. "Likewise. I finally found a time to shop when the crowds aren't huge here."

Stiegel's Grocery did tend to be a little crowded on the weekends. "Yeah, it's a little easier to get around during the week."

"Stiegel's is great, isn't it? They've got a selection of pastry flour you can't get anywhere else except online."

Stiegel's wouldn't have been my first choice for bakery supplies since those supplies were probably cheaper at the supermarket, but maybe Grace needed something special. "That's good. Their produce is outstanding, too."

"Missed you at the banquet Saturday."

I narrowed my eyes, but I couldn't detect any sarcasm in what she said. "I had to leave early."

"It was quite an event. So many people in the kitchen. Reminded me of my days in Las Vegas." She rolled her eyes. "Organized chaos. But somehow it all worked out."

"It helps when people know what they're doing in the kitchen."

Grace's smile dimmed a bit, and I wondered if I was supposed to ask her about her experiences in Las Vegas. "Did you get called out to be congratulated for your dessert?" I asked, since I was pretty sure she had been.

Her smile went back to megawatts. "Oh, yes, it was so exciting. Out there in front of everybody. Just the best."

I nodded and smiled and tried unsuccessfully to

think of something to say. It didn't matter really—Grace didn't need prompting.

"We were all so thrilled. A lot of us went out afterward to the Blue Spot. We even had champagne. It was quite a party." She gave me another smile, but something was off about this one. I couldn't quite put my finger on it, but it made me uncomfortable.

"Well, good luck with your pastry flour." I prepared to push my cart elsewhere.

"Oh, thank you. You'll have to drop by the shop sometime and try a macaron. Since you didn't get a chance to have any at the banquet." She smiled again, and this time I identified the quality in the smile that bothered me. It was sly. As if she was one step away from a smirk.

Was she giving me a jab about Nate? Or was I reading too much into it? Hard to say. And not worth examining at the moment. "Thanks, I'll do that," I said, not meaning a word of it.

I found my sugar and rice, skipping the tortilla chips because I thought I saw Grace in that aisle. I'd ruminate on the possible meanings behind that smile later. For now, I wanted to return to making jam, something I could rely on.

That afternoon I tried the tangerine marmalade, which came together quickly, thanks to the pectin. I put it on the counter to gel and got to work on a large batch of blueberry Earl Grey. The orders had started to come in, and there were a lot of them, gratifying since it meant people were looking at the web site, which was the only place they could find the monthly specials. When Dolce arrived, I put her to work processing the jars in the hot water bath after I filled them. She was a lot happier working on the food side of things than the business side.

For the business side, I had Bridget, who took care of the orders and let me know just how many more jars of blueberry we were going to need. It looked like I was going to have to find a couple more flats of berries, probably from Stiegel's since the manager could most likely get me enough fruit from his supplier.

Thinking of Stiegel's made me think of Grace Peters again, not that I particularly wanted to think of her. I still couldn't decide if she'd been subtly tweaking me over Nate or if it was just my over-active imagination.

"Have you gotten anything at that new bakery on Spruce?" I asked Bridget. I hoped if I avoided mentioning Grace Peters herself it would be less obvious that she was the object of my concern.

Bridget shook her head. "Why would you go anywhere else when you can get stuff from Bianca? Nobody's better when it comes to bread and cookies."

"I guess the new place does French pastry, like macarons and Napoleons and eclairs."

"Who needs macaroons when you've got chocolate chip cookies from heaven?" Bridget asked. I had to admit she had a point, although I was pretty sure she was mispronouncing *macaron* on purpose.

"I've been there," Dolce said. "The macarons were okay."

"Just okay?" I raised an eyebrow. Cooks are very attuned to faint praise.

"I don't know what macarons are supposed to taste like. These were a little dry, but the flavors were good."

I ignored the slightly guilty bit of pleasure I took in

the idea that Grace's macarons weren't exactly Best In Show. That would be beneath me.

Bridget and Dolce left at five, and I had several boxes ready for pickup as well as a counter full of blueberry Earl Grey to go with my tangerine marmalade. I'd been thinking about getting a spare refrigerator or maybe reserving some space in Uncle Mike's oversize refrigerator/freezer, and this day's work seemed to confirm that would be a good idea.

Uncle Mike had already told me he wouldn't be around for supper. I figured that meant he had a date with Madge, but I refrained from asking him to find out what was going on with Nate. He left me Herman, who always felt better if he had physical proof that he hadn't been abandoned.

Uncle Mike's absence meant I was the only one who needed to be fed, and I was just wondering whether to go with lunch meat or peanut butter and some of my abundance of jam, when the phone rang.

I no longer thought it might be Nate; that ship had sailed. So I picked it up without a lot of enthusiasm. I'd already hung up on several people who wanted me to extend my car's warranty that day. "Hello?"

"Hi, Roxy." I recognized Fowler's voice immediately from previous calls, many of them ominous.

"Hello, Chief, what can I do for you?"

"If you can meet me in town, I'll spring for pizza."

I thought of all the possible ramifications of my being seen having dinner with Fowler. Given the currently shaky state of my relationship with Nate, if you could even call it a relationship these days, I didn't want to risk it. "I'm too tired to come to town. Why don't you come out here? And bring the pizza."

Fowler sighed. "I can do that I guess."

It didn't strike me that his coming to the farm was any more of a hardship than my coming into town. "Great. Around six?"

"That'll work. What do you want on your pizza?"

"If you're getting it at Pharoah's, go for the works. It's worth it." A Pharoah's pizza with everything was definitely reward food. I figured I might as well be paid.

"Okay. See you at six."

I found myself hoping Uncle Mike didn't bring Madge to the farm where she'd see Fowler's squad car outside my cabin. But then I decided I didn't care.

If Nate wanted a relationship with me, he knew where I was. Fortunately, so did Fowler.

Fowler hadn't asked me what size pizza to get, but he brought an extra-large, which meant one or the other of us would have pizza leftovers.

"Mike not eating with us?" he asked.

I shook my head. "He's got a date with Madge."

"Madge?"

"Madge Robicheaux. They've been dating for a while." I kept my expression bland, hoping he wouldn't pursue details.

Fowler gave me a long look. "He's out and you're home?"

"Yeah, it happens like that sometimes. You want a beer or wine?"

"I'm driving. Better make it a beer."

I put the pizza in the middle of the table and provided us both with plates and silverware. Herman clicked over to join us, sprawling full-length across the kitchen floor. "Is he allowed to have pepperoni?" Fowler asked.

"Better not. The spices might give him the runs." And since I probably had him for the night, the last thing I wanted to deal with was a dog with indigestion.

We had a pleasant enough dinner. Fowler asked me about the cartons in the living room, and I filled him in on my mail order business. I asked him about current avalanche conditions—a big concern around here—and got an extended rant about idiot backcountry skiers.

Once our pizza eating slowed down, he leaned back in his chair and gave me one of his typical half-smiles. "So I got the DNA results."

The pizza promptly turned to a hard ball in my stomach. Probably a good idea he hadn't told me before we ate or I'd have lost my appetite. "Yeah? What do they say?"

"Well, first I had to wade through a bunch of disclaimers about the results not being guaranteed and some degrees of relationship being difficult to determine and so on."

I controlled my impatience. He was probably trying to be honest here. "Okay, that's understood. But what can they determine?"

Fowler stared down at his pizza, then at me again. "They determined that you're biologically related to Muriel Cates. The kind of relationship is trickier, but there's a good likelihood that the two of you were cousins."

My stomach felt tight again. I wondered if I was going to be sick, but it didn't feel likely. "That's…" I took a breath. "Okay, I don't know what that is exactly. Muriel Cates was Muriel Murphy? One of her folks was related to my mom?" I closed my eyes, gathering my hands into fists.

I heard Fowler lean forward. Then he was resting a hand on my shoulder. "You okay? Should I call Mike?"

The warmth of his hand took me by surprise, and I almost shrugged it off. I also came close to putting my hand on his. *Steady, Roxy. You've already got enough problems.* "No, I'm okay. I'm just absorbing it."

I opened my eyes as Fowler leaned back in his chair. "What happens now? Are you going to try to find my mom's family?"

"I'll check with the New Mexico State Police to see if they have any information on Muriel Cates or Muriel Murphy. They might be able to tell me if she has any family in New Mexico."

"Did she have a current New Mexico license?"

"Colorado. An address in Pueblo, but I haven't been able to find anyone there who knows her so I'm guessing it's no longer valid."

"She must have been living somewhere in town."

"She had a motel room out on the highway, but we didn't find any personal information."

I bit my lip. "Would you mind if I did some checking on my own? Just to find out if my mother's family is still in Clayton?"

Fowler's smirk had returned. "You're actually asking me if it's okay for you to do some investigating?"

I narrowed my eyes. This was a sort of sore point between Fowler and me—he sometimes thought I got in his way when I started checking things out. "Consider it a courtesy request."

"You're free to investigate your family

connections. All I'd ask is that you let me know if you find out anything related to Muriel Cates."

"I can do that. Would you let me know if you find out anything about my mom's family?"

Fowler leaned down to rub Herman's ears. "Assuming it's not information related to the investigation, sure." He pushed himself to his feet again. "Guess I'll take off. Unless you want me to stick around and talk to Mike."

"I can handle it. You want to take the pizza?" There were still three or four pieces left.

He shook his head. "Nope. It's all yours. Good for a family breakfast. See you around."

I watched him go, wondering if Uncle Mike would actually show up for breakfast tomorrow. He probably would, since Madge had a breakfast of her own to run at the café.

I put the pizza away in the refrigerator and considered having another glass of wine. Most of the bottle was left since Fowler had stuck to his single beer. I was just pouring myself another glass when the phone rang.

I grabbed it and checked the number. Nate. I'd pretty much given up expecting him to call, and the fact that he actually was calling sort of threw me. "Hello?" I said tentatively.

"Roxy?" Nate asked. Apparently he didn't recognize the tentative me.

"Yeah. What's up?"

"We need to start getting the food ready for the party at Aldo's insurance place. Could you come by tomorrow afternoon?"

I tried not to be put off by his professional voice.

He had a right to sound like a pro when he was talking about his company. Even if he was—or had been at one time—my lover. "Sure. Are you working in the catering kitchen or the café?"

"The kitchen. Would one o'clock work for you?"

"Yeah, I'll make it work."

"Okay, see you then." He hung up.

Short and not particularly sweet. I felt like dropping my phone from a considerable height, but that was ridiculous since it would only hurt me. I really wanted to drop Nate from a considerable height.

Sort of.

At the same time, I found myself sorry for him and for me. We'd gotten into this mess, and we didn't seem to be able to get out of it. I hoped we could figure it out soon, though. Or maybe just call it a day.

What I didn't want was this kind of twilight we were caught in at the moment, half in and half out of a relationship. We either went all in on loving each other, or we stepped away and said it was over.

One of us had to take the step. I just hoped it wouldn't be me.

Chapter 10

Uncle Mike didn't come down for breakfast, so I didn't have a chance to tell him about the DNA results. I could have called him, but I told myself I needed to tell him the results in person.

I spent the morning trying to make enough jam to get ahead of the orders for once. The tangerine marmalade had turned out well, so I sent an email to Susa asking her to set it up for next month's special flavor. That meant I'd have to find more tangerines.

I was at the point where I could say the blueberry Earl Grey was finished. I'd cooked up all the blueberries I'd gotten from Stiegel's, and I didn't want to buy any more. We advertised the specials as having limited numbers, and I'd decided arbitrarily to set the limit at thirty jars unless we had an unusually large response. As Susa pointed out, there was no point in having a limited time offer if it actually wasn't all that limited.

Bridget and Dolce were supposed to come in midafternoon, after I'd left to work with Nate. I figured I could rely on them to do what needed doing without me being around to organize things. Mostly they'd be filling orders from the stock I was storing in the garage and putting on labels for mailing anyway.

I approached the catering kitchen with some anxiety. I wasn't sure what I'd say to Nate or what he'd say to me. But I'd volunteered to help with this party, and that was what I was going to do, regardless. I stepped inside the building, trying for cheery. "Hi, I'm here."

"Glad to hear it. I'm here too." It wasn't Nate's voice, and I stepped farther into the kitchen to see Coco putting pecan filling into a couple of sheets of her pecan tassies.

"Wow," I said, "those are gorgeous. Are they for the Aldo party?"

"Yeah. Everything's small plate, so I'm doing a couple of two-bite desserts, tassies and ice-cream sandwiches with cookies. Nate's running late. He said for you to go ahead and start peeling and grating carrots." She nodded toward a pile of carrot bags next to the sink.

I pulled off my coat and dropped it on a chair. "What are the carrots going into?"

"Haven't a clue," Coco said cheerfully. "We've had a request for a couple of vegan dishes, so maybe for that."

I grabbed a peeler and got to work. Normally, Nate and I would have discussed the menu and what people needed. But this time we'd had minimal contact with each other. And that was fine with me.

Really. Fine.

"Are you two still on the outs?" Coco asked from across the room.

"I don't know. I guess so. Ask Nate." That sounded about as petty as you'd expect, but I was still annoyed about not having had any input on the menu.

"I'll take that as a yes," Coco said. "Mind telling me what this fight is about? Nate won't say a thing."

I considered telling Coco to butt out, but by now I was tired of the whole thing. Maybe actually putting it into words would help lay it to rest.

"I got called away from the Wine and Food Festival dinner, after we'd finished serving but before we'd gotten everything loaded into the van. My uncle Mike called to say there was an emergency, and I left Nate to do clean-up on his own."

"What was the emergency?" Coco looked concerned.

I paused, trying to figure out how much I could say. But Uncle Mike had told Madge already. "The woman who was killed near our place turned out to have some documents that belonged to my mom, including her driver's license. Uncle Mike thought I needed to know ASAP. It probably wasn't as much an emergency as he thought."

"Wow. I don't know anything about your mom. Is she still living?"

"I don't know. I don't know much about her myself. She walked out when I was three." And I found I didn't want to talk about it much more. I particularly didn't want to explain that Muriel Cates was my cousin.

Coco gave me a kind of stunned look. "I'm sorry, for what that's worth. I can see why your uncle wanted you to come home. And you'd already finished service, so it wasn't that big a deal. Or it shouldn't have been, anyway."

"I should have called Nate that night to explain. I'm sorry now I didn't." Although if he was out at the Blue Spot, he might not have taken the call.

"That kind of fight isn't worth breaking up over. It's a bump in the road."

"It's a big bump. But we'd been having trouble before that. A lot of minor disagreements leading to a big blow-up." The more I'd thought about that, the more I'd decided it was true. There'd been a lot of minor sniping during meal prep and sometimes when we were doing other things. We'd been heading for a crackup for a while.

"Okay." Coco put down the bag of pecans. "I'm going to tell you something that Nate probably would prefer I didn't. But you should know he's under a lot of pressure. A lot. The catering thing has taken off faster than even Mom expected. Nate's being stretched thin between the café and catering. The truth is we need to hire a new cook for the café to fill in so Nate can spend more of his time on the catering side. But Bobby's dead set against it."

Brother Bobby seemed to take the very idea of change personally. "Why? I mean, you guys must have had cooks working the kitchen before Nate came back. It couldn't have been just you and Bobby handling things, given the volume of customers at the café." Bobby had taken over running the kitchen after Nate's dad had died. Coco returned to help a few months later, and then Nate had returned, too.

"Of course, we did." Coco sighed. "We should hire somebody to help now. But Bobby's convinced that only members of the Robicheaux family can cook the menu, which is nonsense. And he's also convinced that the cost of extra help would eat up all the profits, which is also nonsense. We've actually not bid on some dinners for the catering arm because Nate didn't think we could cover them. If he had more time out of the damn kitchen, the catering business would take off even more."

"So Nate's still working a full schedule at the café? I thought he was cutting back to one meal a day so he could work on the catering."

"He was supposed to be cutting back, but then Bobby started arguing that he needed more help at lunch. We've been getting slammed after that article in *5280*."

The café had gotten a nice write-up after a restaurant reviewer had come through town last fall. "That's great, but also not great."

"Yeah, tell me about it," Coco said. "Mom's worried about Nate's health under all of this."

Nate had suffered what he insisted was not a heart attack while he was working in Las Vegas. It had been a serious enough "cardiovascular event" that Madge had come to town and dragged him to Shavano. Robert Robicheaux, Senior, had died from a heart attack suffered in the kitchen of the café, so Madge had a right to be upset.

"Do you think he's having problems?" Nate had seemed physically okay to me, but maybe I hadn't been paying enough attention. Given that I was concentrating more on his attitude than his health, that was likely.

Coco shrugged. "Hard to say. He's working hard and he's not sleeping much from what I can tell. And he's missing you. That's obvious."

"It is?" It wasn't to me, but what did I know?

Coco narrowed her eyes at me. "Give it up, Rox. The two of you are nuts about each other. Nate fell hard the first time he saw you, and he's never wavered. If he's being a jerk now, it's because he's being pulled in eight different directions. Cut him some slack. He needs it. And he needs you. He needs someone who's not a Robicheaux to take him away from all this crap."

I took a breath. Might as well get it all out there. "What about Grace Peters?"

Coco frowned. "What about her?"

"Nate's been out with her a couple of times. While we've been 'on a break.' " That sounded even more small minded than I expected, but I still wanted to know.

Coco grimaced. "Grace Peters isn't even a blip on Nate's radar. Plus, she's a certified jerk."

I picked up another carrot to peel. "Certified by who?"

"By me, among others. She hired a friend of mine to help her part time when she got a big order. Although why anybody would want to order mass quantities of her dried-out macarons escapes me. Anyway, she ended up stiffing Janet. She only paid her half of what they'd agreed on, claimed it was all based on a percentage of her payoff for the order and she hadn't been paid as much as she'd anticipated. Which was total bullshit since she was paid in full. She's a jerk personally. And she's a lousy baker. Trust me, I know. She is absolutely not Nate's type. He's not interested in assholes."

That perhaps settled that. I ignored the slight flush of satisfaction Coco's description gave me. Nate's point of view might be slightly different. And Grace had come across as amiable when I'd met her at Stiegel's, so maybe she'd hidden her less appealing traits around Nate.

I started loading the peeled carrots into the food processor to grate them. Yes, doing them by hand is neater, but I had no intention of spending an entire afternoon grating carrots, and probably my knuckles based on previous experience. Nate came in as I was running the second bunch of carrots through.

He narrowed his eyes. "You going to squeeze the extra moisture out when you finish?"

"Of course." I'd actually been going to ask him what he wanted done, but I wasn't about to admit that. "What are these for?"

"Filo pockets." He glanced at the bulletin board and paused. "I thought I put the menu up there. What happened, Coco?"

She shrugged. "Search me. I'm just the dessert chef."

Nate made an irritated sound and stepped over to the bulletin board. After a moment, he bent down and picked up a piece of paper from the floor. Nobody said anything as he posted it again, securing it with pushpins.

I dumped the carrots into a kitchen towel and wrung them out over the sink. "What else are we doing today?"

"If you do the filo packets, I'll work on the salmon spread. I've already roasted the meat for the beef and horseradish thing. Then tomorrow we can do the sliders and the other stuff. That leaves the crudités and charcuterie, but that we can do on the day."

I nodded. "Okay. Where's the recipe for the filo packets? And the filo."

Nate cast another irritated look around the kitchen, then pulled open a drawer and took out an index card, which he handed to me. "Here."

As I took it from him, I got my first good look at his face. His eyes were more deep-set than usual, and the lines around his mouth had grown more pronounced. He looked tired. Very tired.

I fastened the index card to the metal cabinet door with a magnet and checked the recipe, which looked pretty tasty, all in all. I needed to chop up some onions and peppers and then sauté the veggies before folding everything in filo sheets. I figured all the things I needed would be in the refrigerator, which would save me having to ask Nate. He looked like too many questions would push him over some kind of edge.

Fortunately, I'd guessed right. The boxes of filo were on the top shelf of the refrigerator and the peppers were in the hydrator. The onions were in a bin at the side. I got to work chopping and then sautéing, while Nate worked across from me, chopping up smoked salmon and mixing it into cream cheese.

We didn't say much until I started sautéing the veggies, then Nate looked up, frowning. "Why are you using olive oil? It's supposed to be butter."

"I thought it was vegan," I said.

"It's vegetarian."

"No, it's not," Coco called from across the kitchen. "It's vegan. No butter. Roxy's right."

Nate stood still for a moment, staring down at his salmon spread. "Crap. They won't be able to eat anything else."

"They can eat the crudités," I said. "And we could offer a vegan dip. If nothing else we could just put out a bowl of vegan salad dressing."

Nate didn't move. "Crap," he said again. "I forgot. I totally forgot."

"We caught it. We're good."

He looked like he wanted to beat up on himself a

little more, but I decided not to let him. "How many packets per sheet of filo?"

"Two," he said. "You think that's too many?"

"Not necessarily. We'll see."

Working with filo is a bitch since it dries out at the speed of light. I spent the rest of the afternoon assembling and baking the packets while Nate assembled his smoked salmon rolls and moved on to slicing the beef for the beef and horseradish toasts. Coco left after another hour, muttering something about what a fun afternoon she'd had, but the two of us worked on until five or so.

It was a companionable afternoon, but I could still sense the tension in the air. Tension that came mostly from Nate. When we spoke to each other it was mostly about the food we were working on and the schedule for completion. At one point I thought about asking him over for dinner, but I stifled the impulse. He was caught up in his own miseries, and I didn't want to add to them.

Maybe Coco was right and the problems between us were really the problems Nate was having with the family enterprises. Which didn't make me feel much better.

"What time do you want me tomorrow?" I asked as I got ready to leave.

Nate put down his knife and sighed. "Around the same time as today, I guess. I'll try to get away from lunch service quicker than I did this afternoon."

"Okay. And what time do we start service on Saturday?"

"Five. So we need to get to the building no later than four. It shouldn't take us long to set up if we've got everything prepared."

"Right. See you tomorrow then."

Nate nodded, rubbing a hand across his forehead, then went back to chopping beef.

If I wanted to get any jam made the next day, I'd have to get up early and start chopping up fruit as I made breakfast. Neither Bridget nor Dolce would be around since they both had Friday afternoon commitments. I'd have to sit down and go through my inventory to see what I needed more of based on the orders. And then I'd have to get the frozen fruit ready to go and make sure I had enough on hand to make a few dozen jars.

My life was turning into a constant round of work. And it wasn't even fun work.

That night I made spaghetti and meatballs for supper. Bridget and Dolce had left a nice stack of cartons ready for pickup, although I might add a few more tomorrow if I had time.

I was just warming up a jar of marinara when Uncle Mike came in, running his boots over the door mat. "Snowing again," he said grimly. He was ready to start planting arugula in the caterpillar tunnels so we'd have spring crops, but a major snowstorm would delay everything.

"How much?" I asked.

"Couple of inches so far. Not supposed to be major."

I dumped the bag of frozen meatballs into the marinara. It wasn't gourmet, but it was edible. Uncle Mike pulled a beer out of the refrigerator. "Saw Fowler's car here last night. Business or social?"

Both? But that wasn't something I wanted to

discuss. "He had news." I waited for Uncle Mike to take a seat at the kitchen table. "The DNA results came back. Muriel Cates and I are related. Probably cousins."

"Well, crap." Uncle Mike took a swallow of his beer. "Trust the goddamn Murphys to cause trouble whenever they show up."

That seemed a little harsh, given that Muriel Cates had gotten killed. "Anyway, it gives them someplace to start looking. Fowler's going to check to see if Cates has a record in New Mexico. I'm going to look for Murphys in Clayton."

Uncle Mike set his beer down again. "Why the hell would you want to do that?"

"Because they're my family, too. I don't know anything about them. It's not like I'm thinking of leaving you or anything. I just want to know who they are." I gave him a sort of fierce look.

I did want to know about the Murphy family, but I also wanted to know about my mom. I'd never really wanted to know her, and now I was curious.

Uncle Mike put his hands on his hips. "She's not worth your time, Roxanne. Not even a minute. Trust me."

I grabbed the pan of spaghetti and took it to the sink to drain. "Okay, then, tell me why. I never could ask Dad about her because I knew it hurt him. So now you tell me what I'm not supposed to know." I was pushing him harder than usual, but I needed some answers. Even if I didn't like what I found out.

For a minute I thought he wouldn't tell me. He looked mad enough to stomp away to the main house. Then he took another long swallow of beer. "She cheated on him. After you were born, and she decided she wanted to leave, she started going out and picking up men at a bar in town. Or letting them pick her up—same thing. She'd take you over to that sister of hers, and then she'd head to the bar. She wanted out, and I guess that was her way of telling him how much she wanted out, pushing him to let her go."

I dumped the spaghetti into the pot with the marinara and meatballs. By all rights, I should have sat down with Uncle Mike at the table, but it was easier to listen if I had something to do. "Why didn't he just tell her to get out? If she was so desperate to go, why not let her?"

Uncle Mike snorted. "Damn fool loved her. He thought if he held on, she'd get over it. She loved you, and he thought she wouldn't leave you. And he'd never let you go either. You were the sticking point. He thought if he held on, she'd realize the three of you were a family."

"What happened?" I gave the spaghetti a vicious stir, coating it with marinara.

There was a long pause, and I looked over at him. His expression was grim, and I felt like ice had slipped into my veins. But I had to know. "Uncle Mike?"

"One day he came home from work and found you alone. She'd locked you in your room so she could go out. I guess her sister couldn't look after you or something. He said you were still crying when he found you, and you looked like you'd been crying for a while. You were a mess, all tears and snot and dirty diapers. He didn't know how long you'd been in there by yourself." He stared down at his beer bottle. "Hell, five minutes would have been too long. You were just a toddler, a two-year-old. He took you over to our aunt

Angie's place, and then he went to town and found Linda."

I took a deep breath, trying to loosen my suddenly tight shoulders. "What did he do?"

"You remember your dad. He was a gentle man, couldn't hit a woman—didn't want to. But he said he came as near it as he'd ever come." Uncle Mike looked up at me again. "He told her to go to the house and pack her things. To get out and not come back. He never wanted to see her again, and he'd make damn sure she never saw you again. And that's what happened. She left, and he divorced her."

I wanted to let it go, but I wasn't quite ready yet. "Did she ever try to see me after that?"

Uncle Mike sighed. "Maybe. I don't know. She didn't try for custody, I know that. Steve divorced her and sold his land. He might have paid her off with some of it, but it wouldn't have been much. And then he brought you to Shavano and invested his money in this place."

I started dishing up spaghetti and meatballs. In a way, it wasn't all that surprising. My dad had pretty much covered it by saying *she left us*. But it still hurt.

"You still gonna go digging around?" Uncle Mike asked.

I wanted to say no, to say I didn't need to know any more. But Muriel Cates's murder had opened up a lot of questions. And I still wanted to find the answers. "Probably. Do you remember the sister's name?"

He sighed. "Something with an L. All the women in that family had L names. Loretta? Lorraine?" He paused. "Maybe Lucille. Sounds right. But I'm an old fart, so maybe my memory's playing tricks."

"You're not that old. You're just tough. But I'm still going to look."

"Thought so." Uncle Mike shook his head. "Just like your dad. Stubborn."

Stubborn enough to still want to know what happened to my mother. Stubborn enough to feel like Muriel Cates deserved a better fate.

Maybe stubborn enough to hold onto a relationship until it fell apart in my hands, just like my dad. Maybe it ran in the family.

Chapter 11

Friday was about as chaotic as I'd expected it to be. I got some jam made, although not as much as I would have liked.

I drove into town to finish work at the catering kitchen, but I needed some lunch first. I might have been able to find some things to munch on in the kitchen, but I work better when I'm not famished.

I decided not to go to Dirty Pete's for once, just because I knew it would be crowded. And also, to be frank, because I hated going there by myself. It reminded me of when Nate and I had been okay, which also reminded me of the fact we weren't currently okay at all.

The day was sunny and sort of warmish, that weird weather you get at higher elevations where sunshine is more intense and makes up for very cold air. I decided to grab a sandwich at Millie's, a breakfast and lunch place a couple of blocks from Robicheaux's that had a nice dining deck.

I have no idea who the original Millie was, but her descendants, Concha and Burke Miller, made a rockin' sandwich.

I grabbed a turkey and Swiss with a mustard-based dressing and set myself up at an outside table. I'd just taken a very tasty bite when someone appeared opposite me. Squinting through the sunlight at the vaguely female form, I wondered why a strange woman had decided to approach me when there were still empty tables on the restaurant deck.

"Hi, Roxy. Mind if I join you?" The vaguely female form resolved itself into Sara Jordan.

It took me a moment to recognize her without her apron. I wasn't sure I'd ever seen Sara away from Jordan's Meats before. "Sure, have a seat." I waved my hand vaguely at the other side of the table.

Sara slid in opposite me, pulling her sandwich out of a paper bag. "Nice day, isn't it? Almost like spring."

"Almost. Of course, we're supposed to get snow tomorrow." Weather is the standard conversation topic in the mountains, since forecasts change in a heartbeat.

"Of course." Sara took a critical bite of her sandwich. "Not bad. They're buying our capicola and salami now."

"Oh, yeah? Great."

We munched on our respective sandwiches for a few moments more before Sara put hers down again. "So anything new on that murder investigation?"

I managed not to choke on my sandwich. Sara had that same tense brightness she'd shown when she'd asked me about the investigation before. I gave her a bland smile. "Not much, I guess. They've identified the woman, but that was in the paper. Her name was Muriel Cates."

Sara stiffened a little, but that might have been my imagination. "Did you know her?"

"She came to the house looking for work, but I didn't know her name." I decided to take a chance in order to satisfy my curiosity. "What about you? I thought I saw her downtown one time walking toward your shop. Bianca said she was your assistant." That last wasn't entirely accurate, but it was close.

Sara's expression went blank as she stared at me. Her jaw tightened. I expected her to say no, but instead she shrugged. "My assistant? Muriel Cates?"

I nodded. "As I recall."

"She wasn't my assistant. She was just a gofer, trying to make some cash off the books. She did some errands for us, cleaned up the storeroom. Stuff like that. We paid her by the hour. She wasn't on salary." Sara took another bite of her sandwich. I thought she was trying to come across as relaxed, but not achieving it.

"I didn't realize you guys hired casual labor." It was a small butcher shop, after all. They wouldn't have needed much in the way of help.

Sara shrugged again. "She showed up at the right time. We needed somebody to do a couple of things, that's all."

"Did you tell Fowler about her working for you?"

Sara shook her head, her expression turning mulish. "Why would I? She was only around the shop a couple of times."

"He's looking for information about her, about what she did in town. You could help him fill in the details."

Sara didn't look like she found that possibility attractive. "She was just someone who worked for us a few hours. It wasn't like she was important."

Not important. Just dead. All of a sudden, I wasn't interested in sharing a table with Sara anymore. "I need to go back to work myself. Enjoy your sandwich."

Sara narrowed her eyes like she was trying to find some secret meaning in that statement. "Yeah. You, too."

I finished my sandwich in my truck. I was still trying to decide why I was upset with Sara. She'd been callous, but probably no more than anyone else in town when it came to the murder of a relative stranger.

Except Muriel was no longer a relative stranger. She was a relative. My cousin. And I was trying to figure out how I felt about her, and how I felt about the Murphy family in general. I'd spent most of my life thinking of myself as exclusively a Constantine. Now I was forced to confront the fact that I was also a Murphy. If I'd been able to talk to her, I might have found out more about my mother and the people she came from. Only somebody had killed my cousin before I even knew she existed.

However you looked at it, that sucked.

The more mundane information about Muriel working at Jordan's was interesting, but I wasn't sure if it was worth passing on to Fowler. If she'd only spent a few hours working for the Jordans, they might not be all that helpful. Still, I figured if he happened by sometime, I might give him the information and let him figure out what to do with it.

At two, I parked at the catering kitchen and went inside. I was still thinking about my conversation with Sara, but maybe spending a few hours making meatballs would help clear my head. Since Nate wasn't really speaking to me, I figured I wouldn't have to talk about my family and my mom. Besides, it wasn't information that was important to anyone but me.

Coco wasn't there this time, but Nate was unloading a couple of cartons on the main island. He glanced up as I walked in. "Hi."

I nodded. "Hi. What's that?"

"Cheese wheel. I got it from Marcus Jordan, along with a couple of salamis. We can put it out for people to cut chunks off if they want. Plus, I've got some goat cheese from that place in Antero. And bread from Bianca."

He hefted the cheese into the refrigerator as I wrapped one of the canvas aprons around myself. "What do you want me to do?"

"Sichuan meatballs. Recipe's over there. We can cook them up today and then reheat them tomorrow."

"Do you want a sauce, too?"

He shook his head. "We'll serve them on mini-skewers. A sauce just drips all over when they pick one up."

"Good enough." I got to work mixing mass quantities of ground pork with grated ginger and chopped scallions and Sichuan pepper and a ton of breadcrumbs. Here's a tip if you ever find yourself dealing with a couple hundred Sichuan meatballs: ginger doesn't have to be peeled. Grating unpeeled ginger cut down on a bit of prep time, but it was still the kind of messy work that keeps you focused on the task at hand.

Just what I needed.

By the time I started forming the meatballs with the portion scoop, I was in the zone, laying out row after row of meatballs on parchment lined sheet trays. I wasn't sure whether we were roasting them or frying them, but I was ready to go.

Or I was until Nate turned and asked me, "Are you okay?"

I stared down at the meatballs, wondering if I'd

done something wrong. "Um…sure. Is there a problem?"

"No problem. Just…you looked sort of down."

I blinked. Nate had hardly looked at me over the past couple of weeks, let alone commented on my moods. All of a sudden I felt like crying, but I didn't.

"We found out the woman who was killed out near the farm was my cousin on my mother's side. I'm still trying to process it, I guess."

Nate stared at me. "That's sort of a bombshell."

"Yeah, it is. Like I said, I'm processing." And I didn't want to talk to him about it yet. Not after my last conversation with Uncle Mike.

Nate paused as if he was waiting for me to fill in the details, but I didn't have anything more I wanted to share. After a moment he returned to his roast beef and horseradish sliders.

We finished the afternoon without saying much more. Everything was cooked and packed away in containers to be transported to the party location where we'd heat it again in the kitchen.

"What time do you want me here tomorrow?" I asked as I finished cleaning up.

"Maybe three if you can manage it. We've got a few more dishes to get ready, and then we need to get set up over at Aldo's place."

"Okay, I'll be here at three." That gave me most of the day to do my own work. If Nate and I had still been together, we'd have spent the night at his place and come over to the catering kitchen the next afternoon. One of the effects of no longer being a couple was that it gave me more time to work on jam. I tried very hard to see that as a plus.

I called Susa after I got home and before I started dinner since I wanted to catch her before she went out on whatever date she had lined up for the evening. Susa had known me longer than just about anyone else in town. So she had some idea of my tangled family background.

She listened to my description of what I'd learned from Fowler and Uncle Mike without interruption. "Wow," she said when I'd finished, "that's…a lot."

"I know. I'm still trying to work through my feelings and decide what it all means."

"Do you think Muriel Cates was going to tell you who she was? I mean, she must have known. Was that why she had your mother's stuff?"

I sighed. Yet another unanswerable question. "Maybe. But why did she go through the whole looking for work thing? I mean, why didn't she just say, 'Hi, I'm your cousin Muriel.'"

"Who knows? Maybe Ethan will find out more about her. And I'll help you look for more relatives in Clayton if you want to."

Susa's computer skills were a lot better than mine since she was a pro. "Thanks. I appreciate that."

Susa paused for a moment. "So you're working for Nate tomorrow night?"

"Yeah."

"Anything happening there?"

I thought about the brief moment where he'd been concerned about me. The *very* brief moment. "Nope."

"Hang in there, sweetheart," Susa said. "It'll happen."

"Maybe." But I wasn't counting on it.

After I hung up, I made myself some soup for

dinner. Since it was Friday night, Uncle Mike was off on a date with Madge.

I was just settling in to an evening of TV, when my phone rang. Considering that I'd just talked to Susa and wasn't talking to Nate, I figured it was spam, but actually it was my friend Lauren from Denver.

"Hey, kid," she said, "how's it going? I wondered if you had any more pepper peach jam sitting around."

Lauren was my roommate during my years in Denver. She's still cooking in restaurants there, although now she's a sous chef rather than working the line. After I got her squared away with some pepper peach (of course, I had some around—I always had some around), we settled in to do some catching up on food world gossip. Actually, Lauren supplied the gossip since my access to food world chat is limited at best.

But as we talked, I remembered something I'd wanted to ask her. "How's your cousin doing these days?"

Lauren's cousin was a line cook at Big Tony's, one of the busier Italian places in town. She'd come up to Shavano with Lauren a couple of times. And she hadn't seemed too happy with her job.

"You mean Marigold? She's sort of in a funk right now. Big Tony's is beginning to pall, but she's not sure what she wants to do next. Maybe move somewhere else."

An idea had begun to form at the back of my mind, but I wasn't sure how far to push it yet. "Would she consider coming up here? There might be an opening I could recommend her for."

"In Shavano?" Lauren paused. "Yeah, actually she might. She's a real outdoors type."

"Why don't you have her give me a call if she's interested in Shavano."

"I'll do that. If it wasn't for the salary at my current place, I might be interested in Shavano myself. How's Nate? And Susa?"

"Everybody's fine," I lied. "You going to come up and visit me sometime?"

"Maybe after things get a little more settled at work. This summer?"

"Count on it. Farmers market starts in May."

I wasn't sure whether Bobby was ready to hire somebody else for the café, but Marigold was definitely qualified if he was. And Nate could use some help.

Thinking of Nate made me glum. For the first time, I wondered how long I'd go on working with him. If things weren't going to get any better between us, I should probably just pack it in. Neither of us needed the hassle.

Of course, that would leave him doing even more work on his own when he was already over-stressed. On the other hand, it might inspire Bobby to hire somebody to help Nate out or to fill in at the café.

My leaving might be a good thing for everyone, when you looked at it that way.

But I wasn't ready to look at it that way quite yet.

Chapter 12

I was at the catering kitchen by three, with my chef's coat and pants on a hanger. I figured I could change in the café restroom and then throw my working clothes into my truck. I didn't expect to leave the kitchen at the party tonight, but just in case, I wanted to look professional.

Nate and Coco were both in the catering kitchen, although Coco was just finishing up assembling her ice cream sandwiches. Nate was doing tomato roses to decorate the crudités, so I got to work putting skewers through the meatballs I'd made the day before. We'd warm them up in the kitchen of Aldo's building where the party was taking place. Nate's decision not to use a sauce was looking better by the minute.

It took us around an hour to get everything finished and packed up. Coco patted me on the shoulder on her way out the door. "Have fun. Remember what I said."

I was about to ask her what she'd said that I was supposed to remember, but then I remembered myself: she'd said Nate loved me, and I needed to give him some space. I took a deep breath and blew it out. I'd provided a lot of space, and I hadn't gotten a lot in return. More and more it was looking like it was time to just pack it in and move on. We'd had a good run.

At a quarter to four, I changed my clothes and tossed my jeans and shirt into the truck.

"Ready to go?" Nate asked when I came back inside.

"Sure. You want me to follow you?"

Nate shook his head. "I've got Mom's SUV again. We can just load everything into it and go together."

Maybe he was making sure I didn't run off this time, but driving together was fine with me. Aldo owned a building at the edge of town, a two-story modern with a central atrium where we were going to be serving. The building had lots of glass and fieldstone and it didn't really fit into Shavano style. But it certainly stood out, which was probably what Tony Aldo wanted for his insurance agency.

The kitchen was down a hall off the atrium, which meant we'd have to schlepp the food out on trays. "Who do we have waiting tables?" I asked.

"Donnell and Jase. They should be here by now." Nate's jaw tightened as he looked around the empty kitchen.

"We've got time. We just got here ourselves." I set the first stack of food containers on the counter and went out for more, hoping that he'd calm down and follow me.

Eventually he did. We transferred the ice cream sandwiches from the cooler to the freezer to firm up a bit then got the oven going to warm up the meatballs and the chicken skewers, along with the other small plates. By five we had the food well in hand, and Nate was setting up the tables in the atrium when Donnell strolled in.

Donnell had waited tables at the café for a few years. She was in her forties and looked like it had been a tough forty years. But she was very good at her job, and she appreciated the extra pay, even though it meant working two or three hours in the evening after she'd been on her feet most of the day at the café.

"Where's Jase?" I asked as she stowed her purse under the sink.

Donnell shrugged. "Don't know. I didn't see him when I pulled up."

Given that we were due to start serving in another half hour or so, that didn't sound good. Jase was strictly freelance, a musician who picked up part-time jobs waiting tables in between gigs. I crossed my fingers that he was just late and not totally absent.

"Should I start putting food out?" Donnell asked.

"Let me ask Nate. We may want to wait until the meeting is over and people start coming into the atrium." Of course, they might like to have something immediately instead of waiting for us to bring out the food.

Given that the pre-party meeting was supposed to be a session of back patting and congratulations, I didn't figure it would take long for people to start arriving. As I walked into the atrium, I saw Nate staring down at his phone. When he looked up, I saw his set jaw and burning eyes, and I realized he was furious.

"What's wrong?" I asked.

"Jase has a gig. He said he'd try to make the dinner but he couldn't promise to be here for more than the first hour." Nate turned to lean a hand against the wall. And then he gave the baseboard a vicious kick. "Dammit. Goddammit all to hell. That fucking bastard is going to ruin everything."

Across the room, the bartender looked toward us, frowning.

I put my hand on Nate's arm. "It's okay. Donnell's here. If we get behind, I can help her put food out."

"I'll need you in the kitchen. Now who's going to clear the goddamn tables?" Nate snarled.

"We'll be okay," I repeated. I wanted to tell him to calm down, but I knew how annoyed I felt when someone said that to me.

"We won't. This is a class A fuckup. Just one of many. Just the latest. Goddammit. Just..." He stood for a moment, panting, and he looked like he was having trouble catching his breath.

All of a sudden, I was frightened for him. Madge was worried about his health. Coco said he'd been working too hard. Maybe this latest crisis was something that would push him over the edge into more heart problems, and I didn't want that to happen.

I cupped his face in my hands. "We're okay. We'll handle things. We've been in the weeds before. We've got this." I leaned forward and wrapped my arms around his shoulders.

I felt him stiffen immediately. *Oh, shit. This was a really bad idea.* I started to move away, but then I felt his arms snake around my waist as he pulled me against him. We stood together for a long moment, then he rested his forehead against mine. "Okay," he said. "Okay."

Jase showed up about ten minutes later, looking sort of belligerent. Nate pulled him aside while Donnell and I got the trays of cold food set up on the tables. I figured the guests could eat cheese and bread with a couple of carrot strips while we got the hot food laid out on the warming trays.

People started trailing in as Nate helped get the

burners going beneath the trays and I brought out the first servings of meatballs and chicken and veggie packets. The roast beef pinwheels were served cold, alongside some shrimp spring rolls and the smoked salmon crostini. Donnell had gotten the plates and silverware arranged at some point, and people started loading up with food and drinks.

I escaped to the kitchen, so I could keep the trays of food coming. Nate joined me a few minutes later. "How's it going?" I asked.

"So far okay. Jase is staying until seven. I'll pay him, but if Aldo gives us a tip, he won't get any of it."

"Sounds fair to me."

Jase himself came into the kitchen carrying the first tray of dirty dishes. To tell the truth, I hadn't been sure things would work all that well when I'd told Nate we'd be okay. But as it turned out, I was right. We were fine. Jase and Donnell, and then Donnell alone, kept the food trays filled. They also circulated among the guests, providing them with samples of the small plates they hadn't gotten to yet. Nate and I took turns getting the food ready to go and loading the dishwasher as the trays full of dirty dishes began to accumulate. After an hour and a half, we put out Coco's pecan tassies and ice cream sandwiches, the latter in a cold tray over ice.

As it got closer to nine, our cut-off time, Nate went out to check with Aldo that everything was okay. A few minutes later he stepped into the kitchen. "He wants to introduce us to the guests. Okay?"

We stared at each other for a moment. "Sure," I said. "No problem."

I took off my apron and my ball cap, then rebuttoned my chef's coat as I followed him through the door. The atrium was still fairly crowded, although I noticed most people were sitting at their tables with drinks and empty plates, so we'd probably moved beyond the food end of things. Aldo waved us over to his side. He was a big guy, a former football player turned insurance salesman, and he put an arm around each of us. "Okay, folks, this is the couple who made the food you've all been gobbling up all evening. Nate Robicheaux and Roxanne Constantine. How about a big round of applause?"

He started clapping and everyone else joined in. There were a few whistles and a couple of "yeahs." Nate raised a hand to acknowledge the applause and gave them a smile that would probably have looked genuine to anyone who didn't know him very well. He turned to speak to Aldo again, and I escaped into the kitchen where there were still a lot of dishes to run through the dishwasher.

Nate returned after twenty minutes or so. "We got a bonus."

"Good. We deserved one."

We started dismantling the food trays. Coco's desserts were totally gone. I even saw a couple of people wrapping pecan tassies in napkins to take home. Most of the other serving dishes were also empty, although there were a few veggie packets left. Maybe some people assumed the "vegan" label meant they weren't yummy—their loss.

We dealt with the limited leftovers. Nate had offered the remnants of cheese and salami to Aldo since he'd paid for them, but he'd said we could take away anything that was left over. I was happy to hear that since I hadn't managed to grab anything to eat earlier in the evening. I was pretty sure Nate hadn't either.

Which didn't mean we'd be eating together. Just that maybe we could divide the cheese and salami.

Nate paid Donnell and gave her a chunk of Aldo's bonus after she'd helped unload the dishwasher one last time. "Should I share this with Jase?" she asked.

"Your choice. I wouldn't if I were you, though." I agreed with Nate on that one. Donnell had stuck it out to the end, doing Jase's work as well as her own.

She gave Nate a crooked smile, folding the bills in her purse. "Man needs to learn to prioritize better."

Nate and I loaded up the SUV after Donnell left. I found myself wondering if this would be the last time we worked together. Would he want me to work with him again when we weren't partners anymore? And if I left, would Nate go on doing the catering by himself, or would he pack it in and return to being a line cook at the café?

I hoped he wouldn't do that. The catering had been a way for him to get out of the kitchen and end his constant fights with Bobby. If he went into the kitchen now, it would be a defeat. He might not stay long—Las Vegas or LA would probably hold a lot more charm than Shavano even if he did love it here. In fact, any place might be better than a kitchen run by his demanding older brother.

I climbed into the SUV beside him, trying to remember what kind of groceries I had around the cabin. I was sort of hungry, but not enough to do anything much about it. Probably peanut butter and jelly, which I always had in abundance.

"I miss you," Nate said quietly.

I turned to look at him. He stared ahead at the star-spangled sky over the mountains, making no move to start the SUV.

"What?" I said, although I'd heard him clearly enough.

"I miss you." He turned to look at me, his face dim in the spring darkness. "All this time we've been apart. Every weekend I thought about what a screw-up this was, and how I wanted to get you back, *needed* to get you back. But I didn't know how to get around the distance between us. And yeah, I know I was mainly to blame for making that distance. So I went on missing you."

Part of me wanted to throw my arms around him so much, but I was still sort of pissed. "I've been around." *And you could have called. I would have answered.*

"I know. I know." He reached toward me, slowly, so slowly, letting me turn away if that's what I wanted to do.

I wasn't entirely sure. He'd hurt my feelings, and he'd made me angry. But the bottom line was, I'd missed him, too. Desperately.

He leaned across the seat and brought his lips to mine, his hands cupping my face, lightly. I'd almost forgotten what he tasted like, smelled like, felt like. But it all came rushing back. I put my hands on his chest and felt the thump of his heart beneath my palms. I still wasn't sure if this was a good idea, but on the whole I was inclined to go with it. Bad idea or not, it was what I wanted.

After a few fairly intense moments, Nate raised his head to look at me. "Come home with me?"

There were a lot of reasons not to do that, but more on the other side. The biggest one was that I really wanted to do it. "Okay."

"Do you need anything out of your truck?"

I thought about it. "My normal clothes." Since I didn't want to sit around in my chef's coat all night.

"You've got some clothes at my place."

I'd forgotten about that, but he was right. We'd gotten to the point where he had some of his clothes at my cabin, and I had some jeans and a couple of shirts at his apartment. "Okay. Then no, I don't need anything."

"Good. I don't want to stop."

Neither did I, I discovered.

So we made up. Several times, in fact.

And midway through, we made a great dinner from Aldo's leftovers. I hadn't had a chance to taste the beef pinwheels before or the salmon spread. The meatballs were all gone and so were the desserts. After we'd finished the few remaining small plates, we snacked on cheese and Bianca's bread while we did a postmortem on dinner, just like we always used to do.

"The pinwheels weren't as big a hit as the meatballs," Nate mused. "Plus, they're expensive. I don't know if we should do them again."

I took a meditative sip of the nice merlot Nate had supplied. "You could reduce the horseradish cream. Or eliminate it altogether. Some people don't like it. But most people like roast beef. Maybe just with cream cheese and a little mustard."

Nate narrowed his eyes. "That's a good point. I love horseradish but Coco hates it."

"I love the salmon spread, though. We should keep doing that."

"Yeah, that worked out." He grinned as he picked up the last crostini.

The cheese wheel from Marcus Jordan looked a little seedy since people had been cutting off slices all evening, but it tasted great. "We might want to go with cheese slices instead of a wheel," I suggested. "This looks a little shopworn after sitting out all night."

Nate nodded. "It looks great at the beginning of the evening, though. Maybe go with a half wheel. Or a quarter."

"Cheese wedges would work. And they'd be used up more quickly."

"Good point. I'll make a note."

"Do we have anything else coming up?" I figured we did since the catering company was doing great business. And apparently we were truly a *we* again.

Nate sighed, leaning back to take a sip of wine. "We've got a couple of parties, but I had to turn down a big corporate dinner. It was going to take too much time."

That seemed like a perfect opening to bring up what Coco had talked about. "Are you still working breakfast and lunch?"

Nate grimaced. "At the moment. I'm trying to get Mom to hire a new line cook, but Bobby's fighting it every step of the way."

Bobby was making his brother miserable at the moment because he probably thought Nate wouldn't quit. He could be wrong about that. "What does Madge say?"

"She's on my side on this one, and she's trying to get Bobby to understand the economics involved. We could make a lot more money if we upped the capacity of the catering business, but we can't up the capacity until I have more time to work. Eventually, he'll most likely give in, but right now it's hell. Plus, I'm afraid if we hire someone, he'll make them so miserable they'll quit within a week."

Something tickled at the edge of my memory. Marigold. "So you'd be looking for an experienced line cook to do breakfast and lunch, following the café's recipes."

"Yeah, basically. At some point, we might like somebody who could introduce new stuff, but for now it would just be someone who could make it through a couple of weeks with Bobby without running into the night screaming."

"Let me think about it," I said slowly. "I might have somebody for you."

"Someone you worked with?"

"Something like that." I hadn't worked with Marigold, but I knew what she could do.

"You want to help with brunch tomorrow?" Nate asked.

Before we'd had our breakup, the two of us had usually worked brunch at the café, although my work was mostly pouring mimosas and Bloody Marys. Going to the café would be the final seal on our not being broken up anymore. But I still felt a little hesitant. "Do you want me to?"

Nate moved closer, putting his arms around my waist. "I want you to do whatever makes you happy. But it would make me happy to see you standing next to me in the kitchen with a bottle of champagne. So yeah, I want you to."

"In that case," I said, winding my arms around his neck, "I'll be there."

Chapter 13

I filled Nate in on all the developments about Muriel Cates, including what Uncle Mike had told me about my mother. He gathered me into his arms. "That sucks. *She* sucks. Thank God you had your dad and Mike. I'm pretty sure your mom wouldn't have been a great person to have raised you."

I sighed. "No, you're probably right. Oh, I found out one other thing about Muriel—she was a gofer for Marcus and Sara, at least for a while."

Nate frowned. "A gofer? I might have seen her when I put in the order for the cheese and salami. A woman was cleaning up behind the counter, and it wasn't Sara."

"Blonde? In her forties?"

He paused then shook his head. "I can't remember. Not really. I'm pretty sure she was blonde, though. She had on a Jordan's Meats T-shirt and an apron. I thought she was just an employee."

I remembered Sara's emphatic, *paid by the hour, not on salary* claim. Something about that didn't jive with the snapshot Nate had just provided. Maybe Muriel had bought her own T-shirt, but I doubted it.

"Do you think I should tell Fowler about it?"

"He doesn't know who she worked for?"

"I don't think so. The last time I talked to him, when he brought the DNA results, he was still trying to find out what she was doing in town."

"It wouldn't hurt to tell him. Maybe he's still collecting information about her. You never know what might help."

We headed out to the farm after we'd finished brunch the next day. I wanted Nate to taste my tangerine marmalade. And I figured it wouldn't hurt to check the orders and get a few more jars of raspberry jam ready to go, given that I always had orders for it.

Uncle Mike wandered in with Herman a little after we got there. I suspected he'd seen Nate's car outside and come down to check things out for himself. He greeted Nate with a kind of casual friendliness, as if he'd just seen him yesterday.

Which I appreciated. I didn't want this reconciliation to be a Big Deal. The two of us were still trying to work out just what happened next. I didn't want my uncle and Nate's mom to start planning our wedding and naming the kids.

The café was closed on Mondays, so Sunday nights Nate usually stayed over at the cabin. I wasn't sure if he'd want to this time, but I made the suggestion—very tentatively, I admit.

"Sure," he said. "I'll cook dinner."

As usual, he made the most out of my meager stock of ingredients. I go all out getting the ingredients for my jams, but I don't always remember to stock up on things like pasta and brown rice. Fortunately, Nate had brought along the leftover cheese from Aldo's party, which was primo stuff. He made mac and cheese, using a box of rigatoni that had gotten squirreled away in the back of the pantry. Uncle Mike swung by again and announced that dinner was up to his exacting standards.

Then he disappeared, which I again appreciated. Nate and I still had some making up to do.

The next day we did what we usually did on Mondays: sat around and ate waffles. Nate pronounced the tangerine marmalade a hit. "Has Mom tasted this? It would be great for breakfast at the café, and Coco would go nuts over it."

That was a sort of tricky question since Uncle Mike had taken a couple of jars, but I had no idea what he served Madge when she came to the farm. Their relationship was not a subject for discussion. "I'm not sure," I hedged. "You could ask her."

Nate gave me a dry smile. "Yeah, I'll do that."

While we lingered over our coffee, Nate brought me up to speed on all the catering stuff I'd missed out on over the past couple of weeks.

"We've got an anniversary Friday night. Dinner for fifteen. Mostly family, I guess. Wife came in with a menu very much in mind—apparently, it's got sentimental significance for everybody."

"What is it?"

"You'll love this: meatloaf and mashed potatoes. And peas. She was adamant on that one. Frozen peas. She said we could do whatever we thought was good for the apps, but the dinner was set in stone."

I frowned. "That's kind of lean for a dinner party. How about bread or salad or…I don't know…tomato soup?"

"I can check on the bread and salad. She might loosen up a little on that. But those three items are the dinner. She offered to supply me with her meatloaf recipe, but I said I had one. Now I'm worried that she may not like mine if she's so set on a particular menu for this dinner."

"Make it Best of Breed. Give her the best version of all the things she wants. Meatloaf that's more meat than filler, and maybe has veal and pork along with the beef. Mashed potatoes with warmed cream and sweet butter. Frozen peas…" I paused. What the hell could you do with frozen peas besides heat them up and put a pat of butter on top? "Sorry. I got nothin' when it comes to frozen peas."

"I think it's the fact that they're on the menu that's important. As long as we don't screw them up, she'll be happy."

Screwing up frozen peas would be tough, although not impossible. "What kind of dessert does she want?"

"Cake," Nate said flatly. "I offered to let her talk to Coco, but she's got an order in with Grace Peters."

That put a bad taste in my mouth. We hadn't mentioned Grace Peters, and I was pretty sure I didn't want to. So far as I knew, Nate had hung out with her a couple of times along with several other people. I didn't want to make a big thing out of it.

"I didn't know Grace Peters did cakes." That sounded neutral enough.

Nate shrugged. "I think she's trying to branch out. French pastry isn't in high demand around here."

"I guess that's not something Bianca does. So maybe she'll have less competition. And then there's the cake lady."

Nate's eyes widened. "The cake lady's still in business? She made our birthday cakes when we were kids."

"I think this is a different cake lady. Maybe her daughter. Or her niece. Something like that. Anyway, the cake lady still rules." Which meant Grace's cake had better be spectacular. The cake lady was a local legend. "What do you want me to do for the dinner?"

"Apps, I guess. I'm thinking something sort of traditional. To go along with the down-home dinner theme."

"Onion soup dip with potato chips?" I gave him my most innocent look.

Nate rolled his eyes. "Traditional but classy."

"Pigs in a blanket, with bagel seasoning. Devils on horseback. Stuffed mushrooms. Some kind of crackers and dip. Maybe some deviled eggs. I suppose a cheese ball is too Christmassy."

"I'd say so." He grinned. "I knew I could leave it to you and you'd come up with stuff."

"Still working on it." Visions of fifties buffets danced in my head.

Nate paused, studying me. "God, I missed this. Being able to talk to you about this and get your ideas."

"I did, too."

"I wish we'd done it with the Aldo party. It would have been even better."

We stared at each other for a moment, both of us regretting the squandered time when we might have been together. "Let's make sure we don't do this again, okay?" Nate reached across the kitchen table and grabbed my hand. "Next time we get pissed at each other we'll have a big screaming fight followed by makeup sex."

"Deal," I said, ignoring the trickle of tears. "Absolute deal."

Nate took off in the middle of the afternoon when Bridget and Dolce arrived, which meant I had to endure a few smirks and pointed remarks from Bridget. Worth it, though. Totally worth it.

After Bridget and Dolce left, I took the opportunity to call Fowler. I was a little concerned about getting the Jordans in trouble for not coming forward—they were my friends, after all. Or anyway, Marcus was my friend. But I figured at most it was an oversight they could explain easily enough.

As I expected, Fowler was still at the police station even though it was after five. The man rarely seemed to go home. "I've got some information about Muriel Cates," I began.

"Family stuff?" Fowler didn't sound all that interested.

Maybe he didn't need to hear this after all. "No, stuff about her time in Shavano."

"Go ahead." His interest perked up.

I told him what Sara had said, along with Nate's memory of having seen Muriel Cates at the butcher shop. It was, I had to admit, pretty thin. But maybe it was useful anyway.

When I'd finished, Fowler paused. I hoped it was because he was writing it all down rather than that he was waiting for me to add something to the paltry information I'd provided already.

"She give you any dates?" he asked finally.

"Not really. I might have seen Muriel Cates coming out of Bianca Jordan's bakery, though. She said something about the woman I'd seen being Sara's assistant. That was a couple of days before the murder."

Fowler paused again. "Interesting. Sara Jordan talked to you about Muriel Cates but not to me?"

"Well, she asked me about the murder before I

knew who Muriel Cates was." I'd forgotten about that until now and the sort of weird conversation about Sara's "assistant."

"What did she want to know?"

"She just asked some general questions about the murder—what Cates was doing out there at that time of night, that kind of thing. Except we didn't know she was Cates then."

"She say anything about her employee being missing?"

"No. I asked her about her assistant because Bianca had mentioned her. But Sara said she hadn't worked out." And it had been a weird, abrupt conversation now that I thought about it.

"And neither of you made the connection with Muriel Cates?"

"I didn't. I can't answer for Sara." And I didn't want to try.

"All right, thanks. I'll talk to the Jordans about Cates."

And that was that. I was glad I'd called, but I didn't hold out much hope that this information represented some kind of breakthrough. Still, I was sort of on a roll here, and I decided to push it a little further. After all, I hadn't yet looked for Lucille Murphy in Clayton, New Mexico.

I opened my laptop and spent a few fruitless minutes on Google. There were, as it turned out, a whole lot of Lucille Murphys, including a lot of obituaries. But when I attached the town of Clayton, New Mexico, to the search, I got zilch. On a hunch, I also tried Lucille Cates, just in case that was Lucille's married name rather than Muriel's. But again, zilch.

I tried to think of some other name I could try but came up dry. I'd hit a dead end, at least for now.

Maybe Susa would have more luck. She didn't have the looming familial problems I had, and she was better at searching than I was.

Or so I hoped.

Chapter 14

I worked up a list of possible appetizers for the anniversary dinner we were catering that weekend. I actually had a good time with it, thinking about the kind of down-home apps you'd get at a family dinner in the fifties. I figured if we were featuring meatloaf and mashed potatoes, there was no point in serving foie gras and oysters Rockefeller as a prelude.

Nate and I did a little back and forth and finally settled on a cheese dip with water crackers, some pigs in a blanket, and some deviled eggs with smoked salmon and dill. Yeah, the last one was a little chi-chi, but given how plain the rest of the dinner was, I figured we needed one dish where we could show off a little.

Our client had accepted the need for dinner rolls and salad as long as we didn't go too far. She explained that meatloaf and mashed potatoes was her husband's absolute favorite dish, and she planned on surprising him with a catered version. My guess was her hubs was expecting something like beef Wellington from Robicheaux Catering and dreading it. This dinner was looking like it would be a lot of fun to do.

I went over to Bianca's on Wednesday to order the rolls, hoping she'd have enough time to put something together.

"What kind of rolls do you want?" she asked.

I gave her a sort of outline of the dinner, and it took

her a few seconds to stop laughing. "Oh, man, what I wouldn't give to see the guy's face when he realizes he really gets to eat something he loves. I hope she has somebody with a cell phone camera ready to go with pics."

"Yeah, I'm looking forward to that part of the evening, but I'm not sure what kind of rolls go with meatloaf."

"Lunch lady," Bianca said flatly. "The kind of yeast rolls you find in school cafeterias. Or you used to find them. These days they probably buy them readymade from some big commercial bakery. Always assuming they serve bread at all."

"Oh, that's a great idea. I remember they used to serve them in high school. Huge pillowy yeast rolls. With melted butter on top."

"Damn straight. How many do you need?"

"It's dinner for fifteen. Three dozen?"

She nodded. "That should do it. Everybody gets seconds and the nostalgic ones can take some home."

"Can I pick them up Friday morning?"

"Sure. All you'll have to do is rewarm them at the house that night, although it might be best for you to brush on the melted butter right before you serve them. That way they won't get soggy."

I paid the deposit and started to go when Bianca stopped me. "You got any more of that tangerine marmalade? It was a huge hit."

A message to warm the cockles of my heart. "I should be able to let you have a few more jars. It's the online special next month, so I need thirty jars for that. But I can make extra."

"Do that. I can probably sell a dozen or so." Bianca

gave me a deceptively innocent smile. "So you're working for Robicheaux Catering again?"

"I never left." But I knew what she meant—I was working with Nate again. "Yes, I'm back. Things are going well."

Bianca nodded. "I heard Aldo's big party went okay."

"It did. He was pleased. Your bread was a huge hit."

She shrugged. "Of course it was. You put the right stuff on top of it, and it shines."

I had to smile. Bianca knew exactly how good her stuff was, and she was right. It didn't count as arrogance when you had the tickets to back your judgment up.

The salad for the retro dinner wouldn't take any special ingredients—Nate could order everything we needed from his regular supplier, along with the ingredients for the meatloaf and the potatoes. And I figured the café had lots of frozen peas already.

That night I made spaghetti carbonara to celebrate. I wasn't sure what I was celebrating, but it felt like a good thing to do. Uncle Mike pronounced himself satisfied after two helpings. Not small helpings either. He gave me a slightly tentative smile. "So you and Nate."

"Me and Nate?"

"You're…okay now?"

"We're okay now."

He blew out a long breath. "Glad to hear it. Madge and I were worried."

Which brought up a point. "Actually, I need to talk to Madge. About the café."

"Yeah?" Uncle Mike looked wary all of a sudden. "What about it?"

"She needs to hire a line cook. Nate can't go on working double shifts. It's wearing him to a frazzle."

Uncle Mike grimaced. "She knows that. Trust me, she knows already. She's trying to find somebody, but Bobby's not helping her that much."

"He wouldn't." I didn't hold back the bitterness there. Bobby needed to grow up. "The thing is, though, I think I might know someone who'd be good. She's a cook I knew in Denver, Lauren's cousin. And she's looking for a new gig."

"A woman?" Uncle Mike sounded skeptical. "I don't know how Bobby would feel about that."

"Bobby needs to get a grip. Marigold is a terrific cook. Plus she's worked with some real bruisers. She's tough enough to stand up to Bobby."

"Marigold?" Uncle Mike's eyebrows elevated. "Her name's Marigold? Right there might be a problem."

"Let me worry about that. Next time you talk to Madge ask her to give me a call."

"Okay." He still looked skeptical. But he also looked willing to give me a chance.

Either Uncle Mike talked to Madge sooner than I thought he would or Madge was more desperate than I'd anticipated. She called me later that night. "So who's this cook you know for the café?"

"Her name's Marigold Watson. Her cousin was my roommate when I lived in Denver. Lauren told me Marigold's looking for a new job, and she wants to get out of the city."

"Marigold?" Madge sounded a little wary. "What

kind of cooking has she done?"

I guess it wasn't surprising that people judged Marigold by her name before they met her, but it was still a little annoying. "She's got a lot of experience. Her father and uncle owned a butcher shop in Brighton, so she learned how to break down a cow by the time she was a teenager. Also pigs and chickens, but the cow's the impressive part." Or it had been to me, but then I hadn't had a lot of experience with whole animals.

"So she's a butcher?" Madge still sounded a little cautious, but also more intrigued.

"Along with a short order cook, and she's worked the line at a couple of fine dining joints. Right now she's at one of the big Italian places in Denver, but she's getting burned out. She wants to do something different, according to Lauren."

"Sounds intriguing. Could you have her give me a call? Maybe email me her résumé?"

"I'll call her and see what she says. And I'll get back to you." I should probably have talked to Marigold first, but I didn't see the point in getting her hopes up if Madge wasn't interested.

I called Lauren the next day to get Marigold's phone number. Fortunately, Lauren was pleased. "Marigold would get a kick out of living in Shavano. She's big on outdoor sports when she's not working—hiking, snowshoeing, all of it. We're talking full-time here, right? Because she wouldn't be interested in less."

I bit my lip. I'd assumed the job was full-time, but I hadn't really asked. "Marigold can talk to Madge about the details. All I know is they're looking for somebody pretty hard." Or at least some of the family were. I wasn't sure about Bobby.

Lauren gave me Marigold's phone number and told me she'd be home in the evenings after she got off work. "Better to talk to her when she's sitting at home over a beer than when she's serving up multiple plates of spaghetti and meatballs. Her attitude is liable to be a little more positive."

Thursday I divided my time between jam and appetizers, boiling eggs and chopping salmon in one part of the kitchen, then switching to tangerines in the other. And being very careful not to cross contaminate since salmon and marmalade do not mix happily. After Dolce arrived, I turned the marmalade over to her and started piping the filling into the deviled eggs. Bridget loaded up the mailing cartons with the end of the blueberry Earl Grey, and I can't say I was sorry to see it go. I would probably always associate that jam with my fight with Nate, unfair though that undoubtedly was.

Nate called to check on my progress around five after Dolce and Bridget had both taken off. "I've got the eggs done. And the cheese dip. I figured I'd do the pigs in a blanket tomorrow afternoon so they wouldn't get soggy."

"Great," he said. "Come do them in the kitchen tomorrow afternoon. Then we can head over to the Blavatskys' place after everything is ready."

"Okay, works for me. I'll see you around two."

"While I've got you—did you really tell Mom you could find her a line cook?"

"I told her I knew someone who might be looking for a job. And now that I think of it, I'd better call her this evening and find out how interested she might be."

"Okay. Bobby's likely to snarl at her, but tell her

not to take it personally. He's likely to snarl at anyone who's not a member of the family. Hell, he snarls at us, too, as far as that goes."

"Okay, I'll tell Marigold. She's pretty unflappable, though, and she's worked for a lot of chefs in her time."

"Marigold?" Nate said, inevitably.

"She's tougher than her name. Don't worry about it."

"Okay, see you tomorrow." Nate still sounded dubious, but he'd never met Marigold.

I waited until seven or so when I could be sure she was home from her lunch shift and whatever came after it. She answered after a couple of rings, sounding suspicious. "Okay, who do I know in Shavano? If I don't know you, I'm hanging up, no matter what you're selling."

"Hi, Marigold," I said hastily. "It's Roxy Constantine. Lauren's friend."

"Hey, Roxy, I forgot you live in Shavano. How are things going?"

"Fine." We exchanged a few more pleasantries before we got down to business. "Lauren mentioned you might be interested in moving on from your job. I know of an opening up here, and I wanted to pass it along."

"Yeah, I'm thinking about it. And I was thinking of getting out of Denver for a while. What's the situation?"

I described Robicheaux's—the café, the menu, the crowds for breakfast and lunch, and Nate's situation trying to run both a catering business and a café kitchen.

"Tough," Marigold observed. "So they're looking

for someone to do both breakfast and lunch?"

"Right. There are two other people in the kitchen, including a full-time salad chef and baker. Basically it's working the flattop and maybe preparing some other dishes like pot roast that they use as specials."

"Sounds tempting," Marigold said. "I like Shavano a lot, and being in the mountains is high on my list. Plus it would be a relief to get into basic cooking again. Who do I talk to?"

"The manager is Madge Robicheaux. I already mentioned you. She wants you to send her a résumé and give her a call." I passed on Madge's email address and her phone number.

"Better and better." Marigold sounded like she was smiling.

I hated to spoil things, but I figured she deserved all the facts. "There's a catch."

Marigold sighed. "Figures. What is it? Lousy pay?"

Nate paid me a percentage of the take for the catering jobs, so I didn't know what kind of salaries they paid at the café. "I don't know what the pay is exactly, but I think it's pretty good. Most of their staff has been working there forever." Both of us knew high turnover meant trouble behind the scenes.

"So what then?"

I took a breath. How to explain Bobby? "The guy who runs the kitchen is the oldest son in the family, Bobby Robicheaux. He's been cooking there for a lot of years, both when his dad was still alive and running the place and afterward. He's the kind of guy who hates changes." That pretty much summed Bobby up, although it didn't describe how annoying he could be.

"And you think he'd put me off?"

"Maybe. He can be a real pain in the ass."

Marigold's laugh was as warm as noodle soup on a cold day. "Oh, honey, I've worked with butchers. I've worked with Italian grandmas. I even worked with a guy who garnished his plates with freakin' tweezers and microgreens. It takes a hell of a lot to phase me."

"Glad to hear it," I said with absolute honesty. "Call Madge and see how you like the sound of the job. Let me know if you want to come up and look things over."

"Will do. Thanks for the tip."

I hoped she'd still thank me if she met Bobby, but that was out of my hands. I'd have to leave it to Madge to see if she could rein in her older son's more obnoxious tendencies.

I considered doing some more work but decided not to. I had lots of marmalade on hand, and a couple dozen deviled eggs in the refrigerator. Tomorrow I'd go to the catering kitchen and fix the pigs in a blanket, using the miniature sausages we'd gotten from Marcus Jordan and, yes, frozen puff pastry. I'm only willing to go so far for authenticity.

I felt like I was ahead of the game, more or less. Back on track. Nate and I were together. The catering job was paying off. My jam sales continued to go up and the monthly specials were a hit. And now Marigold might prove to be the solution to the problem of Nate's overworked schedule.

Things were going well overall. I wasn't sure why I had this sudden urge to knock wood.

Chapter 15

I got to the catering kitchen a little later than I'd intended the next afternoon. Uncle Mike had needed my help getting Herman to the vet for his shots. This is a major production every year since Herman is a big dog who's also a total freak when it comes to the vet. It's a tipoff to him when Uncle Mike and I get into the car together with him since usually it's just one or the other of us. This results in howls of anguish from Herm's traveling crate, and I usually end up having to sit with him in the back seat while Uncle Mike drives as quickly as possible to the vet's place.

After we got him checked out and medicated, I had to take a shower so I didn't spend the rest of the day smelling of dog—something I definitely didn't want when I was embarking on a catering job.

I found Nate up to his elbows in meatloaf mix, pretty much literally. He'd already decided to do two separate loaves, given that a single meatloaf for fifteen might be hard to get into and out of the oven, let alone slice at the table. "Are you going to do a glaze?" I asked as I pulled the cocktail sausages and thawed puff pastry out of the refrigerator.

Nate shook his head. "Mrs. Blavatsky asked me not to. Apparently, her husband hates ketchup, so even if we used tomato sauce he'd probably have bad flashbacks to high school cafeterias."

"So what goes on top?"

He shrugged. "Bacon. That'll add some smokiness and keep it moist."

"Sounds good." Nate looked like he was in the groove, so I went ahead with my pigs. I know it's traditional to use crescent roll dough to wrap them, but I like puff pastry dough better, even though it's more work since you have to roll it out thin. Marcus's cocktail sausages were a little shorter and fatter than the ones from the supermarket, but I was betting they were also tastier.

I rolled out the puff pastry, then sliced it into thin strips just the right width to wrap around the sausages. I had a little over two dozen sausages, since Marcus sold by the pound. When I got them all rolled up tight, I gave each one a quick egg wash to make them shiny, then sprinkled on some sesame and poppy seeds for extra crunch.

Nate glanced up as I took them to the oven. "How many do you have?"

"Thirty-two," I said.

He grinned. "Enough to sample."

"Definitely enough to sample. What do you need me to do now?"

"Potatoes," he said. "Peel and dice and throw them in a bowl of water."

"Got it."

We worked in companionable silence until around five. The pigs were great, but I'd known they would be. We had some spicy brown mustard for dipping, but I was going to wait to put it in a bowl until we got to the house. The meatloaf smelled spectacular. Nate was baking it about halfway and then we'd finish it at the house, too. We'd bring the potatoes along to boil them up and smash them on site. And Nate had an industrial sized bag of peas.

We were good to go.

Coco swung into the kitchen as we were loading up the coolers for transport. "All ready for the nostalgia fest?"

Nate shrugged. "We're good."

"What about the cake? Are you supposed to pick it up from Grace?" Something about the way Coco said *Grace* led me to believe she wasn't delighted about Grace having been hired to do the cake.

"She's supposed to bring it by on her own," Nate said. "She did all the arranging with Mrs. Blavatsky directly. I don't know what she's planning."

"You two getting along okay?" Coco asked.

I tensed, unsure which *two* she was referring to.

Nate had the same problem. "You mean Grace and me? We're getting along so far as I know."

Coco shrugged. "Nana Tibbs said she saw the two of you having words at the Blue Light the other night. Said it looked like you were arguing."

That was interesting. Both the fact that Nate was at the Blue Light again and the fact that he'd had a run-in with Grace Peters.

"I was playing pool with Spence," he said with a quick glance my way. "Grace was there with somebody else. We got into a conversation about cooking. I wouldn't say we were arguing. Maybe disagreeing is more like it. Active disagreeing."

"What was it? Did she sneer at your preference for Chipotle over Taco Bell?" Coco gave him a brief smirk.

"She's a typical baker, thinks baking is a higher

kind of kitchen skill. I told her she was full of it. It didn't last long. Just between pool games."

Coco's eyebrows elevated. I was willing to bet she held a very similar set of beliefs since she was a baker herself. "Since when are you unimpressed by baking skills?"

"Since Grace argued that her training at some Paris patisserie put her ahead of people who made their bones in a diner." He gave his sister a level look. The two of them had both started out at Robicheaux's Café, which was, in fact, a very good diner.

Coco shrugged. "So she's an idiot. And now you have to work with her?"

"We're doing completely separate things. All she has to do is show up with her cake before dessert time. And then leave promptly." Nate's smile was sort of automatic.

"Hey, Rox." Coco stepped around Nate. "Have you got any more of that tangerine marmalade? I tried it at Bianca's, and now I'm hooked."

"It's next month's special. I'll save you a couple of jars."

"Great. Good luck tonight, y'all." She stepped to the door that connected to the café kitchen, pausing to give us both a guileless smile before she disappeared.

"Troublemaker," Nate muttered. "A born troublemaker."

"What kind of trouble was she trying to stir up?" I was still a little concerned about Grace Peters, although not enough to be worried.

Nate slid the last container into the cooler, then paused. "There was never anything between Grace Peters and me. Never. She shows up at the Blue Light sometimes, and Spence and I go there to play pool with some of the other guys. But our conversations have been as brief as I can make them. She annoys the hell out of me. And Coco thinks that's funny."

I wanted to ask a few follow-ups but decided to let it go. "You want me to follow you in my truck? We can load the coolers in the back."

He nodded. "That'll work. Mom had to take the SUV tonight for some reason, so all I've got is my car."

"Two vehicles it is. Let's get them loaded."

The Blavatskys lived in one of the new developments toward Mount Oxford. The two-story McMansions in the neighborhood looked a little out of place on the barren high plateau, but the developers had overcompensated when it came to street names. We passed a Spruce Lane and an Aspen Way and a lot of *pine* variants: Pine Tree Street, Pine Needle Ridge, Pine Grove Way, and so on. The Blavatskys lived on Pine Cone Avenue, and it looked like the developers had attempted to plant a few cedar bushes at the street corners for ornamentation. Cedars weren't pines, but maybe they figured nobody would notice.

I pulled in behind Nate in front of the triple garage, hoping we could find a rear entrance to the kitchen. I hated traipsing through the living room carrying coolers, and I was hoping we could keep the secret about the main dish until Mrs. Blavatsky could do her Big Reveal.

The rear entrance led into the family room, but that room was right off the kitchen so it wasn't a bad compromise. Mrs. Blavatsky came in as we were unloading. She looked a little like a fifties movie star, lots of curves in a form-fitting blue dress, along with shoulder-length black hair and generous lips. But she also had the laughing eyes I'd expect from someone who came up with the meatloaf idea.

"Everybody's due to start showing up around six," she said. "If we could have the appetizers out then, we could start munching."

"No problem," Nate said. "We'll warm up the pigs-in-a-blanket, and everything else is cold."

"Great. And the main dish?" Mrs. Blavatsky gave him a roguish grin.

"Just needs to finish cooking. When would you like to serve dinner?"

"Let's shoot for seven. I'll let you know if it's going to be longer than that. And wait until I give the signal to bring it in. I want Art to really be surprised."

Donnell was doing the serving again, so we could get everything ready to go in the kitchen. But I figured I could put out the appetizers on my own before she got there. We had a beautiful deviled egg dish that Madge had found at a yard sale, shaped like an egg with painted decorations to spice things up. I started laying out the eggs so that I could put a bit of smoked salmon and a sprinkle of dill on top. Nate got the pigs into one oven for a quick warm up, then slid the meat loaves into the second oven so they could finish baking.

By five thirty, when Donnell arrived, I had the cheese dip in a bowl and was arranging the crackers in an artistic spiral around the outside. I may not have much of a gift for home decoration, but I can style the hell out of most food.

"Pretty. Do these go out now?" Donnell picked up a stack of appetizer plates and napkins.

"Yeah. There's a big coffee table in the living

room. You can put them there unless Mrs. Blavatsky wants something different." I'd done a quick reconnaissance of the living room to see how things were arranged. I figured the guests would seat themselves on either side of the coffee table and munch away.

Mr. Blavatsky was serving as bartender himself, so there were only three of us from Robicheaux Catering to worry about. I pulled the pigs-in-a-blanket out of the warming oven and started arranging them on the platter. Once they were ready to go, I could work on the salads and brush Bianca's gorgeous lunch lady rolls with melted butter.

Nate was busy with the potatoes and the peas. The timing with the peas would be crucial. We couldn't put them on to steam too soon or they'd be badly overdone. But we also couldn't wait too long or we'd end up serving partially frozen peas.

I dropped the salad mix into a stainless-steel bowl and started whisking the dressing. "Are we going with croutons or sunflower seeds?"

"Croutons," Nate said as he laid the strips of bacon along the meatloaf. "I figured with every other retro thing we're doing, we might as well go with croutons. Coco toasted up a bunch this afternoon."

When she wasn't tormenting her brothers, Coco was a hell of a salad chef. Her croutons were made from torn dinner rolls and hamburger buns, using the café's leftovers, and tossed with parmesan and other seasonings. Coco toasted them in the oven with a little olive oil.

I got the salad plates set up at the side, ready to be placed on a tray when we started serving. Bianca's rolls sat, fluffy as pillows, in their foil pan, and I grabbed the butter to start brushing the tops.

"Hello, there," came a masculine voice from the doorway.

I jumped a few inches, and Nate managed not to drop the potatoes. We both turned toward the door and saw someone who was undoubtedly Mr. Blavatsky.

He was maybe five feet nine or so but built like a railroad tie—very solid and very square. His curly salt and pepper hair surrounded a sizeable bald spot, and he looked like someone who enjoyed life thoroughly. "Art Blavatsky," he said, extending a hand in Nate's direction. "Thought I'd come in and see how dinner's coming." He turned eager eyes toward the stove. "What smells so good?"

We weren't supposed to spoil Mrs. Blavatsky's surprise. On the other hand, Mr. Blavatsky was paying the bills, and not answering didn't seem like an option.

"Um…" said Nate.

"Art, what are you doing here?" Mrs. Blavatsky walked briskly into the kitchen, taking hold of her husband's arm. "Come on. Reggie and Mark just got here. They're dying to see you."

Mr. Blavatsky cast one longing glance at the stove. "Sure smells good," he said as his wife towed him through the door.

Nate blew out a breath, then shook his head, chuckling. "It does smell good. I'll give him that."

"It smells terrific." I slid the foil pan with Bianca's rolls into the warming oven as Donnell breezed in again.

"Eggs are a hit," she said, brandishing the empty egg dish. "Got any more?"

"Yep. How are the pigs?"

"Going well. May need to refill the mustard bowl. Everything's getting snapped up. Hungry people."

"Okay," Nate said, "after you put out the refills, you can put the salads on the table. They're ready to go."

Just then someone knocked very tentatively at the door. Nate had stepped into the dining room to make sure the table was ready, so I pulled it open.

Grace Peters stared up at me from the back step. "Oh, Roxy. That's right. I forgot you worked for Nate."

I was careful not to grit my teeth, even though I wanted to. I did, in fact, work for Nate. Sort of.

Grace stepped into the room, carrying an oversized white carton that was probably the cake for dessert. She placed the carton on the serving island, then began to remove the string that was holding it closed. "Did you bring the ice cream?"

I blinked at her. "We didn't have an order for ice cream. It was our understanding that you were in charge of dessert." I might have put a little extra emphasis on that *our*. So I'm petty. Sue me.

"I'm in charge of the cake," Grace corrected. "That's all. Just cake. It was *my* understanding that Nate would provide a couple of gallons of ice cream from Cobble's."

Cobble's was an artisan ice cream shop in town. Nate had, in fact, bought ice cream from them in the past. But I was very certain he hadn't bought any this time because we didn't have an order for it.

Nate pushed through the kitchen door at that moment. His smile tightened when he saw Grace. "Good, you're here. I assume that's the cake."

Grace's smile was equally tight. "That's the cake, but Roxy says she didn't get the ice cream. What's up with that?"

That time I did grit my teeth. I figured Grace was trying a little blame shifting.

"There's no ice cream," Nate said flatly. "It wasn't part of our dinner order. You need to…"

The kitchen door flew open again, and Mrs. Blavatsky stepped in. "Oh, good," she said when she saw Grace. "I'd begun to worry. Now we've got the cake, and we're all set." She stepped forward to open the carton. "You've all got to see this. It's just the best."

She lifted the top, and Nate and I dutifully stepped forward to get a look. It was indeed a gorgeous cake, round and smooth and decorated with a spill of very realistic looking paste flowers that covered one side.

Mrs. Blavatsky stepped back, smiling. "Lovely. Just lovely."

"I'm sorry there's no ice cream," Grace said quickly. "Apparently, we had a misunderstanding over who was supposed to provide it." The tight smile had returned as she glanced at Nate.

Mrs. Blavatsky shrugged. "Who needs ice cream with this cake? It'll be scrumptious."

Grace's smile was so tight my own jaw ached. "Well, that's very kind of you. I'm still sorry."

"No problem." Mrs. Blavatsky turned to Nate. "Fifteen minutes, okay?"

"Fifteen minutes is fine." Nate gave her another cursory smile as she disappeared into the dining room.

"I guess I'll move on," Grace said. "Good luck with the dinner."

Nate nodded, not smiling at all. "Thanks."

Grace left the kitchen as Nate and I glanced at each other. "She didn't ask for ice cream," Nate said. "Neither did Mrs. Blavatsky. Just so you know."

"I know she didn't. And I know Mrs. Blavatsky didn't either. I'm not sure why she was trying to stir up trouble, but she didn't succeed. This dinner is going to crush. Absolutely crush."

"Damn straight." Nate turned to his meatloaf with new determination.

Things moved along swiftly, and I began to worry I might have underestimated the number of appetizers we needed. But we were approaching our seven o'clock dinner hour so maybe it didn't matter that the eggs and pigs seemed to have disappeared and we were running low on crackers.

I put the rolls into a couple of bread baskets as Nate finished mashing the potatoes and dropped the peas into an inch of boiling water. He sighed. "Frozen peas. At least we've got mashed potatoes and meatloaf to show off our chops."

Mrs. Blavatsky stepped in quickly. "We're going to sit down and have salad. I'll send my son Jess in to let you know when to bring out the main dishes." She gave us a quick grin. "Don't worry. We'll keep Art occupied."

Donnell came in as Mrs. Blavatsky exited. "Okay, what's the deal with dinner? Are we serving plates or family style?"

"Family style," Nate said, pulling the peas off the burner. "And we'll all three carry out a platter or bowl. She wants him to see it all at once."

Donnell looked dubious, but she picked up the two baskets of rolls. "Guess I can get these out there. Might want some bread with their salad."

I had a moment's panic trying to remember if we'd put out the butter, but then I reassured myself that we had. Nate started scraping the mashed potatoes into one of the serving bowls Mrs. Blavatsky had provided, and I grabbed another bowl for the peas.

"Is the meatloaf done?"

Nate nodded. "Bacon's crisping, but it's ready to come out." He tented the potatoes and peas with foil, then opened the oven and pulled out the loaves.

They were gorgeous, if I do say so myself: Perfectly formed loaves draped with crisp bacon slices. Nate had cooked them on racks so that the melted bacon fat didn't make the bottoms greasy.

"Give me a hand," he said. "You hold the platter and I'll do the transfer."

He used an oversized spatula to loosen the loaves from the rack, then slid it underneath the first one, lifting it carefully onto the platter I was holding. "One down."

"Doing great," I said, ever the supportive sous chef.

Nate gave me a quick smile, then lifted the second loaf into place. "Done."

"Gorgeous," I said, and they were. Nate added a sprinkle of chopped parsley and a silver pie server to the platter.

Both doors to the kitchen swung open simultaneously, and I felt a moment's panic that Art Blavatsky had escaped his wife's watchful eye. But it was just Donnell and a youngish guy I figured was the Blavatsky son who was supposed to usher us in.

"Hi," he said. "I'm Jess. Mom sent me to make

sure you guys were ready."

"We are," Nate said. "Is it time?"

Jess stared at the meat loaves, eyes wide. "Oh my God, those look terrific."

"Thanks," Nate said patiently. "Is it time?"

"Oh, yeah, it is," Jess grinned. "This is going to be great."

I hoped so, but a lot depended on getting the food to the table while it was still hot. I handed the bowl of peas to Donnell since I figured it was the coolest of the three serving dishes, then picked up the bowl of mashed potatoes. Nate took the meat loaf platter.

"We'll need you to open the door," he told Jess.

"Right." Jess nodded, suddenly a man with a purpose.

He turned toward the kitchen door he'd come through and we followed him, with Nate bringing up the rear to keep the meat loaf concealed as long as possible. Donnell looked confused but game and I was trying my best to keep a bland smile in place. Jess cracked the door a little so we could hear what was going on.

"You all know this is a very special night, our thirtieth anniversary," Mrs. Blavatsky was saying.

The other people in the room, all apparently relatives, cheered lustily.

"So to celebrate, I went all out. The best catering company in town, the one associated with Art's favorite restaurant, Robicheaux's."

I wanted to look at Nate to see his reaction to being called the best catering company in Shavano, but I didn't want to risk it. I figured as soon as the door opened we were on.

"I told them to give us their very best," Mrs. Blavatsky continued. "Primo everything. A real gourmet dinner. All for Art. Love you, babe."

Now I wished I could see Mr. Blavatsky. I figured his mixed feelings had to be showing. He loved his wife, but he probably dreaded anything labeled *gourmet*.

"Okay, Jess, bring on our gourmet feast!" Mrs. Blavatsky called.

Jess pushed the door open and the three of us stepped into the dining room. The guests watched us expectantly, and then looked a little confused when they saw the mashed potatoes and the peas. But then Nate stepped forward with the meat loaves, and the dining room dissolved in laughter. Someone who was probably a Blavatsky child began clapping, and the others all joined in.

Mrs. Blavatsky's grin lit up the room. She turned to her husband. "As if I didn't know your favorite meal on this good green earth. Happy anniversary, babe."

I stole a glance at Mr. Blavatsky, seated at the head of the table. His face was a rosy shade of pink, and his eyes were suspiciously bright. For just a moment, I worried that he might be angry about being the butt of a joke. But then he was on his feet, giving his wife an enthusiastic embrace. For a moment I was afraid he might embrace Donnell and me, too, which might seriously affect our ability to preserve the mashed potatoes and peas. But then he grinned happily at all the people seated at his table.

"I knew it smelled good," he said. "Real good. Let's eat!"

Chapter 16

The dinner was a hit. A big, massive, absolute hit. Mr. Blavatsky had Nate come out and take a bow, pronouncing his meat loaf the second best he'd ever tasted. The absolute best being the one made by Mrs. Blavatsky herself.

Nate and I retired to the kitchen to start cleaning up while Donnell brought out more mashed potatoes and peas when needed. Apparently, the Blavatsky family was made up of very enthusiastic eaters. They finished off all the potatoes, peas, meatloaf, and rolls and were crying for more. I began to worry that we'd underestimated the amount of food they needed, but Nate assured me he'd followed Mrs. Blavatsky's numbers more or less to the letter.

I really wanted everything to be perfect for the Blavatskys. They seemed like great people, and I only hoped I'd still be as devoted to my partner on our thirtieth anniversary.

Always assuming I had a partner that stuck around for thirty years.

Nate helped Donnell clear the dishes after the Blavatskys had eaten everything in sight. All that was left was the dessert, which wasn't our problem, but I still hoped it was a hit. Mrs. Blavatsky swung into the kitchen a few minutes later looking radiant and slightly rumpled. Maybe Mr. Blavatsky had been expressing his appreciation. "Time for the cake. Can you help me get it to the table, Nate? We'll cut it there."

"Absolutely," Nate said, handing Donnell a stack of dessert plates before he hefted the cake in his hands. It looked a little heavy, but maybe it was supposed to be.

"Okay, then, let's get it out there so people can see." Mrs. Blavatsky swung the door open then stood grinning happily as Nate walked through with the cake. "Just look at this cake, y'all," she called.

Applause echoed from the next room, so it sounded like Grace's cake had been a hit. I didn't begrudge her. Well, maybe a little, but even I had to admit it was a beautiful cake. Although I'd be willing to bet Coco could have come up with something just as scrumptious, given a chance, with half the aggravation.

I started loading the dinner dishes into the dishwasher as Nate did a quick preliminary scrub on the pans. He'd let Tres, the café's dishwasher and general clean-up guy, take care of the actual cleaning, but neither of us was eager to carry dirty pots in our vehicles. Donnell came in with the last of the dinner dishes except for the dessert plates. I finished loading the dishwasher, figuring Mr. or Mrs. Blavatsky could load the dessert plates tomorrow. We promised a clean kitchen when we were done cooking, but *clean* didn't mean *spotless*.

Nate gave Donnell her pay, promising her a cut if Mr. Blavatsky gave him a bonus. Donnell grinned at us both as she folded the bills into her pocket. "Fun night. Wish they were all this easy."

"Ain't that the truth," Nate said ruefully.

We'd just started to load up our various pans and

hors d'oeuvre platters into our boxes when Mr. Blavatsky stepped into the kitchen. "Oh, good, you're still here." He beamed at us both. "I've gotta tell you, that meatloaf was out of sight. Awesome, my kids said. Just awesome."

"Glad you liked it," Nate said. "We had fun putting everything together."

"I know the wife paid you, but that meal deserves something extra." He pressed a couple of bills into Nate's hand. "I always loved Robicheaux's. I knew your dad. Great guy, truly great."

Nate nodded. "Thanks. That's always nice to hear."

"I'll be telling everybody about this dinner. Telling them all to go to you for catering." He patted Nate shoulder enthusiastically. "Thanks for a great evening."

"Glad we could be a part of it." Nate rubbed his arm absently as Mr. Blavatsky walked into the dining room. That pat on the shoulder had been a little overenthusiastic.

"Load up?"

Nate nodded, then handed me one of the hundred-dollar bills Mr. Blavatsky had given him. "Here you go."

"What about Donnell?"

"I'll take care of her out of my share. All in all, a good night's work."

"It was that." I tucked the hundred into my purse and picked up one of the cartons of pans.

It didn't take us long to load up. "Let's get these to the café," Nate said. "Then we can go on to my place."

"Or my place. Are you working breakfast tomorrow?"

He shook his head. "One change Mom pushed

through—I don't work breakfast the day after we cater a dinner. Bobby's not happy about it, but he's adjusting."

"Let's do my place, then. I've got jam. Also wine." I gave him my seductive smile.

"Sold. Jam and wine sound like winners."

We got all the boxes securely fastened in my truck and headed for the catering kitchen. As far as I was concerned, our job was to carry in the boxes and leave them on the worktable. Nate could tell Tres where they were, and Tres could see about getting them washed up. We'd cleaned up the Blavatskys' kitchen, and that was it for the night.

The catering kitchen was a little spooky, with the lights from the parking lot shining in the windows, leaving pools of darkness farther inside. I switched on the overheads as Nate toted in the boxes, stacking them on the floor next to the wooden worktable. I hadn't checked with him to see when we'd need to start working on our next job, but they were usually weekend gigs, so I figured we didn't have to get anything ready right away. Nate checked around the kitchen to make sure nothing was in anybody's way, and then we headed out to the truck, locking up securely on the way.

Nate drove his own car so he could go back to town in the morning. He might have gotten out of doing breakfast, but that still left lunch. To get to the farm, we had to cross Second Street, which is party central in Shavano on Friday night during Spring Break. There were lots of young people clogging the sidewalks and spilling over into the streets, especially around the bars. Shavano didn't get as many Spring Breakers as the big ski resort towns, but we got our share, particularly during March. And right now we seemed to have more than our share of idiot party animals clogging the intersections. Fowler's men were patrolling the streets, trying to keep things under some kind of control, and I thought I saw the chief himself reading the riot act to some very happy frat boys.

We finally got through the crowds and turned onto the county highway that led to the farm. Once we got away from town, things got dark fast, particularly since there was just a sliver of new moon.

We passed the turnoffs to a few farms, most of them marked by yard lights. I'd driven this highway so much it was almost automatic, but that night was darker than usual even with Nate's headlights shining behind me. I told myself to cool it—getting spooked in October was one thing, but getting spooked in March was ridiculous.

Of course, there was always Muriel Cates to think about, dead just a few yards down the road.

We reached the turnoff, and I slowed, turning carefully into the drive. The entrance was masked by pine groves on either side. The first yard light was farther on, closer to my cabin. Again it was darker than usual. I guess I'd never realized how much the pines lining the road blocked out the night sky.

I was just a little way beyond the turnoff, at a point where the yard light was blocked by a curve, when I realized another car was coming up the drive toward us at considerable speed. The drive to the farm is a gravel road that's barely two lanes. It also develops potholes every spring. We fill in the potholes during the summer and every few years we get it graded, but at this time of year, driving it at speed was a very bad idea.

The car racing toward me was a dark shape without headlights, clearly a stranger who didn't know the drive that well. And clearly, even though I had my headlights on, the driver of the other car was either unaware of me and Nate or didn't care that we were on the road, too. The pines at the road's edge made it difficult to get away, but I managed to pull the truck as far to the side of the road as I could without ending up in a drainage ditch. I made it over just in time to let the other car pass a few inches away, with a lot of pinging gravel and spinning wheels. I had only the dimmest impression of what kind of car it was and no impression at all of the driver.

"What the hell..." I began, and then I heard the sound of crashing metal behind me.

I pulled to a stop on the shoulder, twisting to see what was happening. Nate's car had been pushed off the road by the impact. The side was smashed up against one of the pines. Before I could get out of my seat belt, it slid farther downhill and bumped to a stop, the front tires jammed against the outer edge of the drainage ditch.

The other car, whatever and whoever it had been, sped on up the drive either not knowing or not caring about the accident they'd just caused.

I pushed my truck door open and ran to Nate's car, my feet sliding on the gravel and dirt. As I got closer, I could see a large dent in the driver's side, as if the speeding car had bounced off on its way to the point where the drive turned into the county road. Nate's headlights shone down the hillside, outlining the groove of the drainage ditch.

"Nate," I yelled as I ran toward him. "Nate, are you okay?"

I grabbed the door handle and pulled, but the door was jammed shut by the dent. I could see Nate slumped to the side, and for a moment I had a horrible flashback to Muriel Cates. But then he opened his eyes. He still looked sort of bleary, and I could see what looked like blood, dripping down the side of his head.

I yanked on the door again, probably making things worse in my panic. It took me a moment to realize that the bottom of the door was wedged in the dirt beside the car, and after a few more seconds of jerking I managed to get it open.

I dropped to my knees beside him. "Are you okay? Can you hear me? Do you understand?"

I was babbling in panic, desperately trying to get Nate to reassure me. Something he probably didn't feel much like doing.

"Roxy," someone yelled. "What the hell? What's going on?"

I turned to see Uncle Mike trotting up the road followed by Herman. "There's been an accident," I called. "Somebody was speeding up the drive and sideswiped Nate's car."

"Somebody? Who?" Uncle Mike was next to me by then, staring in the open front door. "Oh, Jesus, Nate." Herman rushed by him, whimpering in concern.

I pushed Herman away, figuring the last thing Nate needed was a dog licking his face. "Get your phone. Call 911." I was torn between my need to get Nate out of the car and my fear that I shouldn't move him.

Uncle Mike stared back and forth between us, then dug his phone out of his pocket and punched in the number. I knelt down beside Nate again. "It'll be okay. We're calling for an aid car." *And they'll probably have to get through the mess on Second Street somehow.* That realization made me bite my lip.

I pushed to my feet again and ran to my truck to grab my own phone. Fowler's number was still in my recents. I punched it in quickly. A few seconds later he picked up. "What do you want?"

I guess I shouldn't have expected him to be friendly on a Spring Break Friday night. "Nate's been hit by a hit-and-run driver on the drive to the farm. We need an aid car, and I don't think they can get around Second Street. Can your men help them get through?"

There was a pause. "Did you see it?"

"I was there."

"Okay, I'll see what I can do."

I jammed my phone in my pocket and ran back to Nate. Uncle Mike was kneeling beside him, his handkerchief in his hand. "You need to stay where you are until the aid car gets here," he was saying. "I don't want to make any injuries worse by lifting you around."

"Car's sliding," Nate muttered. "Don't want to go with it." He looked like he was hurting, but he also looked weirdly determined. As if to demonstrate the truth of Nate's observation, the car moved a couple of inches as I leaned on it.

Terrific. Now we really were between a rock and a hard place. But we didn't have any choice if we didn't want him to be hurt even worse. We got his seat belt off, got a blanket for him to lie on, and were just starting to lift him out when the aid car finally arrived, followed by a Shavano police car.

I don't think I was ever so glad to see flashing

lights in my life.

We explained the situation to the EMTs, who got Nate out with minimal stress once they got the car stabilized. Instead of the blanket they loaded Nate on a stretcher and got him into the aid car. Fowler and a Shavano cop had walked down after the EMTs, and they helped to make sure the car didn't slide any farther.

Uncle Mike and I stood at the side and watched. After a few moments, he put his arm around me and held on tight. I realized then I was trembling in pure reaction.

Fowler walked over as the EMTs were getting Nate ready for the drive to Shavano. "Got time for a few questions?"

"I want to follow them to the hospital," I said.

"I need to call Nate's mom," Uncle Mike said.

For God's sake leave us be, we both screamed with body language.

"Of course," Fowler said easily. "Just take a few minutes. A hit and run you said?"

I took a breath, reminding myself that Fowler had probably gotten the aid car through the jam on Second Street. "Yeah. We'd just turned off the county road. I was ahead, with Nate following. A car came up the middle of the drive going at least fifty. I was able to pull over, but he hit Nate. By the time I got out of my truck, he was gone."

"What time was this?"

"Maybe thirty, forty minutes ago." I turned to Uncle Mike, who nodded his agreement.

"Got any description of the vehicle?"

I shook my head. "I think it was an SUV, but I

couldn't tell you more than that. I couldn't see the color clearly in the dim light."

"Maybe Nate got a better look." Fowler turned to Uncle Mike. "Who was visiting tonight?"

"No one." Uncle Mike looked confused. "It was just Herman and me."

"You didn't see or hear any cars?"

"No, but I wasn't in the front of the house, and when I'm in the family room, I can't hear people drive up."

"But nobody came to the door?"

"No." Uncle Mike paused, eyes narrowing. "I remember Herman started barking, maybe ten or fifteen minutes before I heard the crash. He wouldn't shut up. I finally went to the door to check."

"See anything?"

"That's when I heard the crash. I came running out to see what was going on."

"Sounds like you had an intruder," Fowler mused. "One driving an SUV."

"Maybe." Uncle Mike still looked confused, and I felt the same way. The aid car started moving up the drive to the county road.

"Can we go now?" I asked. "I can talk to you tomorrow. Maybe I'll have remembered something more by then."

Fowler sighed, tucking his notebook into his pocket. "Okay. I'll try to catch up with you at the hospital."

Right then I wasn't thinking about that. My main concern was getting to the hospital as soon as I could get my truck turned around.

Chapter 17

Uncle Mike drove off to Madge's house, and I told him I'd call so she'd know what was happening. She didn't pick up, which meant she was probably already in bed. Maybe Uncle Mike had a key, not something I wanted to think about. I tried to figure out what kind of message I could leave. Anything I said was liable to scare her, so I decided to get straight to the point. "Madge, Nate's been in an accident. He's conscious but he's hurt. They're taking him to the hospital to be checked out. I'll probably be there when you get this. Uncle Mike is headed to your house."

Calling the whole thing an accident didn't entirely feel right. That SUV had been racing up the road without paying any attention to who was there. Hitting another car was less an accident than a certainty.

I had to fight through Second Street again, but the number of spring breakers had begun to decline as the evening went on. I pulled into the hospital parking lot, then trotted into the ER, looking for the paramedics who'd been carrying Nate's stretcher. I joined him in an examination room, even though I probably had no right to be there. Nate opened his eyes a little as I leaned close, and I took his hand.

"I called Madge. I left a message. Uncle Mike's going to pick her up."

Nate closed his eyes again. "She'll want to mother

me over this."

"Hell, *I* want to mother you over this." That made him smile a little.

The doctor came in to examine him, and I had to wait in the hall. I was beginning to feel some delayed reaction by then, mainly tears. I dug into my purse and found a tissue to blot my eyes. I was probably looking pretty torn up when Fowler walked into the hall, followed and then preceded by Susa, who dropped into a chair beside me.

"Aw, Rox," she said, putting her arms around me. Which made me cry harder. "How is he?"

"I don't know. He was conscious, but he looked pretty beat up."

"Somebody sideswiped him in your own drive?" Susa sounded outraged.

"Yeah, and we don't know who. Whoever it was didn't even come to the door at the main house."

Fowler folded his arms and leaned against the wall. "I'm just here to find out how Nate is. Your friend here insisted on coming when I told her what happened."

Susa shot him a burning glance. "Of course, I did. You didn't think I'd leave my best friend to do this on her own, did you?"

That prompted more tears from me, but I grabbed my tissue and wiped them away. I needed to pull myself together before Madge and Uncle Mike showed up.

"Did you and Nate have a job tonight?" Fowler asked.

"Yeah. We catered an anniversary dinner, for Art Blavatsky and family."

Fowler nodded. "I know Art. What did you serve?"

I had to stop and think. The Blavatsky dinner seemed like it had happened an age ago. "It was a special menu. His favorite foods: meatloaf and mashed potatoes. And peas."

"That sounds terrific." Fowler had a sort of hungry look, and I wondered if he'd had supper yet.

"It *was* terrific. And it took us most of the evening. We went to the catering kitchen afterward to drop off the pots and the platters to be washed. Then we headed off to my place to grab something to eat."

I paused to catch my breath. Fowler stared at the ceiling. "How long did it take you to get there?"

"We had to fight our way through Second Street. Maybe twenty or thirty minutes all told."

"Remembered anything more about the vehicle?"

I paused. "It was an SUV, and it must have hit Nate's car pretty hard. We were going slow because it was dark and because the drive's rough at this time of year. He smashed Nate's car up against a tree, almost into the drainage ditch. There must be paint scrapings on it to tell you what color the SUV was."

"Could be. We'll see if we can tow it out tomorrow. You sure you didn't get a look at the driver?"

I shook my head.

"You said it was a man."

I paused to think about it. I'd been saying *he* pretty consistently, but I didn't know why. "I don't know that it was. I just said *he* without thinking."

"Did Nate say anything to you about the driver?" Fowler asked.

"No. He was barely conscious, and mostly worried about the car sliding farther into the ditch." Nate most likely wasn't going to remember much about anything.

I leaned against my chair, suddenly more tired than I could say. "It all happened so fast. One minute we were turning into the drive to the farm. The next minute that SUV came out of nowhere and plowed into us."

"You need to find out if someone broke in somewhere on the farm," Susa said. "Why else would they be out there and take off without talking to Mike?"

"Maybe they made a wrong turn and had turned around," Fowler said mildly.

"And pulled out at a high rate of speed, clipping Nate's car in the process?" Susa raised an eyebrow. "Strains credibility."

Fowler shrugged. "Maybe. I need to talk to Nate if he's able."

"He was sort of woozy the last time I saw him. The doctor's still in there."

At that moment, the door of the examination room opened, and the doctor walked out. I pushed to my feet. "Is he going to be okay?"

The doctor nodded. "Looks like it. He's got a mild concussion and he injured his leg getting out of the car, probably a sprained ankle. And he's pretty banged up with scrapes and bruises. Are you his wife? There's some paperwork to sign."

"No, I'm his…friend," I said.

The doctor sighed. "In that case…"

"I need to talk to Mr. Robicheaux." Fowler flipped out his badge. "He's the victim of a hit and run."

"Yeah, I heard. You can talk to him. Have to be tomorrow, though. He's asleep right now—we gave him some medication for the pain."

"Roxy." Madge came hurrying down the hall with

Uncle Mike at her heels. "Where is he? I need to see him."

I gave the doctor the best smile I could manage under the circumstances. "If you need someone to sign papers, this is Nate's mom."

Madge insisted on seeing Nate, even though he was asleep. Then Uncle Mike took her to the nearest waiting room so that she could have a good cry. I went through my story of what had happened and got a blast of indignation from Madge.

"Some stupid reckless driver." Madge blew out a long breath. "Who would be speeding at night on that dark road? It doesn't make any sense."

"No, it doesn't make sense." I yawned then before I could stop myself. I was clearly having a post-adrenaline crash.

Madge reached over to take my hand. "You need to go home and get some rest, sweetheart." She turned to Uncle Mike. "You should drive her home. She shouldn't be on the road when she's this tired."

Uncle Mike was probably about as tired as I was, but he nodded. "Got that right. Come on, Roxanne, let's get you home."

"Oh, but I need to stay. I mean, surely I do. Don't I?" I was sort of woozy, but I didn't want to leave Nate there by himself.

"Neither of us can do anything for him until tomorrow," Madge said firmly. "The doctor says they've made sure he's comfortable. And they'll have nurses looking after him. If something happens they'll call me, and I'll call you. But for now, both of us need to get some sleep or we won't be any help to him tomorrow when they send him home."

My eyes widened. "He's going home tomorrow?"

Madge nodded. "So they say. Assuming nothing else happens during the night. They'll send him home with acetaminophen for his headache and orders to stay off his feet for a while." She gave me a half smile. "I'll be discussing that with his brother first thing in the morning. If not before."

I had a thousand questions right then, the first being who would take care of any upcoming catering jobs. But Madge had a point. Nate would need both of us tomorrow. "Okay, I'll head on home. And I'm all right. You don't need to drive me, Uncle Mike."

"Nope." Fowler stood in the doorway with Susa at his elbow. "You look like you'd be a hazard on the highway. If Mike can't drive you, I'll find somebody to take you home in a cruiser."

Oh, yeah, I really wanted the citizens of Shavano to see me riding in a police cruiser. Again.

"I can do it." Uncle Mike paused, giving me a narrow-eyed look. "Correction: I *will* do it."

Madge turned to Fowler. "What are you doing about arresting this crazy person who hit my son?"

"We're currently investigating the accident. We'll tow Nate's car to town tomorrow and collect what evidence we can."

Uncle Mike rubbed his eyes. "This whole thing is nuts. What the hell was that SUV doing at the farm?"

"We can check on that tomorrow, assuming he left some evidence. And I can drive myself." I gave both Fowler and Uncle Mike my most quelling look. "I absolutely can."

It took another twenty minutes or so before I convinced everyone I was capable of driving the ten miles to the farm. By then I was close to played out, but I was also determined to drive myself home so I'd have my truck tomorrow.

It wasn't a great drive, by any means. I kept myself functioning by playing Brandi Carlile at top volume and singing along. And by the time I got home, I was done. I parked the truck in front of my cabin, grabbed my purse, and stumbled up to the front door as I dug my key out of the inside pocket. Uncle Mike had left Herman in the cabin when he'd gone to Madge's house, and Herman was not at all happy to have been left on his own.

I took him out for a final walk, then settled him with a rawhide chew. I also managed to choke down a peanut butter sandwich before I realized I should probably check to make sure the cabin hadn't been broken into. After all, nobody had disturbed the main house, but Herman had been barking about something.

As far as I could tell, though, the cabin was fine. Uncle Mike had had to unlock the door to put Herman inside, which meant the door had been locked when we got there. And nothing had been disturbed.

Of course, given that my living room was currently full of jam cartons waiting to be picked up, it would have taken considerable effort to make a disturbance.

I considered going outside to look around, but by then I was running on fumes. I'd spent the day on food prep, then a three-hour catering gig, ending with the accident and a trip to the hospital. Whatever reserves I'd had that had made it possible for me to get home, they were long gone.

I stumbled to my bedroom before pulling off my clothes. I didn't even wash my face—just dropped into bed, pulling the blankets up as I turned out the light. A few moments later I felt the bed dip as Herman joined me. But after that I was out for the night.

Chapter 18

By my standards, I woke late the next day, around eight thirty. I still felt tired, but eight thirty was as late as I was willing to let it go. After I got the coffee on, I let Herman out and stood on my front porch, trying to see if anything had been disturbed the night before. As far as I could tell the area around the cabin looked the same as always.

Not that there was all that much to see: my stock tank planters and some wooden lawn chairs I'd covered with a tarp before the winter snows started. Not only could I not see any evidence that someone had been poking around, I couldn't see anything anyone would want to poke around for.

Maybe Fowler had been right. Maybe the intruder was just someone who'd taken a wrong turn and then tried to zip back to the county road again. It had been a stupid thing to do, but I met stupid people all the time.

I figured they'd never let me in to see Nate before nine at the earliest, even assuming he'd be awake by then. In a way, I hoped he wasn't since I wanted him to get a solid night's sleep.

I fixed myself my mainstay breakfast, toast and jam. And then I tried to figure out if I should drive myself in without talking to Uncle Mike, who might well have stayed over at Madge's place for all I knew. I'd just about decided to make some peach jam from frozen fruit as a way to put off making a decision, when my phone rang. I checked the number and saw Bobby Robicheaux listed as the caller.

What the everlasting hell?

I blew out a long breath and picked up. "Yeah, Bobby."

"I need to talk to you about how we're going to cover next week's catering. Mom says you're in charge. Breakfast's over around ten fifteen, and I've got about a half hour before I have to start lunch. Can you be here?"

There were all sorts of questions I needed to ask him, but I figured I could ask them all at ten fifteen. "I can make it."

"Good. Talk to you then." And he hung up.

The fact that we were going to discuss the next catering job meant I needed to find out what that job was going to be. Nate and I had been going to discuss it last night, but then the accident had happened. So now I needed to talk to Nate. I finished my toast, poured my coffee into a travel cup, and headed for my truck.

I found Madge in the waiting room at the hospital, so I guessed we weren't being allowed in to see Nate yet. She looked like she hadn't had any more sleep than I'd had, maybe less, in fact. "Hi, sweetheart," she said, patting my shoulder.

"Hi, Madge, any news?"

She shrugged. "He had a quiet night. They're going to let me in to see him after he finishes breakfast and the doctor has a chance to check him out. You can come, too."

"Thanks, I appreciate that. Would you like some coffee? I can make a quick run to Bianca's."

Madge sighed, running a hand across her face. "I would love some. And a scone if she had any. Let me give you some money."

"My treat." I trotted out before she could argue.

Bianca's place was surprisingly busy, and I remembered then that it was Saturday. Everyone was lining up for muffins and some of her sublime coffee. Bianca herself was at the counter along with her assistants, and when she saw me, she waved me aside, letting them take over.

"I just heard a hell of a rumor. Did you have a hit and run at your place that sent Nate to the hospital?" Bianca made no attempt to keep her voice down.

I didn't know who this information came from, maybe the cops or the EMTs. "Yeah, it happened. I'm here to grab some coffee for me and Madge, and a scone, too, if you've got any. We can't see Nate until he's been checked out again by the doctor."

"Oh, good Lord. Let me give you a couple of muffins, too. Hospital breakfasts are ghastly. Do you think he's had any coffee?"

"I don't know if they'll let him have any. He's got a concussion."

Bianca set about filling coffee cups and pulling baked goods out of the case, all the while muttering about the state of the world in general and Shavano in particular since nothing like this had ever happened in her memory. Of course, Bianca's memory could be considered selective.

She handed me a cup holder tray with a couple of coffees and a bag of pastries. "Just pay me for the coffees. The pastries are on the house. Tell Nate to take it easy. And tell Madge to call me. Or better yet, I'll call her."

Telling Nate to take it easy was simple enough, but getting him to pay attention might be tougher. He looked pale and tired when we finally got into his room, but he also looked determined. "I can't sit around in here. I've got stuff to do."

The doctor, a rangy, athletic blonde with pale green eyes, regarded him without much sympathy. "Somebody else will have to do it for you. You've got quite a lump on your head and a bum ankle. And you need to rest. If you can't do it at home, you'll need to stay here."

Nate's jaw firmed. "There's no way I'm staying here. No way."

"Well, there's no way you're going back to work for a few days," Madge said. "So you can take your pick, Nathan. Either I sign you out and you promise to stay off your feet for two or three days, or I'll leave you here under the care of Dr. Rasmussen and her crew. Which do you prefer?" She gave her son a long, cool look, eyebrows raised high.

Nate sighed, collapsing against his pillows. "Okay, I promise. I won't go into the kitchen. But I've got to be able to work with Roxy. She can't go out on this catering job without a lot of information about what the customers wanted." He glanced at me. "Can you come over to my place to work on it?"

Madge shook her head. "You're not going to be able to use your place. There's no way you could climb those stairs safely with a sprained ankle. You can use your old bedroom at the house."

Nate's pale face became paler. "Aw, come on, Mom…"

Madge folded her arms. "Nathan..."

"If I could make a suggestion," I said quickly, "Nate could come stay at the cabin. I've got plenty of room. And that way he could work on the menu for the catering job while I'm doing jam. And if I had any questions, I could ask him." I wasn't absolutely certain that I had more room than Madge did, but no question Nate would prefer staying at my house to bunking at his mom's place. His expression pretty much told the story.

Madge bit her lip. "You promise you won't let him try to do too much too soon?"

"I promise he won't do anything his doctors don't want him to do before they say he can do it." I was pretty sure Nate would agree to this stipulation, if only to avoid being stuck in his old room at Madge's house.

"Absolutely." He nodded. "I'll take it easy, Mom, I promise."

"All right. I'm not sure what you'll do for clothes, though. I guess I can pack some things for you."

I almost said Nate had some clothes at my place already, but I managed to keep my mouth shut. I wasn't sure how Madge would feel about that information.

"Okay," Dr. Rasmussen said. "I'll check you again around noon. If you're still doing all right, I'll let you go with the understanding you're going to rest for two or three days."

"Right," Nate said. "I'll do whatever you say."

I had a feeling that promise had been delivered with crossed fingers, but I had no intention of letting him overdo. On the other hand, I figured he'd be dying to do something by the second day of enforced inactivity. He might even be delighted to chop apples for jelly.

Madge went off with Dr. Rasmussen to get the details of what Nate was and wasn't supposed to do. I stayed where I was. "So what catering job do we have this week? Bobby wants to talk to me about it."

Nate frowned. "Why does he want to talk to you? He could just phone me."

"I think he thinks I might need to do this one on my own," I said carefully. In fact, I didn't know why Bobby wanted to talk to me, but my guess was he didn't think Nate would be up to cooking and serving whatever we had on deck. And he might well be right.

Nate's frown grew deeper. He wasn't delighted to hear his brother considered him incapable of doing his job.

"Just tell me what we're supposed to do. That way I'll have something to say. I don't want him to think we need to cancel."

Nate rubbed a hand across his forehead, looking tired again. "We don't cancel. Ever. It's a company cocktail party at a real estate agency on Aspen Way. Not as big as Aldo's, but I think we got the job because Aldo talked us up. Anyway, it's just heavy hors d'oeuvres, maybe crudités and a dip. They didn't want charcuterie. I was going to go over some possibilities with you last night."

"When is it?"

"Thursday night. It's the only thing we've got going next week. His estimate was thirty people, give or take."

"So thirty-five to be safe?"

He nodded, then closed his eyes. Nodding was probably not a good idea.

"How do you feel? Really."

"Like shit," he said slowly. "I've got a hell of a headache. I'm supposed to get some super ibuprofen that'll take care of it, but that'll probably knock me out after I take it. I'm not going to be good for much today."

"Okay, I'll get you to the cabin, and then you can sleep for a while. I've got jam to make to fill orders for next week. We can work on the menu tonight or tomorrow."

"Yeah. Sounds…doable." He reached out and took my hand. "Thanks, babe. I'd never be able to get anything done if I was in my old room at Mom's. Besides, it would feel way too weird to have you visiting a room that still has my basketball team picture on the wall."

I gave his hand a quick squeeze. "Glad to do it. But don't kid yourself—I'm not going to let you overdo it either."

"Right now I don't feel much like overdoing it. Or even doing it. But I'll get myself pulled together by Thursday, honest."

Just looking at him, I didn't think that was likely. But I figured we could discuss it later, after he'd had a couple of days to regroup. I headed off to find Madge and the doctor, and to hear what exactly I had to do to make sure Nate didn't have a relapse.

I pulled into Robicheaux's parking lot around ten twenty. I might have been a few minutes late, but I had a good excuse. Bobby didn't look like he was inclined to accept any excuse, good or otherwise. He very pointedly looked at his watch as I walked in.

"Sorry. I was at the hospital with Nate and Madge." Which was my way of telling Bobby to cool it.

"What's going to happen with this thing on Thursday? Can you handle it on your own if Nate's not up to it?"

I'd been thinking about that on the way over because it didn't look like Nate was going to be up to it. Not unless he made a miraculous recovery over the next couple of days. "I can handle it, if you'll let me use Coco."

"Use Coco?" Bobby gave me a dark look. "I'm already down one person. I can't make it two."

"If you'll let her work with me doing prep on Wednesday and Thursday and then maybe working the party on Thursday night, that's all I need." Nate might be on his feet by Thursday, but I figured it was best to plan for the worst and be pleasantly surprised when it didn't happen.

Bobby still looked dark, but maybe he always did. "You talked to Coco about this?"

"Not yet. I wanted to talk to you first." I figured a little ego massage wouldn't hurt.

Bobby looked slightly mollified. "Okay, if she thinks she can handle her regular work and this, it's okay with me."

In reality, the decision was mostly Coco's since Bobby wasn't her boss. But I figured it didn't hurt to let Bobby believe he had some say in this.

I found Coco in her corner of the kitchen, prepping a large bowl of tuna salad. She gave me a quick smile. "How's the invalid? Mom has him at death's door, but I assume it's not that bad."

I shrugged. "It's a concussion and a sprained ankle, along with bruises and scrapes. He's got a major headache and he's supposed to stay off his feet for a while. I'm going to take him to my place so he has a chance to rest."

"Yeah, he's more likely to be resting at your place than with Mom. She goes into mothering overdrive when one of us gets sick." Coco's expression was grim. "Jesus, what a mess. Any news on the driver?"

I shook my head. "Fowler's going to tow Nate's car to see if they can find any evidence about the SUV that hit him. I didn't see it well enough to tell him anything, and I'm guessing Nate didn't either."

Coco grimaced. "And, of course, it would be an SUV. Everybody in town owns one, including me."

Coco's SUV was sort of small, but it still qualified as all-wheel drive. I had the other Shavano alternative with my pickup truck. "Maybe we should alert everybody to be on the lookout for an SUV with a big scrape on the driver's side. I don't think he got off without any damage."

"That's a thought. If we let all the cooks in town know, that's a formidable group right there."

I glanced at the clock and realized I'd let more time slide by than I realized. Time to finish up. "I wanted to ask if you could help out with the catering this week. In case Nate still isn't back on his feet by Thursday."

"Sure. What's the main course, and how can I make it involve pastry?"

"It's a cocktail party with heavy hors d'oeuvres, so no main course. But if you want to make something like cheese puffs, that'd work for me." And I was pretty sure it would work for Nate, given that he wouldn't be doing any of it.

"Cheese puffs. Or maybe tartlets. Little mini-quiches. I could do the shells on Wednesday and then fill them Thursday. Yeah, that would work." She stared off into space, maybe dreaming of puff pastry.

"Okay, I'll get back to you after I go over the menu with Nate. Thanks, Coco."

"Sure, any time." She paused. "I mean that. Any time I get a chance to stretch a few baking muscles, I'll be glad to help."

I went back to the hospital to pick up Nate, musing over what Coco had said. If we had a dedicated group of observers keeping track of damaged SUVs around town, it might help nail down the hit and run driver a lot faster, assuming he or she was still in Shavano. It was worth a shot. And Coco and Bianca could spread the news a lot more effectively than I could.

I arrived to find Nate being helped into a wheelchair for the ride down to my car. He wasn't happy about it, but he seemed to be putting up with it anyway. Anything to get out of the hospital.

He was still wearing a T-shirt Madge had probably found for him since his shirt from the day before had been streaked with blood. Madge gripped a large garbage bag with his clothes to take with us as if she was getting ready to fight off anyone who might try to take it away. I wasn't about to argue with her.

"They're saying I have to ride down in this thing," Nate said grumpily. "Believe me, I can walk."

"Never pass up a chance to ride, babe." I started pushing him down the hall, hoping Madge would follow.

At the hospital entrance, Nate insisted on walking to the truck. At least I'd parked it close. Madge pressed a sack of pill bottles into my hands. "He needs to take these today. And probably tomorrow, too. The doctor said to take them whenever he felt like he needed them. Oh, and he's not supposed to take ibuprofen or NSAIDs because they can promote bleeding and there's a chance he might have a brain bleed." She looked a little faint.

"Mom, she said a 'very slight chance.' I don't have a brain bleed." Nate looked like he was gritting his teeth.

"Probably not. Knock on wood." Madge gazed at me again. "Are you sure…"

"It'll be okay. If anything happens, I'll call. And you can stop by and see him if you come out to see Uncle Mike."

That possibility apparently hadn't occurred to Madge before. She gave me a slightly tremulous smile. "I can, can't I?" She reached over and gave Nate a fierce hug. "You do everything the doctor told you to do. And everything Roxy tells you to do. And make sure you get plenty of rest."

Nate closed his eyes, rubbing his mom's back. "Okay, okay, Ma. We'll be all right. Don't worry."

No chance of that, but I got Nate to the truck without mishap. Madge stood in the doorway watching us drive away, Nate's blood-stained T-shirt still clutched to her chest as if it was a stand-in for her son.

I'd never felt so guilty about rescuing someone in my life.

Chapter 19

Nate reclined in his seat, leaning against the headrest as he closed his eyes. "Did you talk to Coco?"

"Yeah. She's okay with helping. She wants to do mini quiches."

Nate sighed. "Fine with me. She's always loved doing pastry apps. She should have a great time. How did Bobby react?"

"He's okay with it, too. A little grumpy about being understaffed, but maybe this will make him more open to hiring a new cook."

"Always possible."

I glanced at Nate as I turned out of town. His eyes were still closed, and he might have been asleep. Chances were good he'd been keeping up appearances in front of Madge, but he was ready to let it all go with me. Maybe he could finally get some rest.

Not a problem. I pulled into my parking space next to the cabin a few minutes later and wondered if I needed to wake him. He opened his eyes slowly. "That was fast."

"Not much traffic." I wondered if there was some subtle way I could come around the car to help him into the house.

But he read my mind. "Don't worry. I can make it into the cabin on my own." He opened the door and climbed out of the truck, leaning heavily on the cane he'd been given at the hospital. I grabbed the bag of clothes from behind my seat and followed him to the door.

The cabin was small, but it did have two bedrooms. "I'm putting you in the spare room so you can sleep when you want to." I kept my tone brisk. "Do you want to take some of these painkillers?"

"I already took some at the hospital. That's why I'm so woozy." Nate paused, staring down the hall. "Where is the spare bedroom?"

My cheeks heated. When he'd been here before, he'd always been in bed with me. "Down the hall to the left. Let me check to be sure the bed's made up."

I opened the bedroom door and put Nate's bag of clothes next to the small dresser. The room was a little Spartan with just a bed, a dresser, a bookcase where I stuck books I was through reading but wasn't ready to give away yet, and a rocking chair with an afghan I'd bought at a charity crafts show a few years ago. But the window faced the west and the room got lots of sunlight.

Nate stepped through behind me and surveyed the lack of amenities. "I know it looks a little bare bones," I said. "But the bed's comfortable if you want to rest."

Nate sighed. "Believe me, that's all I want to do." He sank down on the bed, pulling off his shoes. Then he stretched out and closed his eyes.

I resisted the urge to spread the afghan over his legs. He was a grown man, and he could decide what he needed.

"Don't worry about me, Rox," he said without opening his eyes. "I'll be fine. I just need to get some sleep."

"Right. Yell if you need anything."

I actually got a lot done that afternoon since I was trying to find ways to keep myself from going to check on Nate. I scrolled through the online orders and figured out how much jam I needed to make for them, along with my usual customers like Bianca and the Made In Colorado shop. It looked like we were going to need a fair amount of marmalade, which took a while. Fortunately, I had a few pounds of tangerines already on hand. I got set up and made a couple dozen jars. I figured the more jam I made right now the better, since I'd be working on the catering job next week.

I had frozen peaches out thawing for the next round of peach jam when Uncle Mike wandered in with Herman. Herm must have sniffed Nate's presence because he started whimpering immediately. Uncle Mike grabbed hold of his collar before he could bolt down the hall. "Nate sleeping?"

Madge had probably told him I'd brought Nate to the cabin. I nodded. "He took some painkillers from the hospital. He's in the spare room."

Uncle Mike stabbed his fingers through his hair. "I don't know what the hell's going on around here. First that Murphy woman gets killed up on the county road, and then some fool hits Nate on our own drive. I mean, we never had trouble out here before."

I paused in my labors. "You think what happened to Nate is connected to Muriel Cates?"

"Nope." He gave me a narrow-eyed look. "Do you?"

"I hadn't until you brought it up." That wasn't entirely true. I'd been thinking about Muriel Cates as I started down the drive last night. "I guess it is unusual for the farm to have two mysterious things going at once."

"How much does Nate remember about what happened?"

"I haven't had a chance to ask him yet. You were there when I opened the car door. He was out of it."

"Has he talked to Fowler yet?"

"Not that I know of." I felt a little guilty about that. The doctor had shooed Fowler out of the hospital last night with the promise that he could talk to Nate today. And then I'd taken Nate away before Fowler got there. On the other hand, Madge could tell him where Nate was, and I certainly wouldn't stand in the way of a conversation.

As long as I got to be there, too.

"Okay, well, guess I'll go up to the house. You want me to leave Herman?"

Herman might be a pain in the neck since I'd have to take care of him and Nate both. But he might also be good company for Nate, assuming he wanted company. "Okay. If he gets to be a problem, I'll call you."

Herman settled into his usual spot between the kitchen and the living room where he watched me cautiously as I made peach jam. Using frozen fruit can be tricky. I sometimes get jam I'm not happy with, but I usually sell it to Bianca for fruit-filled pastries since you wouldn't use first-class stuff for those anyway.

I had the kettle on and boiling with peaches, sugar, lemon juice, vanilla, and a few tablespoons of bourbon when Herman staggered to his feet, his tail wagging briskly. I peered down the hall and saw Nate shambling toward me, leaning one hand against the wall. At least he wasn't staggering, although it wasn't a robust walk.

He stepped into the kitchen, inhaling deeply. "Hi. Whatever that is, I want some of it." He nodded toward the jam kettle.

"That's not ready for tasting, but I've got some from a previous batch. You want toast? Peanut butter? A jar and spoon?"

"Toast sounds good." He stepped around to the living room door to pet Herman, who wasn't allowed in the kitchen when I was working. "Hey, Herm, how's it going?" Herman rubbed against Nate's leg in a paroxysm of joy as Nate scratched his ears. I was a little afraid Herm might knock him over, but Nate kept hold of the doorjamb.

"I thought Herman might be good company for you while I'm doing jam. He's not much of a conversationalist, but he's love personified." I removed the jars from the canning kettle, then dropped a couple of pieces of Bianca's sour dough into the toaster.

"I can always use a little love." Nate stepped back to kiss my cheek. "Hi, beautiful. Did I remember to thank you for letting me crash here?"

"You did, but it's always good to hear. And I'm glad to have you."

The toaster popped, and Nate grabbed a plate. Since he knew where everything was in my kitchen I let him fix his own bread and jam while I lined the jars I'd taken from the processor out on the counter where they'd cool down. I figured having me fuss over a piece of bread would only annoy him. It would have annoyed me if I'd been in his place.

Nate and Herman settled at the kitchen table with Nate's toast and the *Shavano County Sun*. I'd just finished putting the last batch of jars onto the counter to cool when someone knocked on the door. I was pretty sure I knew who it would be.

Fowler stood on my doorstep, looking slightly annoyed, a kind of perpetual expression when he's around me. "Nate awake?"

I nodded. "Come on in. I'll fix coffee."

Nate looked resigned when he saw Fowler. "Hey, Chief. I figured I'd need to talk to you sooner or later. Sorry it wasn't sooner."

"Me, too." Fowler studied Nate's plate of toast and jam. "Don't suppose there's any more of that around?"

"Sure. There's always jam here." I dropped another couple of pieces of sour dough into the toaster. "You want whiskey peach or raspberry? Or I've got some tangerine marmalade, too."

"Marmalade, please." Fowler dropped his Stetson under his chair, then turned to Nate. "You up to a few questions?"

"Sure. I'm okay. Just a headache and a tendency to drop off to sleep every couple of hours, courtesy of the pain killers they gave me."

Fowler nodded. "We need to go over what happened last night, along with some other things that may or may not be related."

Nate started to nod and then thought better of it. I took a seat near the stove, so I could get the toast when it popped. Fowler gave me a long-suffering look. "I don't suppose there's any way I could get you to go find something to do elsewhere."

"No way in hell," I said, as pleasantly as I could.

Fowler sighed but turned to Nate. "So what do you remember about last night?"

Nate took him through the sequence of the dinner

at the Blavatskys' house. Fowler nodded at the end. "Yeah, I got that from Roxy. What happened when you came back here?"

"We had to drop off the dirty dishes at the café so Tres could wash them. Then we headed for the farm. I took my car instead of riding with Roxy because I was supposed to work lunch today. It took us a while to get across Second because of the crowds."

Fowler nodded. "Right."

"When we got to the county road, there was a lot less traffic. In fact, I don't remember seeing anybody until we got to the drive up to the farm." He gave me a questioning glance.

I shook my head. "No, I don't either."

Fowler took a swallow of his coffee. "And then?"

Nate closed his eyes to think. "We turned in at the drive. It was dark—I could barely see the yard light at the cabin. Roxy took it slow, and I was following her taillights, trying not to hit the potholes, when I heard a car coming up the drive. I thought it was Mike at first, but then I realized it was coming fast, a lot faster than Mike would have driven."

I let my hands form into fists and worked on keeping quiet, even though I was suddenly furious. Fowler looked like he heard about idiot drivers all the time. Maybe he did. "What happened then?"

"I saw Rox pull way over, and I tried to do that, too, but he was coming too fast. The next thing I knew he was on top of me."

"He hit you then?" Fowler was making notes.

"Yeah. His car plowed into the side of mine, and my rear end bounced off into one of the pine trees. I got thrown around pretty good, even with my seat belt on."

I took a deep breath and blew it out, telling myself it could have been a lot worse if he'd been moving, too. It didn't make me feel much better.

"What do you remember about the vehicle?" Fowler was carefully keeping his focus on his notes, probably concerned about influencing Nate's memory.

"It was big and black," Nate said. "Full size SUV. Sort of like the one we use at the café only a different make and model."

Fowler paused. "You know what make and model it was?"

Nate shook his head carefully. "One of the great big ones. We use ours to pick up supplies at the café and to carry food to catering jobs. A lot of people around town have them."

"If I showed you some pictures of SUVs, do you think you could identify it?"

Nate sighed, rubbing his eyes. "I could try. But I can't promise anything. It was dark, and it happened fast. I saw the shape and the size, and that's about it."

"You said it was black."

Nate paused to think again. "I think it was. Either black or dark blue. Something that looked black in the darkness."

"Did you get a look at the driver?"

My shoulders tensed as I watched Nate. If he could identify the driver, things would be a lot easier.

"Not really," Nate said. "Just a pale face in the darkness."

"Male?"

He shrugged. "Maybe. I couldn't see for sure."

Fowler nodded, making another note. "We towed your car to the city impound lot this morning so we could check it for evidence. Your insurance people will want to see it."

"Terrific. I'm pretty sure it's totaled. Anything else I can tell you?"

"You said some other people in town drove the big SUVs. Who would that be?"

Nate frowned. "I don't remember exactly. I just know a lot of restaurants have big SUVs or pickups to haul stuff around." He glanced at me. "You remember anyone?"

I rubbed a hand across my eyes, thinking. "I think the Made In Colorado store uses one. And maybe Jade Garden. Dirty Pete's uses something like that, but it might be a panel truck now that I think of it. I think I've seen one at the barbecue place, too."

Fowler closed his notebook. "Okay, I'll bring some pictures around for you to look at. If I think of any other questions, I'll give you a call. Are you going to be here for a while?"

Nate glanced at me, then shrugged. "For a while, I guess."

"Good enough." Fowler picked up his Stetson again, smiling his typical half-smile at both of us. "Be seeing you around."

Chapter 20

A kind of bubble of silence remained after Fowler had left, as if both of us were waiting for the other to speak first. "Did you see more than I did?" Nate asked finally.

I shook my head. "Less, actually. I could tell it was an SUV, but not much more. Who else has an oversize SUV?" I gave him an innocent look, but he saw through me.

"Yeah, Bobby has one, but he doesn't use it for anything except going into the back country. And it wasn't Bobby who ran into me."

"No, of course it wasn't." I was confident about that since I'd seen Bobby this morning, and he showed no ill effects. I figured the person who'd been driving the fugitive SUV had to have a few bruises, too. "Will Fowler find out, do you think?"

"Probably. But I didn't feel like giving him a head start. If he questions Bobby, he'll find out he couldn't have done it."

"But he may come here and snarl at you."

Nate shrugged. "I can take a few snarls."

I sighed, settling into my chair. "I've been trying to think of other people who drive big SUVs. Bianca's got one. I've seen her driving it around town."

"Marcus uses it sometimes, too. I've seen him."

I bit my lip. If Marcus used the SUV, so did Sara.

And that raised some possible unpleasant links with Muriel Cates.

"A lot of people have them," Nate said. "Fowler's in the best position to find out who owns them around here. He can hit up the DMV."

I took a good look at him then and saw the dark circles under his eyes. He wasn't in any shape to be sitting around talking about fugitive vehicles. "Would you like some dinner? I've got soup." That was a sort of clumsy attempt to change the subject but the best I could do. I really wanted him to eat something and then go to bed.

Nate gave me a dry smile because he saw right through me. "Soup sounds good. I probably need to take another pill."

We didn't talk any more about SUVs that night. Nate went off to his room to sleep after we finished dinner.

Sunday was quiet, except for my jam-making juggernaut, but Monday was hopping. Madge came to see Nate around mid-morning. The café was closed on Mondays, so she could spend as much time as she wanted with him, which was probably more time than he wanted. But he was a dutiful son and put up with Madge's pampering. Uncle Mike came over around noon and brought lunch, which we all ate together. He took Herman with him and Madge, which was probably a good idea.

Bridget and Dolce arrived mid-afternoon, so Nate retreated to let us get the orders put together. Bridget wanted the details about the accident and was sort of put out when I couldn't give her much.

"Goddamn crazy driver," she said, scowling. "You

were going down your own drive to your own house at night and you got broadsided. Who does that kind of thing?"

I didn't have any answer for her. Or any answer that made sense. We went back to our usual gossip about people around town.

"Heard Grace Peters did the cake for that dinner you did last week," Bridget said. "How was it?"

"I didn't taste it. But it looked great."

Bridget gave me a crooked smile. "Hell, City Market cakes look great. They just don't taste like much of anything. I hear Peters is scrambling—her stuff isn't selling well. Maybe that's why she's getting into the cake business. There aren't too many good cake bakers in this town."

"There's the cake lady," Dolce said. "She's terrific." Kids always loved the cake lady—for good reason.

"Bless the cake lady's heart," Bridget said. "But she probably doesn't do fancy frosting like a pro. There's also a difference between cake decorating and cake baking. You can make a cake look great, and it might still taste like crap."

Or if you were good, you might be able to do both. But I wasn't sure Grace Peters was in that category.

Nate padded up the hallway after my assistants had left. "Let me help with dinner. I'm going nuts just sitting around."

I'd been going to make spaghetti with jarred sauce, but Nate took over and did something with eggs, spinach, and hamburger that was absolutely delicious.

"What is this?" I asked after several bites.

"Joe's Special. One of the specialties at Ned's

Place, the restaurant where I worked the line in Las Vegas. I started thinking about it this afternoon, and I wanted to fix it for you."

"It's great. You should offer it as a main dish, either at the café or for catering."

Nate shrugged. "It sort of falls between stools. It's not fine dining, but it's probably more trouble than the café would want to go for. You have to make up each serving individually. It's best for a late-night supper, after you've been drinking a lot or gambling a lot or both. That's what Ned's specialized in." He passed me the breadbasket where I'd sliced up a baguette I'd had in the freezer. "I knew Grace Peters in Vegas. Did I tell you that?"

I figured he must have heard us gossiping earlier in the afternoon. "Nope. Was she baking at one of the restaurants?"

"She was an assistant at a French bakery in one of the hotels. One of the more chi-chi places. Something she was pretty proud of. You couldn't have a conversation with her without hearing about her time in Paris, and how American French bakeries just couldn't get the same ingredients. You know bakers."

I knew some bakers could be a pain in the ass. Much like some chefs. "She worked in Paris?"

"Trained there, she said. Some kind of pastry school and then a stage at a French patisserie."

"Were you friends?" I thought about Nate and Grace at the Blue Spot. I wasn't nervous about the two of them, but, well, I wanted some details.

"We hung out some. We were both scraping along, sharing apartments with other people who worked on the Strip. But like I said, she considered herself higher up the ladder than I was. And she was probably right. I was a line cook, but she was an assistant pastry chef."

Something about the way he said *we hung out* made me think there had been more to it than just a friendship. But I wasn't going to get worked up over a relationship in Nate's past. Not much, anyway.

"Do you miss Las Vegas?" I'd asked him before, but maybe the question had a little more direct relevance now.

He paused before taking another quick bite. "I do and I don't. I miss the challenge. When you've got a half-dozen dishes all going at once and you're fighting to stay out of the weeds. That's exhilarating when it isn't terrifying. Usually, it's both. And I don't get that rush much anymore. But I like being in charge of my life, and I didn't feel that way in Vegas. And I didn't realize how much I missed Shavano until I got here."

"It's slower," I said.

He nodded. "Yeah, and sometimes that's frustrating. But I still love the place." He reached out and took my hand. "You're part of Shavano, Rox. Part of what I love about the town."

That came close to taking my breath away. I wished I had something equally meaningful to say to him, but I didn't. "I'm glad you're here," I said, because that was part of what I was feeling.

"I'm glad I'm here, too. Although as soon as my ankle heals, I can move to my apartment."

I wasn't sure how I felt about that. I sort of liked having Nate nearby where I could talk to him whenever I wanted to, although he seemed to be getting better by the hour. "Do you want to move back?"

"Eventually, I'll have to. But I like being here with

you. And it gives Bridget something to talk about."

I had to laugh at that. "Not that she needs more than she's already got. The woman knows more details of everyone's life than anybody should."

Nate grinned. "You want to talk menus? Or is this a streaming night?"

"We need to talk menus. I've got to start prepping tomorrow. And make sure Coco's working on her end. How many dishes are we in for, and what did they request?"

"They wanted the smoked salmon pinwheels and the filo packets—they've got some non-meat eaters in the group. Beyond that they were flexible, and we need maybe two or three more dishes."

"Crudités and dip for one of them," I said. "Heavy on the carrots and light on the broccoli."

"Right. And no Brussels sprouts." Nate grabbed a pad and pen from my kitchen desk and started making notes. "Coco's doing the mini-quiches and you can probably get her to do the filo packets, too. That leaves one more."

"The pigs-in-a-blanket went over big at the Blavatskys. Maybe we could do them again here." Although the idea of talking to Sara again made me uncomfortable. Particularly now that I knew she sometimes drove a large SUV.

"Let me check on the cost first. Those sausages from Marcus were pricey, and these guys aren't paying that much."

"Okay. We need something with meat, though. Just to balance things out. Maybe the Sichuan meatballs with ginger and scallions?"

"Yeah, that'll work. And we can do the pigs again

sometime if we can keep the cost down—maybe cheaper sausages."

I hated to give up Marcus's sausages, but we could if we had to. And not having to give the order to Sara had a lot of appeal. "Okay."

"Let me run some numbers. I need to call Coco, too, and get the final cost on the quiches." He pushed himself to his feet, and I bit my lip.

"Would you like me to do it? I mean, are you sure you don't want to rest after dinner?"

"I've been resting for two days, and I'm going bonkers. This is what I need to stay sane."

"Okay. I'll load the dishwasher while you work with your accounting stuff." I was secretly relieved. I did cost analysis for my jam business, but it had been a while since I'd done any cost per plate estimates, and I hadn't enjoyed them much when I'd done them at culinary school.

By Tuesday we had the menu in hand: salmon pinwheels, mini-quiches, filo packets, crudités and dip, and meatballs. I went over to City Market to pick up the ingredients we didn't already have on hand, then to the catering kitchen to store my purchases and start working on the prep I could do in advance, like the meatballs and the salmon spread for the pinwheels.

Coco was already in the kitchen working on the quiches. She was going to prebake the shells, then do the filling and the final bake on Thursday afternoon before we went to the job.

"So are you okay doing the filo packets?" I asked her.

Coco shrugged. "Sure, fine. Low stress. Do we have any filo?"

I'd actually bought a couple of packages of filo at the store, assuming the café wouldn't have any on hand. "Yep. Is this okay?"

"Sure, put them in the refrigerator so they'll thaw."

I put the salmon spread and meatball recipes on the refrigerator with magnets. "I'll get started on this today, then do the crudités and dip tomorrow. That means final prep on Thursday afternoon."

"Right. Do we know who our waiter is?"

I paused. Nate usually took care of that. Had he remembered to do it this time? "I don't know. I'll call him." I started digging for my cell phone.

"Or you could just wait and ask him over dinner." Coco gave me a Siamese cat kind of smile.

But she had a point. I tossed my cell into my purse. "How's the kitchen doing with one less cook?"

Coco shrugged. "We're okay. Not great but okay. Bobby's sort of conceded that he can't do everything, which is a major concession, believe me."

"Are you working breakfast?" Usually Coco stuck to lunch, although she baked some of the breakfast pastries and wanted to bake more.

She gave me another of those smiles. "Yep. Bobby is actually letting me use the flattop. He's conceded that my pancakes ace his, and my French toast is the bomb, as I could have told him if he'd ever bothered to ask."

I frowned. "Do you want to go on doing breakfast?" The café did a big breakfast business, but they started serving at eight, which meant showing up in the kitchen at six thirty every day except Sunday when they shifted to ten o'clock brunch.

"Not necessarily. I wanted to make a point, and I made it. And Bobby's slowly accepting the concept that another cook wouldn't be a bad idea. Mom said you'd recommended someone, and she's going to come up and look us over soon."

"Marigold's coming to Shavano?" That was definitely news I wanted to pass on to Nate.

"Marigold?" Coco narrowed her eyes. "Her name is Marigold and she's going up against Bobby?"

"Don't underestimate her. She used to be a butcher."

Coco threw back her head and laughed. "A butcher is what we need. Tell her to bring her largest cleaver."

We finished for the day around four, and I drove to the cabin. It seemed a little weird to be coming home to Nate, but weird in a good way. I might want to think about the ramifications of the whole "coming home" thing sometime, but I decided this wasn't the time to do it.

I gave Nate the receipts from my grocery buying trip so he could keep track of the expenses. He'd already gotten the figures for the supplies we'd taken from the café's pantry, like the flour and other ingredients for Coco's mini-quiches and the hamburger for the meatballs I was fixing.

"Are we actually making money?" I asked him after he'd entered the expenses into his accounting software. "I mean, is the catering working out the way Madge hoped it would?"

"We're doing better than Mom expected. If we keep up the volume we've got now, we'll end the year with a healthy profit. If we increase the volume, we'll be even healthier than that."

"And to increase the volume…"

"We need more people," Nate said flatly. "I can't

go on dividing my time between catering and the café, and once the farmers market opens, you won't be able to do as much as you're doing now."

"Well, there's Marigold. She's coming up to look the place over sometime soon, according to Coco."

Nate rapped his knuckles on the kitchen table. "Here's hoping she likes Shavano, and here's hoping Bobby doesn't scare her off."

"Here's hoping," I agreed.

Supper that night was festive. I retrieved some of Marcus's pork chops from the freezer, along with some fingerling potatoes and early asparagus from someplace other than Colorado, where it would be another month or two before asparagus started showing up in the farmers markets. Nate wasn't taking his super acetaminophen anymore, so he tried a glass of wine. We talked about menus and asparagus and who was running for mayor of Shavano. We didn't talk about Bobby or the café or Grace Peters or the phantom SUV.

That didn't mean they didn't cross our minds—they did, particularly mine. But it was as if we had a temporary agreement to stay off serious topics.

Nate poured himself another half glass of wine and took a cautious sip. "I am so ready to be back to normal."

"You're still supposed to take it easy." I was channeling Madge.

"I am taking it easy, trust me." He sipped the wine carefully. "But I'm a lot better these days. Maybe I could help you get ready tomorrow."

"You'd have to be on your feet for a couple of hours," I said doubtfully.

"I'm tired of being off my feet." Nate gave me a

mutinous look.

"It would be okay with me, but I think your mom won't like it." Which was a definite understatement.

Nate sighed. "Okay, what if I sit down to work? It goes against the grain, but I can do it. There are a couple of stools in the catering kitchen."

"We can probably set something up. But you do need to take it easy. For Madge's sake if not for yours." Actually, working in the catering kitchen might give him some idea of the limits on his stamina. I didn't want him running the catering job, since that would be a stretch.

The next afternoon, Nate set himself up at one of the counters, working on the crudités. I was glad to have him help out since trimming veggies has never been my strong suit. Nate, on the other hand, makes gorgeous tomato roses.

Coco tried a couple of sly digs at her brother, but she mostly kept her peace, working on the filo packets. The three of us got a lot done so we wouldn't have to do too much on the day of the event, which was the idea, after all.

But by four, Nate had begun to droop. I knew he'd never admit it, but he was tired even though he'd been sitting all afternoon. We got things cleaned up and put away, and Coco stepped in front of her brother. "You're not coming tomorrow, right?"

Nate gave her a slightly rebellious look. "I could handle it."

"So can we. It may not run as smoothly as it would if you were at the helm, but we can do it. And you need to take the time off, bro. It isn't just this thing with the SUV hitting you. You've been pushing way too hard for weeks. Go to Roxy's place and put your feet up. Rely on us to get it done."

It was the longest speech I'd ever heard Coco deliver, and the only time I'd ever heard her talk to her brother as if she cared about him.

Nate looked almost as surprised as I did. "I'll…think about it. And yeah, I'm sure you two could handle it without me there checking on everything."

"We can." Coco nodded decisively. "You've got us a waitress, right?"

Nate nodded. "Donnell. She knows her stuff."

"Yep. Then I'd say we're set. And you can stay home and get your strength back. I mean it, bro. Stay home." She leaned forward and kissed his cheek, then turned to wink at me.

As I drove to the farm, Nate leaned into his seat, staring out the window at the beginnings of spring greenery. It takes a while for spring to hit the mountains, but you can watch it slip in, little by little. "I guess Coco's right," he said finally. "I need to take the whole week. It pisses me off, but she's right."

"We can do it. Honest."

"I know you can. I just don't want to know it." He gave me a tired smile.

"Give us a chance." I pulled into the drive that led to the cabin. I could see Uncle Mike's car up at the main house, and I thought I could see another car parked next to his. If it was Madge, I sort of hoped Nate didn't notice.

We were home, both Uncle Mike and me. And maybe Madge and Nate were part of whatever *home* consisted of these days.

Nate followed me inside. We'd grabbed a pizza

from Moretti's on the way, and I set it on the counter. "You want to try some wine again? Or maybe beer?"

He nodded. "Definitely beer."

I pulled a couple of bottles out of the refrigerator, while Nate set the table and pulled the pizza out of the box. It was sort of weird how normal this was becoming. I decided I probably shouldn't let myself get too used to it, though. Nate would be leaving soon, and I'd be back on my own again.

"No salad. I meant to pick some up at the market. Sorry." We'd spent a large part of the afternoon trimming vegetables, so maybe salad was less necessary than I thought.

"That's okay, pizza's good." Nate paused. "Come on, Rox, sit down. You've been on your feet all day."

I put a hand on the counter, suddenly more tired than I'd realized. "You're right; I have." I let myself slump against the counter for a moment.

Nate stepped up and put his arms around me, resting his cheek against my hair. "You need to rest too, babe. It's been a long week."

I closed my eyes, enjoying the warmth of his body against mine.

"If I stop bitching and let you guys do your thing, can I have a reward?" Nate ran his hands in circles on my back.

I let myself lean against him. "Depends. What did you have in mind?"

"That I don't have to sleep in the spare room anymore." He pulled away to look at me. "Your bed's warmer."

I managed to keep my grin within bounds, but only just. "I think that can be arranged. In fact, that can definitely be arranged."

Chapter 21

I spent Thursday morning making marmalade, with Nate's help. He'd seen me make jam before, but the marmalade was something new and he was curious. I set him to work on the tangerine rinds, and he produced thin, elegant ribbons that put my usual rind toothpicks to shame.

After lunch, I packed away the jars we'd made so they could gel and got ready to go to the catering kitchen, with a quick stop at Bianca's to pick up some flatbread for the pinwheels. Nate leaned in the doorway as I grabbed my chef's coat and a pair of black pants along with my ball cap.

"I emailed the guy who's in charge of this shindig. His name's Alan Adamo. It's his place, Adamo Real Estate. Anyway, he's expecting you and Coco. He'll get you set up in their kitchen. They're having the party in their lobby, so you may have to climb some stairs to get the food in and out."

I wished we had a busboy for the evening. "What time are we supposed to show up?"

"Five. The party's supposed to start at six, but he said the bar's going to open at five-thirty. My guess is we should at least have the crudités out so people don't get plastered too soon."

"Got it. Crudités and maybe salmon pinwheels. Then we can get the rest of the stuff warmed up and out at six."

"Sounds good." He sighed. "You're sure you don't want me there?"

"I'm absolutely certain. I want you to stay here and figure out next week's menu. Is there a job next week?"

"Yep." He leaned forward and kissed my cheek. "Have fun. Don't forget to pay Donnell."

"I won't. Donnell won't let me." Which was all to the good.

Truth be told I was sort of nervous about this. I had no problem serving as Nate's sous chef, but I'd never been lead on something like this before. If it hadn't been for the accident, I'd have been easing back on my participation in the catering business. The farmers market was due to open in another month or so, and once it did, I'd probably be swamped trying to keep up with my online orders and my in-person sales.

Instead, here I was, leading a catering crew for a cocktail party. It felt weird. But I didn't have time to worry about the weirdness.

Bianca was at the front counter of her shop for once, and she brought out the bag of flatbread Nate had ordered. "You may want to warm this up. Maybe a couple of minutes in a microwave, much as I hate them."

"It's for salmon pinwheels. They should be fine cold." I paused, remembering something I'd been thinking about. "Do you use a full-size SUV for deliveries and picking up supplies?"

She shook her head. "It's in the shop right now. Sara borrowed it and said there was a problem with the fuel pump."

I took a deep breath, trying to find a way to ask her

if she'd actually seen it before it went into the shop. Was she absolutely sure the problem was a fuel pump and not a gouge along the side?

"Anyway, it's getting sort of rickety. I may replace it next year. Why? You in the market?"

I shook my head. "Not yet. Maybe when my truck gets too old." I beat a hasty retreat, wondering if I should call Fowler and deciding that would be sort of nuts. He'd probably be checking for large SUVs on his own, without my help.

At the catering kitchen I started working on the salmon pinwheels. I spread the flatbread with cream cheese and scallions, sprinkled the chopped smoked salmon, and scattered fresh baby spinach for some color and crunch. I rolled up all the loaves and then put them in the refrigerator to set. I'd slice them when we got to the location. The crudités were already prepared, so next I worked on the sour cream and herb dip to go with them. By then it was mid-afternoon, and Coco joined me, filling her mini-quiche shells with cheese custard and then baking them a sheet pan at a time.

I started scooping up the meatballs from the bowl of mix I'd made yesterday. "Do you need any help with the filo?" Filo's a bitch to work with and the packets were the last thing we had to do.

Coco shook her head. "I'm done with the quiches. All I have to do is put the filo packets on a sheet pan and bake them—I got the filling roasted off yesterday."

We worked side by side for another hour or so, not saying much, concentrating on our various tasks. "What time do we go over there?" Coco asked finally.

"Nate said five, but I think four thirty might be a better idea. They're opening the bar at five thirty."

"Oh, yeah. We'll need to put something out. Otherwise they'll either fill up on stale peanuts and skip our food or they'll be half shitfaced after thirty minutes because there's nothing to eat."

"Do you want to ride with me?"

Coco shook her head. "I'll drive myself. That way I can go home instead of coming here."

I'd have to come there to drop off all the paraphernalia we'd used to cook and serve, but that was the nature of the job.

Adamo Real Estate was in a three-story building in a strip mall. I hoped their kitchen had a microwave at a minimum. The building didn't look particularly promising. I made sure the cover on my pickup was locked over all the food I was carrying in the back of the truck and went in search of Alan Adamo.

His real estate agency actually occupied the entire building, which made me feel a little more optimistic about the facilities. Adamo turned out to be a portly fifty-something in a well-cut suit. He had his PA show me the way to the kitchen.

It was depressing, but no worse than I expected. The kitchen was next to a classic office lunchroom. It had a sink, refrigerator, and microwave that I feared would smell like fish. Fortunately, they also had a dishwasher.

"Looks like the cleaning staff's been through." The PA smiled brightly. "Need anything else?"

"Could you show me the way to the lobby from here—the room where they're holding the party?"

"Oh, sure." She took me down a flight of stairs to a large open room with some ficus and palm trees I suspected were phony and a nice selection of leather couches and coffee tables. Looked like setting up would be relatively simple.

The PA gestured toward a couple of long tables draped with white tablecloths. "The bar's going to be right over there," she said. "We thought you could put the food on the table next to it."

Normally we would have scattered the food on tables around the room, but putting it all on one table would probably make it a little easier to serve and keep track of.

"Anything else?" she asked.

"Nope, that's fine. Thank you."

"Okay, see you in a bit. Can't wait to see what you're serving us." The PA gave me another bright smile, then went up the stairs.

I figured the next step would be getting our food into the kitchen. I was picking up the first hotel pan of meatballs when Coco pulled in. She'd changed into her own version of a chef's outfit, an immaculate white shirt and pants with a black apron. "How's the place?"

"Grim kitchen, decent party room. Can you bring the quiches?"

She nodded. "Got 'em. Let's go."

We managed to get the things that needed to be kept cool into the refrigerator by rearranging the collection of lunch sacks and yogurt containers already there. Coco transferred her mini-quiches to a plate and opened the microwave.

"At least it's clean," she said. Also full size, which made our life easier. If it had been a mini we'd have been in deep trouble, considering how much food we had to heat up.

I checked the lobby. The bartender had set up at the

table he'd been given, along with a couple of washtubs loaded with ice. It looked like he was mostly going to be serving beer and wine, but I saw a bottle of Bloody Mary mix and what looked like a pitcher of margaritas.

I went to the kitchen and started laying out the crudités on a large plastic platter from the restaurant. It wasn't gorgeous, but it held a lot, and I didn't figure the partygoers were going to be paying much attention to the serving ware as long as the food looked good. Thanks to Nate's tomato roses and some gorgeously fresh veggies, the crudités looked very good indeed. Balancing the large platter on my arms while going downstairs was a little tricky, but I managed it. Maybe I'd use the elevator from now on.

Donnell was standing in the lobby watching the bartender when I came in. "There you are. I was about to go on a search."

"Kitchen's upstairs," I said. "Come on, I'll show you."

She followed me up the stairs, grumbling. "Gonna be a pisser getting stuff up and down these stairs. And we don't have Nate to carry."

"I'll carry. And we can use the elevator once it's free." I figured most of the employees who weren't going to the party would have cleared out by six.

From then on, things went faster. I sliced up the first of the pinwheel loaves and gave them to Donnell to take out to the lobby, using the stairs since the elevator was currently full of people. She looked dubious about balancing the tray down the stairs, but she took off as Coco got the next plate of her mini-quiches into the microwave. I lined up the meatballs to go in next. We'd warm the food in the kitchen and then set it out on warming trays in the lobby.

Normally we'd have sent out one platter at a time so people could finish one app before another one arrived. But since everything was going on a single table, I figured we might as well get them out there all at once.

I was setting up the warming trays for the meatballs and the quiches while Donnell arranged the napkins and forks alongside the plates when people began to trail in, first in ones and twos and then in larger groups. We'd planned for thirty-five, and I hoped Adamo hadn't decided to ask a bunch more people at the last minute. Most of the guests were clustered around the bar, but a few wandered over to our table to load up their plates with some veggies and a salmon pinwheel or two.

I sprinted up the stairs and got the first hotel pan of meatballs. Coco grabbed a pan of quiches and followed me. This time we used the elevator.

Donnell had set up a tray stand and tray at the side of the room where people could leave their dirty plates. She and I would have to tote the loaded trays up to the kitchen, but I figured we could use the elevator for that. No way was I risking a tray of dishes going down the stairwell by accident. The elevators weren't in heavy use anymore, so we could use them full time.

We had everything out on the table by six, and I withdrew to the side of the room. I figured Coco could handle the kitchen, but Donnell might need help getting the tables cleared. Besides, at large parties Nate usually stayed out in the party room for part of the time so the clients could find him if they needed to. And I was channeling Nate, however inexpertly.

Most of the guests looked like employees, but there were a few people who seemed to be potential customers, given the amount of time Adamo spent with them. I divided my attention between the guests and the food, leaving a couple of times to replenish the meatballs, which were definitely a hit.

The mini-quiches were flying off the warmer, too. But the crudités and the filo packets were taking a little longer. I figured that was predictable—we'd labeled the packets *vegan* and a lot of people think that means *tasteless.*

I grabbed the first tray of dirty dishes after about twenty minutes. It wasn't full, but I wasn't sure I could carry a full one. I hoisted it onto my shoulder and started for the elevator just as a group of guests disembarked. They looked around expectantly, and I recognized a couple of them.

Apparently, Marcus and Sara Jordan were customers of Adamo's, since I doubted they were employees. When Sara caught sight of me, her eyes widened and she looked away. But friendly Marcus broke into a grin. I had no intention of having a conversation with either of them while I was carrying a moderately heavy tray of dishes. I nodded in their general direction, then detoured around the group and caught the elevator before the doors closed.

In the kitchen, Coco was warming meatballs and quiches. "How's it going?" she asked.

"Fast. Meatballs and quiches are flying. Pinwheels, too. Crudités and packets are taking a little longer." I set the tray of dishes on the counter near the dishwasher. "If you can load these, I'll get the next round of food down there."

"Right." Coco and I switched places so that she could get to the dishwasher and I could lift the pans of meatballs and quiches she'd finished warming. This was an elevator load.

When I got to the lobby, I saw Donnell circulating the room with a plate of filo packets. Good idea. After people tasted them, they'd probably want more. I added the meatballs and quiches to their respective pans and checked on the dirty dishes.

Already filling up. Given the amount of toting and carrying I was doing, I was going to deserve a shoulder massage when this evening was over. Fortunately, Nate was gifted in that area.

"Hi, Roxy. I didn't realize you were doing the catering."

I'd forgotten all about Marcus Jordan in the chaos of getting food onto the table and getting the dishes to the kitchen. I wasn't exactly delighted to see him, although I like Marcus normally. I didn't have time to be sociable. "Hi, Marcus. I'm sorry, but I can't talk. I'm working." I turned and headed for the elevators, balancing the tray of dishes on my shoulder.

"I could carry that for you." Marcus trotted along beside me. "It looks heavy."

The last thing I wanted was for a guest to start toting dish trays for me. "Thanks, Marcus, I can handle it." I ducked through the door to the elevator.

I wondered if other guests were nervous about me carrying trays of dishes. I'm a big girl, but I'm still a girl, and some people get antsy when they see women do heavy lifting. I could tell Nate he was definitely missed.

I swung into the kitchen again. Coco turned, eyes

narrowing. "What's up? You look stressed."

Shake it off. "It's nothing. One of the guests wanted to carry the tray of dishes for me because I'm such a fragile flower."

"Who was it?"

"Marcus Jordan. He's here with Sara. They must know Adamo."

"Oh, Lord, Sara Jordan." Coco grimaced. "She's such a grouch. Marcus is super nice, but geez, he can't carry trays if he's guest."

"Tell me about it. Where are we on the food?"

"Warming up another round of meatballs as we speak. Donnell took the tray of pinwheels up a few minutes ago."

I grabbed one of the trays the dirty dishes had been sitting on. "Has this been rinsed?"

"Yeah."

I started toward the elevator again, hoping Marcus wouldn't be waiting for me. I had stuff to do. But I could maybe avoid him if I used the stairs this time. I turned back and climbed down the staircase quickly then pushed the door at the bottom more energetically than I needed to. A couple of people standing nearby gave me raised eyebrows, and I realized that could have been a disaster if someone were standing where the door swung out. Fortunately for me, they weren't, but it was a wakeup call. I needed to concentrate on the job.

I walked across to the dirty dishes, placing the new tray next to the tray stand and hoping Donnell would put it in place. I picked up the rapidly filling tray and headed for the elevator. Fortunately for me, no one seemed to be interested in following me this time around. Maybe Marcus had found someone else to talk to.

In the kitchen I put the tray down on the counter then realized I hadn't checked the food table to see what we needed. I might be trying to channel Nate, but I wasn't doing a very good job of it.

"What do we need?" Coco asked. She started adding the dirty plates I'd brought in to the load in the dishwasher.

I closed my eyes trying to remember the last time I'd looked at the table. "Quiches, meatballs, pinwheels. We'll probably need more filo packets, too since Donnell's circulating the tray around the room. Basically just about everything."

"Take the meatballs and the filo packets. Quiches still need to warm."

I grabbed both pans and headed for the elevator. No time to pause and think. We had stomachs to fill. People were scattered around the lobby now, most of them holding plates and glasses. The volume level wasn't quite to max yet, but it was energetic.

Donnell loaded a few more dishes onto the tray as I delivered the meatballs and filo packets. The filo was moving now. And the crudités tray looked a little picked over. We probably needed to refresh it.

"How's it going?" Donnell asked, doing a quick survey of the table.

"We need more veggies for the platter," I said. "Go up and get some from Coco. Then just fill in the platter where it seems thin."

Donnell looked dubious, but I didn't have time to reassure her. Maybe Nate would have done it himself, but he had more help than I did.

I checked the dish tray, but it didn't look ready to

take up yet. The mini-quiches, on the other hand, were looking thin. I trotted toward the staircase again.

We were approaching the caterer's dilemma. You don't want to have less food than people expect, but you don't want to have too much food either, particularly if you want to make it to the end of the evening. Adamo had said thirty people, and we'd prepared enough food for everybody to have a few bites of a lot of things. But now we were running low on the most popular dishes. The quiches were almost gone, and the meatballs were running low. There were probably enough pinwheels and filo packets to last the rest of the evening, but people might get a bit miffed if their favorites disappeared.

I checked my watch to see how much longer we needed to have food on the table and was amazed to discover it was almost seven. That hour had flown by, which meant we only had another thirty minutes to go.

In the kitchen, Coco had the dishwasher going. "I just sent Donnell down with some veggies. Does the dip bowl need refilling?"

"Most likely," I said. "I'll take down the dip and the end of the quiches. Once those are gone, I'll bring the warming pan and get everything out for the last half hour."

"Go for it, kid. We're doing good." Coco gave me a quick smile and turned to the meatballs and filo.

I hefted the last pan of quiches and added the container of dip to the load, then went out again. I was trotting down the hall toward the elevator when I heard voices coming from the stairwell. As far as I knew, we were the only ones on this floor at the moment, but I supposed it was possible some of Adamo's employees were using the stairs to go up and down if the elevator was too slow.

I pressed the elevator button then paused. One of the voices sounded loud, but then I was standing close to the door. I couldn't make out the words, but the voice seemed familiar. The more I listened, the more convinced I became that it was Sara Jordan. I couldn't make out what the other person was saying, but Sara definitely sounded annoyed.

"I told you that plan was insane," she was saying. "Why the hell did you want to go out there anyway? Now I've got to come up with excuses for the shape the van's in."

For a moment, I stood riveted to the spot. I listened as hard as I could, but the other person spoke softly and I couldn't make out the voice.

The elevator arrived just then, and I balanced for a moment, trying to decide what to do. I had to get the food to the lobby. We had thirty more minutes to get through. But I had good reasons for my opinion that Sara Jordan had something to do with both the death of Muriel Cates and perhaps the accident with the SUV. And now she seemed to be talking about the latter with the person who was maybe driving on Friday.

First things first. I took a deep breath and sprinted down the stairs to the lobby. I dumped the quiches in the warming pan and refilled the bowl of dip quickly. Then I stowed the hotel pan and dip container under the table where they were mostly hidden from view by the tablecloth.

"You gonna take that dish tray up now?" Donnell asked.

I checked, and she was right. It needed to go. "Just

a sec," I said and trotted over to the door to the stairwell.

I couldn't hear any voices, but the noise in the lobby was pretty loud. I opened the door as cautiously as I could and stepped inside.

The voices were still there. Sara was most likely standing in the stairwell outside the door to the floor above the kitchen, and she was still having a very loud conversation with somebody. "How the hell am I supposed to explain this to my mother-in-law?" she was saying. "She already hates me."

Okay, that was maybe confirmation that Sara's van was the one who'd hit Nate. I needed to pass that on to Fowler.

I stepped out into the lobby again, then trotted across the room to pick up the dirty dishes.

Someone grabbed my arm, and I jumped, turning to see a guy in a gray business suit. "Got any more of those meatballs?" he asked.

I took a deep breath, willing my pulse to return to normal. "I'll see what I can do," I said and trotted for the elevators.

Once the elevator reached the second floor, I sprinted down the hall, hitting the door to the kitchen at a run.

"Whoa," Coco said. "What's up?"

I put the tray of dishes on the counter, then leaned forward to catch my breath. "Sara Jordan's having a very loud conversation with somebody in the stairwell. About the accident. It sounds like it, anyway. Bianca's van was the one they were using. And Sara's involved. She's talking to the driver."

"What the hell?" Coco pulled off her apron. "Call

the cops. Call Fowler. You know him, right?"

"I want to make sure I heard what I think I heard first. Plus, if I call Fowler, there could be a lot of cops swarming around here screwing up Adamo's party, which won't make him a happy customer. I need to make sure I'm right."

Coco glowered at me, then nodded. "Okay, let's go. You could use a witness for whatever she's saying."

We sprinted down the hall. At the door to the stairwell, I motioned for Coco to be quiet, then opened the door as silently as I could.

For a moment, I thought Sara was gone. Then I heard someone speaking in a low voice, probably the driver of the van. There was a long pause, then Sara spoke more quietly than she had before. "You'd tell him? After everything I did for you? Jesus."

The other person said something else I couldn't hear. "All right," Sara said. "All right. I'll keep quiet, and you keep quiet."

Coco frowned up at me, and I shrugged. What she'd heard wasn't all that incriminating, although it seemed to indicate Sara was hiding some secrets. Maybe the other person was blackmailing her, which opened up some interesting possibilities. It was always possible that Muriel Cates was involved in blackmail, too.

I started to step forward so that I could maybe see who the other person was when the door on the lobby floor swung open with a crash.

"Roxy," Donnell called, "we need more pinwheels."

Everyone in the stairwell froze for a moment, and then I heard the sound of frantic footsteps and a door opening above me. Coco jumped forward to try to see up the stairwell, but the upstairs door slammed shut.

"Dammit," I snapped. "Dammit, dammit, dammit."

"Roxy, did you hear me?" Donnell called, but I was too busy running up the stairs to worry about pinwheels right then. I pulled open the door to the third floor and stepped out. The hall was empty. Sara and her blackmailer had taken themselves off. They'd probably rejoined the crowd in the lobby, and I'd never be able to figure out who Sara had been talking to.

I stepped back into the stairwell again to see Coco talking to a clearly pissed Donnell. I took a deep breath. Time to go back to work.

Chapter 22

The rest of the night was uneventful, although I suppose compared to the scene in the stairwell anything would have been uneventful. I got the pinwheels out on the table and mollified Donnell, although she was still annoyed with me. She'd probably welcome Nate with open arms, which should make him feel good.

The party wound down around seven thirty, as advertised. I didn't see Sara Jordan after the incident in the stairwell, although I saw Marcus standing around with a beer and a couple of meatballs. He didn't seem to know anybody at the party, and I wondered why they were there.

I brought in the last tray of dishes and helped Coco load them up. "Any luck finding the person who was talking to Sara?" she asked.

I shook my head. "I didn't even find Sara. She's keeping a very low profile."

"You're going to tell Fowler about that, right?" Coco narrowed her eyes.

"Right. Maybe he can check out Bianca's SUV in the shop before he questions Sara. Then he'd have her dead to rights." Which was an unfortunate turn of phrase.

Coco and I got the pans and platters loaded into the boxes we'd used to carry everything. I'd pack it all into my truck when we were done, but first I needed to run down Alan Adamo to get the balance of our fee.

He was standing in the lobby talking to a couple of people while he watched the bartender break down the bar. The leftover liquor would probably go home with him. We didn't have any leftover food to speak of, so it wasn't an issue.

Nate always handled the financial side of things, but he'd given me an invoice to present to Adamo. He'd already paid fifty percent, and the deal was he'd pay the rest at the end of the evening. "Don't let him give you any crap," Nate warned me. "He's been a little slippery about what he owes."

I stood a few feet away, waiting for Adamo to finish his conversation, but he seemed to be ignoring me pointedly. He must have known what I was there for, but maybe he thought I'd be too shy to approach him. In that case, he thought wrong.

"Good evening," I said, pasting on my blandest smile. "I have the final paperwork for you."

Adamo frowned, but he took the invoice and checked it over. "I thought Robicheaux was going to be here to be paid."

"Nate was in an accident earlier this week. I'm filling in for him." Which Adamo undoubtedly knew already, but I didn't mind refreshing his memory.

"Service was kind of slow." He gave me a disapproving glare.

The service had been decent, although probably not up to Nate's standards. Still, we'd delivered the food on time and no one had gone hungry. "I'm sorry if people were inconvenienced," I said.

"I'll have to look this over," Adamo said, tapping the paper. "I'll get back to Robicheaux next week."

No, you freaking won't. "According to the catering contract, we were to be paid the remainder of our fee this evening after service was finished. If you feel you've been charged incorrectly, you can talk to Nate tomorrow, but I need to pay my crew now." Donnell constituted *crew,* after all. I figured Nate would settle up with Coco later.

I was aware of people watching us, and Adamo was, too. After another moment he sighed and reached into his pocket, pulling out a check. "Here. I'll be talking to Robicheaux about the service."

I took the check and gave him a teeth-gritting smile. "Thank you. I'll let him know you'll be calling." I turned on my heel and went toward the kitchen.

Nate had actually given me Donnell's pay in advance and told me to split any bonus with her. It was pretty clear no bonus was going to be forthcoming, but I passed on the cash.

Donnell pulled on her coat. "Sure hope we don't do another one here. Going up and down those stairs was a bitch."

"Yeah. And Adamo turned out to be a jerk. My guess is we won't be working with him again."

"His loss." Donnell tucked her pay into her purse. "Tell Nate I hope he's feeling better."

Coco had pulled off her apron and the scarf she'd tied around her hair. "Do you need help with anything else, or can I take off?"

"Take off. I'll load the pans in the truck and bring them back tomorrow. Right now, I want to go home and put my feet up."

"Sounds like a winner. I'll help you carry them out."

The two of us got everything out to my truck, packing it all away in the back so I could lock the tonneau cover over it. Adamo's building was in a dark corner of the parking lot, the nearest light ten or twelve feet away. I was antsy about getting out of there.

"Okay," Coco said. "I'm off. See you tomorrow or sometime."

I nodded. "Definitely tomorrow or sometime." Coco headed toward her car, and I climbed quickly into the cab of my truck.

And stopped cold.

Someone was sitting on the passenger's side, slumped down so that she hadn't been visible until I was in the driver's seat. "Who the hell…" I started.

Grace Peters sat up straight and I saw the gun in her hand for the first time. "All right, enough screwing around. I need that package and I need it now."

I stared at her blankly. "What package? I have no idea what you're talking about."

"Don't give me that. She was your cousin, and she told me you were in on it. You know, goddamn it." Grace lifted the gun higher. "I need that package. And you're going to give it to me. You're going to drive me to your house and get it. If you do that, I'll consider not shooting you. If you don't, it won't even be a question."

I was still staring at her, but the penny had dropped. "You're talking about Muriel Cates."

"Of course, I'm talking about Muriel," Grace snapped. "Muriel and that little blackmailing scheme the two of you cooked up. And if you're thinking of stalling, just remember what happened to your cousin when she tried to double-cross me. You could easily be found dead here in the parking lot. It doesn't matter to me. Now are you going to drive or am I going to mess up your clean windows?"

I turned the key in the ignition, trying desperately to think of alternatives. There had to be some, didn't there? I decided to lead with the truth. "I didn't even know Muriel Cates was my cousin until after she was dead. And I have no idea what she was up to in town. I only spoke to her once."

Grace snorted as I pulled onto the county road. "Bullshit. Muriel told me she came to town to see you. When she recognized me, she told you all about it. You agreed to help her take me down. And if you know what's good for you now, you'll give me everything she gave you. I know you've got it at your place."

I thought about telling her that she could have anything Muriel left for me if she could find it, but I figured that wouldn't be helpful. My best bet was to turn toward the farm and hope Nate or Uncle Mike saw what was happening. And didn't get shot themselves if they tried to stop it.

"Were you driving the SUV that hit Nate?" It seemed pretty clear she had been. She was also most likely the person who'd been talking to Sara.

"We're not having a conversation. Drive. I'll give you ten minutes." She settled against the door, pointing her gun directly at me.

Ten minutes was barely enough time to get to the farm from Adamo's office building. I sped down the road five miles over the speed limit, taking all kinds of chances. But then I was already taking all kinds of chances by having a not-entirely-sane woman pointing a gun at me. I just hoped it didn't go off by accident if I hit a pothole.

Finally, finally, we reached the turnoff for the farm. It was even darker than it had been the night Grace had hit Nate's car. She must have been hunting for her elusive package and tried to run when she heard us coming down the drive.

I still hadn't figured out what I was going to do when we got to my cabin, other than hope against hope that neither Nate nor I would get shot. My hands were shaking as I gripped the steering wheel, and I was breathing so hard I was afraid I'd hyperventilate.

I pulled to a stop a few feet from my normal parking space at the cabin. Maybe Nate would look out the window before coming out to see what was going on. For some reason the yard light wasn't on, so he might not be able to see where I'd parked the truck. "Now, what?"

"Now you get out and get me that package." Grace sat up, still pointing the gun in my direction. "Get out of the truck. Slowly. And you don't try anything cute. I'll be right behind you."

I'd never felt less cute in my life, and I had no idea where I was supposed to find this mythical *package* that Grace kept telling me to fetch. I opened the driver's side door and climbed out carefully. Grace slid after me, gun still pointed at my head.

I took a couple of steps toward the cabin since I couldn't think of anything else to do when the yard lights suddenly blazed on. Not just the single yard light at the cabin, but all of them from the main house across the yard area and the storage sheds nearby. The contrast was so dazzling I actually raised my arm to shade my eyes. At the same time, I heard someone shout, "Drop the gun, and raise your hands. Police."

If I'd paused to think, I'd probably have frozen in place. But instinct had me dropping to the ground and rolling beneath the truck. I glanced back and saw Grace in the spotlight, twisting with her gun. In another moment, she'd probably figure out where I'd gone. I scrabbled farther underneath, hoping the undercarriage might protect me.

The disembodied voice came again. "Drop it, I said. Get those hands up. You're covered." And I heard the unmistakable sound of a shotgun being racked.

Well, damn. I knew who that voice belonged to.

Fortunately, Grace didn't. She dropped her gun and raised her hands. A figure quickly stepped behind her and kicked the gun away while Uncle Mike emerged from the darkness holding his trusty Remington. I'd never seen him use it against anything other than beer bottles and the occasional thieving raccoon, but he couldn't very well miss at this range.

I doubted very much he'd be willing or able to shoot Grace, however much she might deserve it.

The other figure turned out to be Nate, who yanked Grace's wrists behind her. "Don't suppose you have any handcuffs."

Uncle Mike shook his head. "Not much call for them out here."

Grace twisted hard, but Nate held on. I rolled out from under the truck, then climbed into the cab and pulled a piece of rope from my glove compartment. "Here," I said, wrapping the rope around Grace's wrists.

"Get your hands off me," Grace snarled. "I'll have you arrested for assault."

"Yeah, good luck with that," I said. "Tell me the

cops are actually on their way."

"They are," Nate said. "Well, Fowler is. But Mike and I didn't want to wait for him to get here."

"And I'm really grateful you didn't." I felt like my knees were about to give way, but I managed to stay upright. I pulled the rope tight around Grace's wrists.

"You're hurting me," she said. "When the cops get here, you'll be the one they arrest."

Uncle Mike snorted. "Right. You were the one with the gun, missy."

More cars were turning down the drive now. I recognized Fowler's cruiser, which was followed by Coco's compact SUV.

Which explained how Uncle Mike and Nate had been prepared for Grace and me.

They both pulled to a stop next to my truck, and Fowler climbed out, with Coco close behind him. "Are you okay?" she called. "Did she hurt you?"

"Coco saw Grace in the cab of your truck, and she thought she saw a gun in her hand," Nate said. "She called me. I called Mike. We both called Fowler."

"I'm okay, thanks to you," I said and gave Coco a very fierce hug.

"All three of you called me, as a matter of fact." Fowler walked toward us, pulling his handcuffs off his belt. "Did she have a gun?"

"Yeah," Nate said. "I kicked it away after she dropped it. It's somewhere over there."

"This woman assaulted me," Grace said. "And these two men threatened me with that shotgun. I want to press charges against all three of them." She tried to twist out of Nate's hold again. "Let go of me, you jerk."

I had to give Grace credit for chutzpah. Although

that was all the credit I was going to give her. I turned to Fowler. "On the way over here, she told me she killed Muriel Cates. And she threatened to kill me if I didn't give her whatever Muriel was using to blackmail her. I have no idea what that was, but she thought it was out here."

Nate's eyes widened. Coco and Uncle Mike looked properly outraged.

"Interesting." Fowler untied Grace's wrists, then snapped on the handcuffs quickly. "Any response, Ms. Peters?"

"I'm not saying anything more until I talk to my attorney. But I'll be suing for slander and false arrest." Grace raised her chin and gave us all a burning look.

"Right." Fowler didn't sound impressed.

Another squad car had arrived by then, with two uniformed cops. Fowler used their flashlights to locate Grace's gun, which hadn't gone very far, and put it in an evidence bag. Then he turned Grace over to the uniforms. Fortunately, their cruiser had a cage for transporting prisoners. I wouldn't have trusted Grace in a normal car.

"I just thought she was a lousy baker," Coco muttered. "I didn't realize just how lousy she really was."

"I need statements from all of you," Fowler said. "We'll do formal statements tomorrow down at the station, but I need a clear idea of what happened this evening."

So we told him. I told him about Grace hiding in my truck and threatening me with her gun after she'd admitted killing my cousin. Coco told him about seeing Grace in the cab of the truck (although she hadn't been sure it was Grace—just someone with a gun) and calling Nate. Nate told him about calling Mike and planning a strategy if I came to the farm that involved turning off the yard lights and then switching them on when we got out of the truck. Uncle Mike explained about the shotgun, after he'd removed the shells.

When we were finished, Fowler stared at me. "And you've got no idea what she was after?"

I shook my head. "Just some kind of hold Muriel had over her. Grace said Muriel knew her, recognized her. And Muriel lied and told her I was in on it, so Grace must have figured I could give her whatever Muriel had."

Fowler narrowed his eyes. "And Muriel didn't tell you anything like that?"

"I never had a conversation with Muriel. She asked me for a job without identifying herself as my cousin. When I said no, she left. I didn't see her again until we found her body." That sent a quick shiver up my spine.

"So we're right back where we were, except we know who killed Cates." Uncle Mike looked annoyed, but I wasn't sure if he was annoyed at Grace or Muriel. Probably both.

"One more thing," I said. "Grace was driving the SUV that hit Nate. It was Bianca's, and she got it from Sara Jordan. Sara was at the dinner tonight and I heard then arguing."

"Well," Coco chimed in, "we heard Sara arguing. At the time we didn't know Grace was on the other end."

Fowler stared at me. "Bianca Jordan's SUV? Did she know about this?"

I closed my eyes. Poor Bianca. "Sara said no. And

Sara told her the SUV was in the shop because of a broken fuel pump, not because the side had gotten banged up. I guess you could check that out."

"I guess I could." One corner of Fowler's mouth edged up in one of his sardonic smiles. He sighed, tucking his notebook into his pocket. "All right, looks like Grace Peters was out here looking for whatever it is Cates had on her. When she didn't find it the night she hit Nate, she may have decided to go for broke and grab Roxy. I doubt Muriel Cates had time to hide her blackmail material out here, but Peters thought she did, so it's worth a look. I'll send a search team out tomorrow."

"We'll take a look around ourselves," Uncle Mike said. "Roxy knows what's supposed to be here. And what isn't."

Fowler wasn't pleased. "What we're looking for is evidence of a crime, a murder. To make it stand up in court, I need a clear chain of evidence. Let us do it."

I shook my head. "I see your point, but nope. That woman killed my cousin and tried to kill me over something that's hidden here, in our home. We need to look for it."

Fowler sighed. "I'll make a deal with you. If you find anything that looks like it might be what Peters was looking for, yell for the guys who'll be out here searching. And if they're gone, call me before you touch it. Give me a chance to document it before it's disturbed."

"Okay. That we can do. We won't start looking until tomorrow when it's light anyway."

Uncle Mike looked like he was ready to start looking right then, but I wasn't. In fact, I felt like I had all I could do to stay upright.

Nate put his arm around my shoulders. "She needs to get some rest. We all need to get some rest. Grace is in custody, and I don't think anybody else will come out here to look around. Tomorrow's soon enough." He started nudging me gently toward the cabin.

"Tomorrow it is." Fowler nodded. "I'll have people here searching bright and early."

"Terrific," I mumbled. Right then, *bright and early* sounded pretty grim.

Chapter 23

Fowler's men did start searching relatively bright and early the next morning. Bright and early enough that Nate and I were both a little bleary when they arrived. I made coffee and toast, and two guys searched my house, although I was pretty sure they wouldn't find anything.

I supposed it was possible that Muriel had found a way into my cabin, but the locks were pretty good. When you live out in the country like we do, you pay attention to security. At this time of year, I kept my windows closed and latched, and both doors bolted. In fact, the back door still had a small pile of snow in front of it, which probably ruled it out as a point of unseen access unless Muriel knew how to levitate.

The searchers were thorough and, fortunately, neat. They put everything back the way they'd found it, said thanks, and walked up to the main house, which seemed even less likely as a target for Muriel. Nate sighed, then finished the last of his coffee. "If it's here, I think it's got to be outside somewhere. Getting into either of the houses would be too tough and too risky. Plus, she'd be thinking about retrieval, and getting in a second time might be a problem."

"I agree. But I don't know where she'd hide stuff outside unless she buried it somewhere. And if she did, we'll probably never find it."

"Don't you think she would have marked the spot somehow, just so she could find it again? Particularly if it snowed after she buried it."

I paused, considering. "Maybe. Or maybe she put it near a building or some equipment so she'd have a landmark."

That gave us a starting point, at least, and we fanned out to look across the spaces that were closer to buildings. I'd never thought about how many structures there were on the farm: equipment sheds for the tractors and the other machinery, a storage building for the hand tools and bins for harvesting, a cement-block structure that used to be an icehouse where the produce was sorted and packaged, even an ancient barn from when the farm featured cattle and horses. Uncle Mike meant to restore the barn as a guest house sometime, but he hadn't gotten around to it yet. Nate hiked off to check around the sheds since they were closest.

Muriel could probably have tucked stuff anywhere around any of these places if she'd come out after dark when no one was around to see her.

But would she? That was the stumbling block for me. To bury something near one of the outbuildings, she'd have had to leave her car somewhere on the county road and then hike down the drive and across a lot of open area. And it wasn't easy going. There were several working fields close in, complete with caterpillar tunnels at this time of year. Walking across them would have been a bitch, even with frozen soil. If I were Muriel, I'd want something easier, somewhere I could reach more quickly if I needed to move things around.

I looked up the drive toward the road. There were

all those pines at the entrance. She could probably have stashed something next to one of them. And if she had, I figured she'd have marked the tree in some way so that she'd be sure to find it when she needed it.

It took me an hour or so to convince myself she hadn't done anything of the sort. One of the trees had been badly scarred when Nate's car had crashed into it, and the ground near it had been torn up. But I couldn't find anything else that looked like it had been marked. And there were no signs of any disturbance in the carpet of wet pine needles and old snow along both sides of the road near the entrance.

Yes, she could have gone farther away from the drive. But I didn't think she would. It seemed out of character for someone who wasn't big on unnecessary labor. And given that Muriel had apparently been making her living via blackmail, I was guessing unnecessary labor was something she'd avoid.

I walked down the drive again, trying to study the farm through Muriel's eyes. Had she been thinking about blackmailing us, too? Was that why she'd come to my door pretending to be looking for work? Or was she just curious about the relatives she'd never met? And why had she brought my mom's license along?

Maybe if Uncle Mike hadn't shown up when he did, she would have told me who she was. And maybe I would have found out more about my mom and her family. But I was guessing not. Muriel was running a con, and having actual relatives in town might have gotten in her way.

The farm probably looked like easy pickings to her. We had Herman and Donnie's dog Lulabelle running around the place, but they weren't much of a threat as watchdogs, particularly since we took both of them in at night. Muriel could have slipped in and out easily enough without being seen or heard. Assuming she hadn't been leading Grace on a wild goose chase, which wasn't at all a safe assumption, where might she have hidden whatever she had to hide?

I walked toward my cabin, narrowing my eyes, still trying to see things as Muriel might have seen them. It was the building closest to the drive, easiest to access, flanked by trees that partially concealed it from the main house. And while I was around most of the day, I was frequently gone at night on catering jobs.

All Muriel would have needed would be a rundown of my catering schedule. And Sara might have been able to help with that since we ordered lots of stuff for the jobs from Marcus's shop.

I did a slow circuit of the cabin, looking for anything that appeared to be disturbed. If she'd buried something before a snowfall, I probably wouldn't find it until all the snow finally melted. But would she have gone to the trouble of burying something at all, particularly if she wanted to be quick?

After a half hour or so, I was satisfied that Muriel hadn't buried anything nearby my cabin. Not surprising. So where else could she have tucked something? I checked the siding and the foundation to make sure there weren't any gaps where she could have slid an envelope or two, but I didn't see anything promising.

Once I'd returned to the front porch, I paused to take stock. And saw my planters.

They were small, galvanized steel stock tanks, placed at right angles to the front walk. In the summer I planted them with petunias and geraniums. Right now, they were full of soil and a few streaks of dirty snow, all that remained of the last flurry. I walked around them, trying to see if there were gaps at the side where an envelope or a bag could be tucked, but I didn't find anything. The soil reached to the sides of the tank, and when I tried pushing my fingers into it, it was hard to dislodge. I checked carefully, but I didn't see any signs of digging. The soil was packed down hard, a uniform gray surface stretching from side to side.

I sighed. It had seemed like a good idea. The planters were easy to access but not obvious. The pines beside the cabin probably screened them from the main house. If Muriel had been there at night when I wasn't home, she could have easily dug a quick hole and buried her materials before anybody knew any better. If I were Muriel, that's what I would have done, dammit!

I stared down at the ground, trying to think of other hiding places. Which was when I noticed that one of the planters was ever so slightly out of place. I could see the outline in the dirt where the planter had been. It looked as if it had been moved a couple of inches to the side.

My heart did a quick thump. I considered calling for help, but I decided to see if I could move it myself first. Muriel had been smaller than I am. If I couldn't move the planter, chances were she wouldn't have been able to either.

I took a deep breath and took hold of the planter, lifting with all my strength, but that turned out not to be necessary. Even filled with dirt, the planter didn't weigh that much. I moved it aside and saw a bundle of papers wrapped in plastic.

I knelt down carefully beside it and pulled the plastic taut, trying to see what was inside. It looked like a couple of photographs and a few pages of text, although I didn't see anything about Grace Peters. I debated opening the package, but I couldn't justify it. I might as well haul Fowler out to the farm. If I called him and it turned out to be nothing, he'd have only himself to blame. After all, he was the one who'd told me to call.

When I finally got through, Fowler sounded marginally interested. He told me not to move the bundle until his men had had a chance to take pictures. I figured as soon as those pictures had been taken, Muriel's package would disappear into one of those evidence bags, and we'd never find out what it contained.

"I won't mess with it, but I want to know what's inside. Once your men have taken their pictures, I'll need to open it to make sure it's not related to the farm."

Of course, we both knew that was crap. If this was Muriel's blackmail bundle, it had nothing to do with us. And nobody on the farm would tuck important documents under my planter. I could hear his sigh all the way from town. "I'll be there in a half hour or so. Don't touch anything, Roxy."

I texted Nate and Uncle Mike as soon as I hung up. No, we wouldn't touch anything, but the more of us who were around, the harder it might be for Fowler and company to pick up the bundle and disappear.

"Fowler told me to leave it alone, so I'm not opening it," I said as soon as they got to me.

Nate and Uncle Mike both did the same thing I'd

done, smoothing down the plastic to try to see inside. "Some pictures," Uncle Mike said. "Can't say of what."

"And some printed stuff. Looks like a magazine article." Nate narrowed his eyes, trying to see through the murky surface of the plastic.

"We could just open the plastic to see inside. Not disturb anything." Uncle Mike looked hopeful, and I knew how he felt. But I also knew Fowler would go ballistic if we did, and he had a point.

"We can't." I sighed. "We can justify touching it because we had to make sure it was what the cops were looking for and not just random junk. But we need to leave it to Fowler to open. Remember, he's trying to prove Grace killed Muriel. Which she did."

Uncle Mike looked like he was considering some counter arguments, but the two cops who'd been searching the place showed up just then, and the matter became moot. They took lots of pictures but didn't open the bag until Fowler got there.

It was less than thirty minutes when he pulled up, and I think everybody was relieved to see him, even the cops. He leaned down, frowning as he inspected the package. Then he put on a pair of latex gloves and picked it up.

"You going to open it?" Uncle Mike asked. He'd most likely block the drive if Fowler tried to leave without opening it in front of us.

Fowler glanced at us, then shrugged. "Okay. Let's go inside."

My living room was fairly crowded with both cops, Fowler, and the three of us, but we all managed to arrange ourselves around the coffee table. Fowler opened the sealed plastic bag with gloved hands (after taking another shot of the sealed edge) and lifted the contents out.

I saw several printouts of pictures taken with a phone and an article that looked like it had been clipped from a low-end magazine—lots of dense type and a couple of black-and-white photos.

Fowler spread them out on the table, and we crowded around to take a look. The photos were easier to see than the article. The ones closest to me were of Grace Peters, but she didn't seem to be doing anything nefarious. One was a shot of the main window of her shop, with Grace dimly visible inside. The other was of Grace standing behind her shop counter helping a customer.

"What the hell?" Uncle Mike said. "Why would Peters have been paying her for those?"

Fowler blew out a breath. "No idea." He moved the pictures of Grace aside so we could look at the ones underneath. Those were considerably more like blackmail material.

"That's Sara," I blurted out because it obviously was. But Sara wasn't alone in the pictures, and the man she was with wasn't Marcus. Judging by what was going on in the pictures, the two of them were a lot more than friends.

"Anyone recognize the guy?" Fowler asked.

"I do," I said. "I catered a dinner for him last night. Alan Adamo."

"Who turns out to be a jerk in more ways than one." Nate rubbed a hand across the back of his neck. "I guess that explains how Muriel ended up working for Jordan's Meats."

"Yeah. Wonder what else Muriel squeezed out of

Sara?"

"Money most likely. And Peters might have used the threat of the pictures to get Sara to loan her the SUV," Uncle Mike mused. "Bianca sure wouldn't have loaned it to her directly. They're competitors. Sara must have gotten it for her."

Nate sighed. "Well, damn. Wonder if Marcus knows."

Fowler glanced around at all of us. "This goes without saying, but I'll say it anyway. Nothing about any of this leaves this room. Got it?" He fixed his stare on the two cops.

We all nodded, including the patrolmen.

"What's that other thing?" Uncle Mike asked.

Fowler returned to the printed pages, flipping them over. "Looks like something from a newsletter or a magazine."

I squinted at the headline on the first page. It read "New Program Provides Prisoners With Second Chance." But what program? And why would Muriel be interested? I skimmed through the first few paragraphs. "This article's about a culinary program at a state prison somewhere. I wonder if Grace was one of the instructors?"

Fowler was reading on his own. "If she was, she isn't listed here. There's only one name mentioned, and it's not her." He paused. "At least I don't think it's her."

Which was a good point. Was Grace Peters really Grace Peters?

Nate frowned, staring down at the picture. "They must have taught baking. Looks like they're making cinnamon rolls."

I stared at the picture, too. It showed a middle-aged

woman in a chef's coat and beanie standing next to another woman in a canvas apron over a T-shirt and pants. Other women worked behind them, placing rolls on sheet pans for the ovens. One of them glanced toward the camera, as if she'd been caught off-guard.

I narrowed my eyes. "Is that…?"

Nate put his hand on my shoulder, leaning closer to the picture. "It sort of looks like her."

Now all six of us were leaning in, trying to see. Uncle Mike grabbed my magnifier from on top of the TV. "Everybody back," Fowler snapped, then leaned closer to the picture holding the magnifier over the face. "It's her. Younger and plumper, but her."

"Holy shit," I murmured. "Grace learned to bake in prison?"

"Long way from a Parisian patisserie." Nate grimaced. "She must have made it up. The whole thing about her French pastry background."

Fowler stayed where he was, still studying the photo. "And if she was in prison, her fingerprints will be on file. Where is that prison anyway?"

One of the patrolmen pulled out his phone and started typing. "Idaho," he said after a moment.

"Good enough. We should be able to get her real identity and some real background." He gave us all a slow smile. "Come on, gentlemen, time to pack up and go."

By the time the police had cleared out, it was late afternoon. Uncle Mike drove to town to check in with Madge. I wasn't sure how much he could tell her since Fowler had sworn us all to secrecy, but he could let her know the mystery had been more or less solved.

Nate and I settled down with a very late lunch or

early dinner and a couple of beers. "Poor Marcus," Nate murmured after we'd eaten most of our sandwiches.

"Yeah. I hope he finds out about this on his own. It's going to be hell keeping it quiet if we know and he doesn't."

"Sara's got to know it's all going to come out now. I figure everybody in town has heard about Grace—at least that she threatened you and got arrested for it."

I nodded. "If Sara has any sense, she'll tell Marcus herself and take her lumps. She could probably make it look better than it will if he hears it from somebody like Fowler."

"Or Bianca. If Bianca finds out before Marcus does, Sara's a goner." Nate took a swallow of his beer. "Bobby called me while I was out looking for buried treasure."

"Yeah? What did he want?" I'd forgotten all about Bobby, the catering business, and making jam. For the day, anyhow.

"He wondered if I was coming to work tomorrow. So I'm doing lunch."

I frowned. "Are you sure? Can you stay up on your ankle that long?"

"I'm sure." He gave me a quick smile. "Trust me, I'm ready to be doing stuff again. And the ankle's mostly okay. I can handle it. Then I'll help with brunch Sunday."

"I'll be there." I paused. "Maybe." Usually, I helped with brunch when I stayed over at Nate's on Saturday night. But since we'd just spent the week together, I didn't know how eager Nate was to have me at his place.

"I was hoping you would." He slid his arm around

my shoulders. "Counting on it."

"Okay, then I'll definitely be there." I leaned back against the couch, letting my head rest on his shoulder. "Do we have any catering coming up?"

"I'll have to check. I think we've got a party a week from Saturday."

Well, great. I was afraid we were going to slide right back into the routine we'd had before with Nate working himself to exhaustion and me worrying about what would happen when the farmers market opened up.

"One more thing," Nate said. "Your friend Marigold's coming for an interview Sunday afternoon. I forgot until now."

"Yeah?" I turned to look up at him. "Sunday after brunch?"

He nodded. "So I hear. You want to stick around for that?"

I settled down again, smiling this time. "I wouldn't miss it."

"I figured as much." Nate took another pull on his beer. "Do you honestly think she can keep Bobby from running all over her?"

"Trust me," I said. "Just trust me."

Chapter 24

On Saturday, I got to work on jam. Susa was supposed to post tangerine marmalade as the flavor of the month next week, and like I say, marmalade takes a lot of time.

When Dolce came in, she started slicing the softened rinds into toothpicks. Hers weren't as elegant as Nate's but they were serviceable. I tried to make sure I got the right amount of pectin for the larger batches we were doing so we could make it to our quota of thirty jars, with a few more for in-town sales. Maybe fifty in all.

Bridget came in a little later so she could get us up to date on our order fulfillment. That meant I'd get to live with stacks of cartons for the next couple of days until the delivery guy came by to pick them up. I needed to do something about a storage shed of my own since I had no intention of carting all the boxes over to one of the existing storage sheds with its load of farm implements.

"Heard they got Grace Peters in the slammer," Bridget said. "Did she really try to shoot you?"

I guess it was too much to hope that the news hadn't gotten out. "Yes, she did. And yes, she is. She jumped me at the event we catered on Thursday."

"How did the catering go without Nate?" Dolce said quickly.

Bridget looked like she wasn't through quizzing me about Grace, but I was good with letting it go.

"It was okay. The place wasn't set up for a party, though. We had to go up and down some stairs to get to the event space from the kitchen. Sort of a pain. I wish we'd had Nate to help us carry dishes, but Donnell and I managed."

"Where was it?" Bridget asked.

"Alan Adamo's agency. Out in the strip mall on the north edge of town."

Bridget wrinkled her nose. "Alan Adamo. What a sleaze."

"Yeah?" I tried not to sound as curious as I was. "Why do you say that?"

"His wife's a sweetie. Carol Adamo. She runs that outreach agency for rural poverty, works with farmers who are having problems. You know her, right?"

"Yeah. I'd forgotten about that." Bridget was right—Carol Adamo was a sweetie. Which meant Alan Adamo was a sleaze.

"So why does that make him a sleaze?" Dolce asked. "Carol's nice, and he's married to her."

Bridget looked uncomfortable, but she'd brought it up in the first place. "He cheats on her. I've seen him with women at High Country, and believe me, it's not business."

Dolce's cheeks turned pink. "That's awful. Somebody should tell her."

"Somebody probably has. She may have decided it's better to be married to him. They've got a couple of kids." Bridget focused on the computer for a few silent moments. She had a couple of kids herself, along with an ex who hadn't been a model husband.

It figured that whatever was going on between Sara and Adamo hadn't been serious, but I hoped Marcus didn't get hurt. Unfortunately, that depended on Sara and her willingness to come clean. And I had little faith in Sara after discovering she'd supplied Grace with the SUV.

Dolce took off around two for a basketball game, and Bridget left soon after to get ready for evening service at High Country, leaving me to thread my way among cartons while I tried to arrange a Monday pickup. I'd just finished cursing the online service app when someone knocked at my door.

This time I was alert enough to check the peephole. Grace Peters might be in jail, but who knew who else was lurking around here?

The woman on my front porch didn't look like much of a lurker. Her gray hair was cut short around her face, and she wore knit pants and jacket, along with a turtleneck that looked like it had been through a few wash cycles. I'd never seen her before.

I opened the door. "Can I help you?"

The woman stared at me for a moment, blue eyes wide. She seemed shocked to see me, and I wondered if she'd come to the wrong house. "Are you Roxanne?" she asked.

"I'm Roxanne Constantine." If she was selling anything, she wasn't going about it in the right way.

She licked her lips. "I'm Lucille Decker. Used to be Lucille Murphy a while ago. I think I'm your aunt."

I was so stunned, I fell back a step. Then I moved to the side to let her in. "Come in. Please. Would you like some coffee?"

Lucille nodded. "Coffee would be fine." She

followed me into the kitchen, which I'd just finished cleaning, fortunately.

I got us coffee and a plate of cookies, then sat her down at my kitchen table. Lucille was staring at me again. "You look a lot like your dad," she said finally. "But I can see Linda, too. Your eyes look a lot like hers."

"Do you, well, talk to her?" I really wanted to ask if my mother was still alive, but that was a little stark.

Lucille shook her head. "I haven't seen her in ten years or so. I didn't like what she did to your dad. He was a good man, didn't deserve that. Linda and me fought over it. And over her walking out on you. We didn't have much to do with each other after that. Just letters now and then."

"You don't know where she is?"

Lucille shrugged. "I kept her address. She came to Clayton a few years ago and asked about you. I told her where you were, but I don't know if she ever came up this way."

"Not so far as I know." The news that my mother had asked about me started an uneasy feeling in my gut.

"She regretted it," Lucille said flatly. "In the end, she knew she'd done wrong. That's my opinion."

Which didn't mean her opinion was true. "What happened to her after she and Dad got divorced? Do you know?"

"She was married for a while when she was living in Phoenix. Darryl Wright his name was. Then they got divorced, too. No kids that time. After that she moved to Nevada. Henderson. So far as I know she's still there. That's where I send the Christmas cards, anyway."

If I knew where my mother lived, I could have Susa find her for me. Or not. I swallowed hard. "Are you in town for…" I didn't know how to tactfully ask her if she was there to take her daughter's body to New Mexico.

"For Muriel," she said. "To bring her home."

That was so huge I didn't exactly know what to say. "I'm so sorry," I mumbled finally. "About everything." I put my hand on hers.

Lucille nodded, pressing her lips together. "I'm sorry, too. Muriel shouldn't have come up here in the first place. And she should have told you who she was when she did. She was a lot like Linda in some ways. Always trying to find an easy way to do things."

"She had my mother's driver's license. Do you know how she got it?"

Lucille shrugged again. "Linda left a lot of stuff behind when she moved. I put it all in a box upstairs. Muriel could have found it there."

"I'm not sure why she brought it with her."

Lucille took a sip of her coffee. "Muriel was always curious about Linda. And about you. You're the only cousin she had—my husband was an only child. Maybe she wanted to prove the two of you were related."

And maybe she planned on using that relationship to further her own schemes, but I'd never know for sure. "Do you have any other children?" It was too sad to think of her coming to Colorado to take her only child back to Clayton.

She nodded again. "I've got my boys, Harold and Fred. They wanted to come with me, but I didn't want them to take off work." She glanced around the kitchen.

"I heard Steve died a few years ago. You live here with Mike?"

"Dad died when I was sixteen, but he left me his half of the farm. Uncle Mike lives up at the main house. We have dinner together most nights."

"That's good," Lucille said. "You tell him I said hello."

"I will." I wondered if I should call Uncle Mike down so he could see Lucille before she left, but she didn't seem anxious to talk to him.

Lucille slid to the front of her chair, preparing to get up, and suddenly she looked a lot older than I'd thought. My only aunt. "Could you come and stay out here with us? Uncle Mike has lots of room. We'd be glad to put you up as long as you need." At any rate, I would be. Uncle Mike had still seemed a little pissed at the Murphys.

Lucille shook her head. "Thanks, but no. I wasn't going to stay long in town. I'll be leaving early tomorrow."

"Oh." I didn't know what else to say. I had too many things I wanted to ask and no clear way to ask them.

"It's all right," Lucille said softly. "It must be a shock, having family drop in out of nowhere. Especially when you didn't know you had any. I'm glad I got to meet you, though."

"Yes. Me, too." I stepped forward then, without thinking much about it, and gave her a hug. She felt small and birdlike in my arms. After a moment, she hugged me back.

Lucille leaned away to look at me. "I used to take care of you when you were a baby, you know. Linda worked in town part time, and she'd drop you off with me." Her lips curved up. "I'd say you've grown some."

"Yes, ma'am, I'm sure I have." When you're six feet tall like I am, you get used to people commenting on your size. And Lucille was entitled.

Just then I heard my front door open. "Roxy," Nate called. "Are you here?"

"In the kitchen."

Nate stepped through the kitchen door, then paused. "Sorry. I didn't know you had a visitor."

I took a breath. "This is my aunt, Lucille Decker. Muriel's mom. Aunt Lucille, this is Nate Robicheaux, my…"

Nate stepped into the gap, shaking Aunt Lucille's hand. "I'm pleased to meet you Mrs. Decker. I wish it were under better circumstances."

Lucille smiled back because Nate's the kind of person who makes it easy to smile. "Nice to meet you." She turned to me. "I should go. Good talking to you, Roxanne."

"Could I have your address? So I can send a Christmas card, too?"

Aunt Lucille's cheeks turned pink. "Oh, well, of course."

She wrote down her address and phone number, and I gave her one of my Luscious Delights cards. That led to a quick discussion of my business and a box of jam to take back to Clayton. We hugged again on my doorstep, and I watched her car wend its way up the drive to the county road.

"Well," Nate said.

"Well." I blew out a long breath. "I have two cousins in Clayton, but no half-brothers or half-sisters so far as I know. My mother's probably living in Henderson, Nevada, but hasn't kept in touch with her family. And Muriel the grifter was a lot like her aunt Linda, a.k.a., my mom." I bit my lip, which had begun to tremble.

Nate gathered me into his arms, rubbing circles on my back. "Are you going to tell Mike?"

"That she was here? Of course. I invited her to stay, but she said no. Maybe things are still a little tense between the Constantines and the Murphys in that generation."

"Did you ask her how Muriel got your mom's license?"

"She said she had a box of Linda's things at the house and Muriel could have gotten it there. Lucille thought Muriel might have wanted something to prove she was my cousin, but Muriel might have been thinking about another scam, even if she didn't end up running one. I don't think Aunt Lucille knew Muriel's plans."

"Probably not." He stepped inside again. "You want to come to my place tonight? That way we'd be on site for the Arrival of Marigold."

In the shock of seeing Aunt Lucille, I'd forgotten all about Marigold. "Sure. Just let me get my purse."

"And I'm your young man," he called after me.

"Say what?" I grabbed my purse and turned around.

"You didn't know what to call me to your aunt. Just tell her I'm your young man. That's safe."

I paused. "So, if you were describing me to someone, would you call me your young woman?"

He shook his head, suddenly serious. "If I

described you to someone, I'd say you were the love of my life."

I stood blinking, while Nate put an arm around my shoulders and herded me toward the door. "Come on. I told Harry we'd drop by Dirty Pete's to try out his new version of a Manhattan. He's calling it a Shavano."

"Okay." I managed to inhale. When your young man takes your breath away, sometimes it's hard to get it back.

Chapter 25

Dirty Pete's was jumping with Saturday crowds. Harry's Shavano Manhattan was a lot like a normal Manhattan except it used Colorado whiskey. It was still tasty, though. Through the crowd I saw Bianca sitting at a table with Marcus. Definitely not a conversation I thought I needed to join.

"We should talk to her soon," Nate murmured. "We need to know if she's found out about Sara and Adamo and Grace using the SUV. Otherwise, we'll be walking on eggshells around her."

He was right, and that was a problem. We ordered a lot from Bianca's shop. We couldn't avoid her even if we wanted to, and I for one didn't want to. After a few minutes, Marcus got up and walked out, not even glancing our way. Nate sighed. "Should we go over there?"

I took a quick survey of Bianca. She looked somewhere between furious and sad. "Yeah, let's do it."

Bianca glanced up as we approached her table. She tried for a smile, but then gave up. "I'll warn you, I'm lousy company."

"That's okay. I'll just remember all the times you were great." I sat down opposite her, and Nate grabbed a chair at the side. "What's up? Can we help?"

"Marital problems," she said shortly. "Marcus and

Sara. They're separating. Or something. Marcus wasn't clear on that. He still loves her, which means they'll try to work things out. So I'm biting my tongue full-time."

"I'm sorry to hear they're having problems." I took a quick sip of my Shavano Manhattan in hopes I'd look more believable.

Bianca stared at me for a long moment, then narrowed her eyes. "You knew already. How did you know already?"

I sighed. I'm bad at duplicity. "Some stuff came out in the whole Grace Peters thing. We thought Sara and Marcus might be having trouble."

Bianca narrowed her eyes. "Does everybody know?"

"No," Nate said quickly. "Fowler swore us to secrecy, and we've honored it, so help me."

"Good. Marcus has already had to put up with a lot of bullshit, like that piece of crap inviting him to his party so he could get a little slap and tickle with Sara." Her eyes narrowed. "Lord, you were there, weren't you?"

"I was. Nate stayed home for that one. That's where Grace tried to kidnap me."

Bianca grimaced. "Okay, clearly, you had your own problems that night. I just feel bad for Marcus. It would be a real shitshow if everybody in town finds out what Sara's been up to." Bianca squinted at my drink. "Those any good?"

"Not bad. If you like Manhattans."

"Maybe I'll have Harry make me one. To go."

Bianca lived close to downtown so she was probably walking home. Just the same, I was a little worried. "You want to join us for dinner? Caroline said the special is chicken tinga tacos."

Bianca smiled a little sourly. "Thanks, kid, but I'm okay. Just worried about Marcus. Guess I'll go home and call his dad. Maybe he'll have some ideas for how to get him through this."

Marcus's dad lived in Geary, a few miles away. I was pretty sure he and Bianca were divorced but not absolutely certain.

Bianca pushed herself to her feet. "Thanks for the company."

"Any time," Nate said. "Let us know if we can help. I mean that."

Bianca nodded. "I know. I appreciate it."

We watched her wend her way around the other tables. "Sara's got a lot to answer for," I said. "A broken marriage and a broken SUV."

Nate shrugged. "Maybe it'll make her pull herself together."

For Marcus's sake I hoped so, but I didn't think anyone could count on it.

We ordered dinner because it was a little late to cook and neither of us wanted to order pizza again. Caroline was setting our plates on the table (enchiladas for me because why order something else when Pete's enchiladas are perfection?) when I saw the chief wander in.

Fowler never really looked off duty, but this was as close as he came. He wore jeans and a denim shirt with a leather jacket. He glanced our way.

"Should we invite him over?" I asked.

Nate sighed. "Sure." He raised his hand.

Fowler didn't look all that excited about sitting with us, but he wasn't the type to look excited, period.

"Evening. What's the special?"

"Chicken tinga tacos." I nodded toward Nate's plate.

Fowler narrowed his eyes. "I'll go with enchiladas."

"What's new? Assuming you can tell us."

"Peters has lawyered up, although she's not Peters. Real name's Gail Pettus. She served three years for embezzling money from her employer in Idaho. That much will be in the papers tomorrow." Fowler signaled to Caroline and put in his order. Caroline brought him a Dos Equis when she came over. Obviously, he was a regular.

"How did Muriel find out about her? Any ideas?" I was still more interested in Muriel than Grace. Or Gail. Or whoever she was.

"Turns out Muriel served some time there, too. She was in that same culinary program, although I don't think it took with her."

"Well, she did get a job at Jordan's Meats." Nate took a bite of his taco.

"Yeah, I'm guessing that didn't have much to do with her culinary training."

I took another bite of my enchilada, trying to decide how to frame my next question. "Is Sara in trouble?"

"With me or her husband?" Fowler raised his beer.

"Yeah, she's got trouble with Marcus. But is she in legal trouble, too? She gave Bianca's SUV to Grace."

Fowler gave me one of his blank looks. "Sara says Grace asked for the loan of the SUV to make a delivery. As a fellow Shavano restaurant professional, she complied."

The fact that that fellow Shavano restaurant professional was looking for blackmail material on them both and that Grace had earlier taken care of that blackmailer herself had probably had something to do with it. "Grace would have known we weren't there because she saw us at the Blavatskys' house when she delivered the cake," I mused. "Maybe she figured it would take us longer to get to the farm than it did."

"Or maybe she figured we weren't coming to the farm that night," Nate said. "Maybe she thought we'd go to my place since we had to go to town to drop off the equipment at the kitchen."

If that was true, Grace was probably already annoyed when she barreled into Nate with Bianca's SUV. "Do you think Sara knew Grace killed Muriel?" It was a question I'd mulled for a while. "Is there any chance they were in it together?"

Fowler raised an eyebrow.

"Off the record. Not for attribution," I said. "Personally, I think she suspected and didn't care. But I doubt she was in on it. I don't think she'd have done anything that extreme. And I don't think Peters would have worked with a partner."

"That's...possible," Fowler said slowly. "Muriel Cates was blackmailing both of them, although it's still not clear how Muriel got the pictures of Sara and Adamo."

Nate shrugged. "Probably took them herself. If she was a professional blackmailer, she'd be on the lookout for anything she could use. And it doesn't look like Sara was all that discreet."

"What was Muriel doing out at the farm that night anyway?" I asked. "How did she end up getting killed out there?"

Fowler gave me another blank look and sipped his beer. "I don't know for sure. That would be speculation."

"Okay, I'll speculate. Maybe Muriel thought Grace was going to pay her off. And maybe that was the night she hid the stuff at my cabin. Risky because we were inside having dinner, but less risky because we'd have been in the kitchen. She parks her car on the county road, comes down and hides the stuff, then goes back to her car and meets Grace, who's supposed to have brought however much money Muriel was demanding." I paused.

"And Grace shot her," Nate finished.

I bit my lip. My speculation was probably accurate, but it made me think of Aunt Lucille, who'd come a long way to take her daughter home for burial.

Nate gave me an apologetic look. "Sorry. Your Aunt Lucille didn't deserve to deal with that."

"You met Mrs. Decker?" Fowler asked.

I nodded. "She dropped by. I didn't even know she existed."

"Family feud?"

"Something like that."

Fowler shrugged. "As far as your speculation goes, I can't say whether it's right or not. I don't know, and Peters isn't likely to tell us. But it fits."

"Yeah. It fits." I returned to my enchiladas.

Fowler looked up over my shoulder, his expression shifting to blank. Susa stepped next to our table. "Hey, Rox, you okay? I was going to come out today, but I got hung up at work."

"I'm good. Grab a chair and join us."

Susa gave Fowler a cool look, then shrugged. "Sure."

Fowler might have left except Caroline appeared just then with his enchiladas.

Susa turned to Caroline. "Gee, Caroline, those look great. Why don't you bring me a plate of my own. And a margarita." She gave Fowler a feline smile, as if she was daring him to leave.

He settled in his chair with a stony look in his eyes. I figured they could spend the evening sniping at each other, but I wouldn't stick around to referee. Not that either of them would appreciate my services.

Nate and I ducked out soon after that, leaving Susa and Fowler on their own for better or worse. They could take care of their own love lives, and I'd take care of mine.

Or maybe Nate would.

We had the rest of the evening, after all, and his apartment was just down the road.

Chapter 26

Nate had a better mattress than I did, but my bed was bigger, so it was a tossup as to whose bedroom was more comfortable. Besides, lying next to Nate automatically made any bedroom better.

I was half-asleep and thinking I should just give up and slide all the way, my head resting against Nate's chest. Through the curtains I could dimly see snow falling in his backyard. Tomorrow might be messy with slush, but right now everything felt cozy and warm.

"Hey?" Nate said, rubbing his hand slowly along my arm.

"Mmmm?" I was so close to asleep, I almost hated to say anything.

"I've been thinking," he said tentatively, dropping his hand to my hip and pulling me a little closer.

I moved my head a little so I could see his face in the shadows. "About what?"

"About how much I liked seeing you every day last week. Even if I was hobbling around half the time." His grin flashed in the darkness. "Being around you at breakfast and dinner. It was cool."

I settled down again, snuggling close. "It was nice. I liked it, too." Liked it particularly when I had him there to rescue me from Grace.

"Yeah." He nodded. "So I was thinking…" This time he paused for a long moment, like he was pulling some ideas together.

"You were thinking…" I prompted.

"Maybe we should try moving in together."

My eyes snapped open. Talk about an idea being totally unexpected. "Move in?"

"Yeah, I mean…" He paused again, which might have given me a chance to jerk my own thoughts together, except they were scattered all over the landscape. "If we hire somebody else at the café, I won't have to do breakfast all the time so I won't have to be there so early in the day. So I'd have time for breakfast with you. And I could come home to you in the evening." He took a breath. "Is this weirding you out?"

I shook my head. "No. Not at all. I just have to catch up." I wasn't weirded out, but my heart was hammering hard, and I was trying to figure out why. I wasn't frightened or worried—I knew that much. So why?

Maybe it was hammering because I was in love with Nate. And this was beginning to tiptoe closer to marriage. I closed my eyes for a moment, taking another in a series of deep breaths. It wasn't a surprise. I was in love with Nate; therefore, I wanted to be with him. Moving in together made a lot of sense, even though I hadn't thought about it up until now.

Besides, the thought of moving in together made me feel good, even while my heart hammered away. We got to see how we fit together before taking any legal steps.

"We've got two houses. Have you thought about which one we'd move into?"

Nate sighed, sliding down a little farther in bed.

"That's something else I've been mulling over. I could make a case for either place. If you moved in here, you could use your place as your jam kitchen full time."

Which meant I'd only be cooking jam in my cabin. No more dinners or breakfasts with Uncle Mike and Herman. It wasn't like Uncle Mike couldn't fend for himself—we only ate together a couple of times a week. But the thought of not doing it at all made me sort of melancholy.

I snuggled closer. "If you moved into my place, we'd have more room overall since it's a bigger space. I know right now it's sort of crowded with the jam cartons, but I've been talking to Uncle Mike about getting a storage shed where I could keep them until they're picked up."

Nate nodded. "I know you've got more space. On the other hand, your place is a few miles out of town, which means more of a drive to get to the café. Of course, if we hire Marigold or somebody else, the drive to town won't be an issue. If we don't, and I'm doing breakfast, it would be easier for me if I were living here."

He had a point, but now that I'd had time to think about it, I had to admit I wasn't all that excited about moving into Nate's apartment, even if it meant living with Nate. It was a single room, separated by partitions. Very efficient, but not particularly comfortable. Besides, I had an emotional attachment to my cabin and what it represented for me. I just wasn't sure how to explain it to him.

"Talk to me," Nate said. "What's going through your mind right now?" He ran his fingertip along my cheekbone, and I closed my eyes.

"The thing is, that cabin means something to me. I moved into it when I came back from Denver, when I was really hurting." When I'd run away from being assaulted and then being fired at a trendy Denver restaurant. Something it had taken me months to get beyond. "Uncle Mike wanted me to stay in the main house, but I just couldn't. I wanted to be alone for a while but still close. And the cabin gave me that. It was my hiding place, sort of. I was trying to figure out what I'd do with the rest of my life, after I gave up on working in restaurants."

"And?" Nate leaned back to watch me.

"And I tried all kinds of stuff—baking cookies and making salsa and hot sauce. Everything I could think of. Nothing was right." But it had been a process. One I'd needed, so I could work myself back into the kind of life I wanted to live. And then I'd hit on what I was searching for. "Then one day I took a flat of raspberries home from Pergosian's farm stand and made jam. And it was just…a revelation."

I could still remember the smell of raspberries and sugar, the taste of fresh jam from the pot, once it had cooled down so that it was no longer like lava.

"You found your calling," Nate said softly.

"My calling." I paused to take a breath. "Definitely my calling. Maybe it's sentimental, but that's what the cabin means to me. At least right now. It was freedom, and it was finding myself again so I could move forward. What does your apartment mean to you?"

He lay silent for a while, his hands folded behind his head. "Privacy, I guess. Mom would have been happy to have me in the house when I came back from Vegas, but that felt like failure. Like I'd been out on my own and couldn't hack it. The apartment was independence."

And he'd still been close enough for Madge to check on him now and then, given that he was recovering from that heart "incident." My guess was it had been a compromise that had worked for the two of them.

Nate sighed. "To tell you the truth, I've never been that attached to this place. I always meant to find someplace else, like Coco and Bobby did. But I just never got around to it. And then I found you. After that I had a lot more interesting things to do with my time than look for another apartment."

He turned to look at me. "That settles it, I guess. Your place. It means more to you than mine does to me. But this all depends on what happens at the café. If we hire somebody to work in the kitchen, and I don't have to work breakfast every day, I'll move in at the farm. Deal?"

I nodded. "Works for me."

Nate paused for a long moment. "Are you okay with this? Really okay? I don't want you to feel like I'm pushing you into anything."

"It's okay. Beyond okay, in fact. I'm happy. Please allow me to demonstrate just how happy I am that you may be moving into my place."

And I rolled him over on his back and spent a very enjoyable time demonstrating.

Brunch service started at ten on Sundays, which meant we got there around eight thirty to get everything set up. Bobby was there already, but by now I was used to that. He always liked to be in position before anybody else so he could give us all annoyed looks when we trailed in.

Coco came in five or ten minutes after we did and ignored Bobby completely. He seemed to be gritting his teeth, but he didn't say anything. After all, his sister was a partner in the café, just like he was. Still, he normally would have made a comment or two, and this time around he'd let us all wander into the kitchen with nothing more than dirty looks.

My presence in the kitchen was strictly voluntary. On Sundays I made the mimosas and Bloody Marys that were the only brunch drinks served beyond the usual coffee and tea. Bobby and I had had occasional run-ins on just how much champagne I was putting into the mimosa glasses, but this particular morning he was too distracted to pay me any attention. He didn't even check the Bloodies to make sure I was putting in smallish celery sticks rather than cucumber wedges.

It finally occurred to me that he was nervous about Marigold's meeting with Madge. Change was hovering over Bobby's head, and if there was one thing he hated, it was change. But to be honest, I was nervous, too, and for pretty much the same reason. If Madge hired Marigold, my life would change almost as much as Bobby's would.

I wasn't afraid of that change. Not really. I loved Nate, and I loved the idea of waking up next to him every day, of having him around for dinner every night. All of it. But I couldn't pretend it wouldn't be a massive adjustment. We'd both been on our own for a long time, and moving in together would mean major alterations for both of us.

Nate didn't seem to be thinking about that. In fact, he was surprisingly chipper as he ran the flattop. His omelets were terrific, but he also did a nice job with simple fried eggs and what the café called "scrambles": scrambled eggs with a variety of fillings, including one with serrano chilies, chopped tomatoes, Monterey jack cheese, and a sprinkling of cilantro that was my favorite.

Coco was happy, too, humming as she did waffles and French toast. The three-hour brunch period ticked away with Bobby and me looking fraught and Nate and Coco looking Zen. The last few customers got their orders and Bobby pulled off his apron. "That's it. Kitchen's closed."

I breathed a sigh of relief, although we had a half bottle of champagne left. Usually Bobby would have complained about that, even though the champagne they used for mimosas was exceedingly cheap. Today he didn't even appear to notice.

Nate tossed his apron into the laundry, then put his hands on the small of his back and stretched. "Not too bad today."

"They cleaned me out on cinnamon rolls and waffles. Maybe next week I'll try some donuts." Coco gave Bobby a challenging smile since he always argued that fresh donuts were too labor-intensive and not cost effective, but he didn't seem interested in quarreling with her either.

After a few minutes of cleaning up and a little meal prep, it was clear we were all waiting around for Madge and Marigold. When the door to the kitchen opened, we all wheeled around to see. However, it was just Madge.

My heart dipped down. If Marigold hadn't taken the job, Nate couldn't move in. If I'd had any doubts about the whole living together thing, my sudden jolt of disappointment took care of them.

I wanted him to move in. Fancy that.

Madge was smiling, then she paused and turned to the door. "We're in here," she called.

A moment later, Marigold walked into the kitchen.

I hadn't bothered to describe her to anyone because I wasn't entirely sure she still looked the way she had the last time I'd seen her. Marigold's style was pretty fluid. But I should have had confidence in her allegiance to personal idiosyncrasy.

She was taller than Coco, but not as tall as I am. Her hair was always a shade of platinum so pale it was almost white, but she dyed her forelock something different each time I saw her. Right now it was a violent purple, dipping down over her brilliant blue eyes. Marigold wasn't fat, but she was definitely solid, lots of muscle from being a butcher and then a line cook. She was wearing what probably passed with her for polite fashion: khaki slacks and a knit shirt. Of course, the knit shirt had *Wacker and Son Meats* embroidered on the back.

And then there were the tattoos.

A lot of chefs have tattoos—Nate had a couple, crossed knives on one biceps and a chef's hat and whisk on the other. He also had a private one on his lower back that made my temperature rise. Coco had a star on her wrist and a cupcake on her shoulder, and maybe more in more concealed areas. I have a butterfly on my shoulder blade, and I hate needles, so getting it had been a major accomplishment. Marigold put us all to shame.

She had a range of tattoos on both arms, extending down to her hands: meat diagrams and knives, *Born to*

Braise in Gothic script, carrots and tomatoes dissolving into slices. On one hand the backs of her fingers said COOK, and the other they said CHEF. At the moment she was wearing that short-sleeved knit shirt even though the temperature was in the forties. I figured she'd decided to give Madge an indication of her artwork, just in case it made a difference.

Apparently, it didn't.

"So this is the kitchen," Madge explained. "We've got a smaller one for the catering business next door. And this is the family. My son Nate and my daughter Coco. And you know Roxy. She's a member of the family, too."

Marigold grinned at me. "Hey, Rox, long time."

"Good to see you, kiddo." I gave her a quick hug. Nate and Coco both grinned widely.

"And this is my older son, Bobby," Madge went on.

Bobby wasn't grinning, but then he also wasn't scowling. In fact, he appeared to be sort of dazed, maybe even dazzled. He nodded at Marigold, eyes wide. She nodded at him, looking faintly amused.

"Marigold's accepted the job offer," Madge said happily. "She'll be starting week after next. I promised to help find her a place to live here in town before then."

Nate grinned. "I think I can help with that."

Oh, my. He was going to offer Marigold his apartment. Which was great. And he was going to move in with me. Which was even greater. My heart gave a mighty thump, and I found myself grinning as widely as he was.

Coco gave Marigold a hug of her own. "Welcome

to Robicheaux's. I can't wait for you to start. It's going to be so much fun." She glanced at Bobby under her lashes, giving him one of those sly smiles.

I checked Bobby again, a little apprehensively. He could still mess up the deal if he treated Marigold like crap. He was still staring at her, but he didn't look angry or hostile. In fact, it was tough to define just how he looked.

Stunned. Staggered. Thunderstruck. In a good way. Bobby looked like someone who'd just seen his future unfurling before him. A future he didn't exactly know what to do with.

Oh, Coco was absolutely right. This was going to be so much fun to watch!

Nate put his arm around my shoulders. "It's great to meet you, Marigold. Glad you're joining us. Let us know if there's anything we can do to help."

Marigold nodded. "I'll do that. Thanks."

We walked out to the parking lot. Nate was still using Madge's SUV since he hadn't gotten the check for his totaled car yet, and I had my truck.

Nate paused. "How do we do this? Make a formal announcement or just let everybody figure things out for themselves?"

"I vote for letting them figure it out. You're going to offer Marigold your apartment, aren't you?"

He nodded. "I'll talk to Mom about it, but it makes sense. Housing's scarce up here. And it's a good apartment for a single person."

I took another of those deep breaths that seemed to clear my head. "Why don't we start moving stuff over today. We can load up my truck and your SUV. It should give us a good start."

Nate studied me for a moment, the corners of his mouth creeping up. "You're ready for this?"

"Oh, hell, yes." I wrapped my arms around his neck and gave him a fast kiss. "Very ready. Very, very ready."

"Okay, then," he said. "Let's do this."

"Let's." I turned toward my truck, my heart suddenly as light as one of Nate's omelets. Like the guy once said, after you figure out who you want to spend the rest of your life with, you want the rest of your life to get started ASAP.

Because the rest of my life—our lives—was definitely going to be interesting.

A word about the author…

Meg Benjamin is an award-winning author of romance. Along with her Luscious Delights series for Wild Rose Press, she's also the author of the Konigsburg, Salt Box and Brewing Love series. Along with these contemporary romances, Meg is also the author of the paranormal Ramos Family trilogy and the Folk series. Meg's books have won numerous awards, including an EPIC Award, a Romantic Times Reviewers' Choice Award, the Holt Medallion, the Beanpot Award, and the Award of Excellence.

Thank you for purchasing
this publication of The Wild Rose Press, Inc.

For questions or more information
contact us at
info@thewildrosepress.com.

The Wild Rose Press, Inc.
www.thewildrosepress.com

Milton Keynes UK
Ingram Content Group UK Ltd.
UKHW021613050624
443649UK00016BA/859